"I'm no stranger, Letty Sue," the man with the gun stated.

Realization dawned quickly. Those eyes, she'd never forget them. They were the color of cold hard steel and had been stowed away in her mind.

Chase Wheeler.

"Remember me?" he asked, lowering his gun but directing his razor-sharp gaze toward her.

Speechless, she nodded. She barely remembered the boy with the Cheyenne name, Silver Wolf. But he was a man now, with strong features—dangerous eyes, aquiline nose, rigid jaw, tall in frame and she assumed a powerfully competitive opponent to any who crossed him. He was dressed in white man's clothes, a plaid work shirt, chaps over his trousers and a black Stetson that seemed to cover up rather longish ink-black hair.

He drew in a deep breath, his eyes once again taking her in. A cold shiver ran down her spine.

Oh Lordy, Letty Sue.

CHASE WHEELER'S WOMAN

CHARLENE SANDS

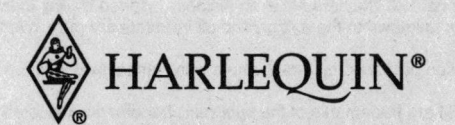

HARLEQUIN®

TORONTO • NEW YORK • LONDON
AMSTERDAM • PARIS • SYDNEY • HAMBURG
STOCKHOLM • ATHENS • TOKYO • MILAN • MADRID
PRAGUE • WARSAW • BUDAPEST • AUCKLAND

ISBN 0-373-29210-4

CHASE WHEELER'S WOMAN

Copyright © 2002 by Charlene Swink

This edition published by arrangement with Harlequin Books S.A.

® and TM are trademarks of the publisher. Trademarks indicated with ® are registered in the United States Patent and Trademark Office, the Canadian Trade Marks Office and in other countries.

Visit us at www.eHarlequin.com

Printed in U.S.A.

Available from Harlequin Historicals and
CHARLENE SANDS

Lily Gets Her Man #554
Chase Wheeler's Woman #610

Please address questions and book requests to:
Harlequin Reader Service
U.S.: 3010 Walden Ave., P.O. Box 1325, Buffalo, NY 14269
Canadian: P.O. Box 609, Fort Erie, Ont. L2A 5X3

To my talented son, Jason, my web master,
tech support and the greatest son a mother could have.

And to my sweet, beautiful daughter, Nikki,
the heart of my heart whose journalistic ability
is a source of great pride for me.

You have the world at your feet—
tread wisely and follow your dreams.
I am truly blessed to have you both in my life.

Special and sincere thanks to my editor, Patience Smith.
You are the very best.

Chapter One

Sweet Springs, Texas 1881

Letty Sue Withers stormed out of the house with picnic basket in hand, her straw bonnet falling off her head and cascading down her back. She yanked at the ribbons, freeing herself of the disturbance. "Please, Albert, let's just go."

Albert Milner took hold of her bonnet, then helped her up onto the buggy. "Are you all right, Letty Sue?"

"I will be, as soon as you get me off the Double J. I need…I need cooling off time, is all."

Albert shot her a curious glance, then handed her bonnet back before boarding the buggy and picking up the reins. With a flick of the wrist he coaxed the horse to a fast trot.

Wriggling her backside to get comfortable in the seat next to him, she noted beads of perspiration break out on the young assistant banker's forehead. He was handsome in a book-learned way, she thought, eyeing his light blond hair and fine brocade suit.

This was the fourth time he'd come courting. Today he was taking her on a picnic. He was a pleasant companion—the precise tonic she needed to keep her mind off disagreeable subjects, like Mama leaving the ranch in the hands of a stranger.

"Care to tell me what's got you so blustered?" he asked. The ranch house was just a dot on the horizon now. Albert slowed the horse to a steady walk.

"Oh Albert. Mama just informed me that she and her new husband, Jasper, are going on a honeymoon. To the East! Chicago, St. Louis, New York, all the places I long to see. Why, just about everybody this side of Louisiana knows how much I've dreamed of traveling East. It's been a notion of mine since I was just a girl. Mama's abandoning me to go off for a high time for three entire months, and that's not the worst of it."

Albert's eyes gleamed. "You mean you'll be alone at the ranch all that time? I could—"

"No, that's just the point. I won't be alone. Mama saw fit to hire on a new foreman. Seems Sam Fowler isn't good enough to help me run the ranch, although he's been with us the longest. Mama says he's smitten with me and I'd just get his socks in a knot. But that just plain isn't true. Why, Sam is the best friend I have on the ranch."

Albert cleared his throat. "Joellen might have a point there, Letty Sue."

"Oh, not you, too, Albert. Isn't it bad enough Mama saw fit to hire a half-breed to run the ranch?"

"Why would she do that?" Puzzled, Albert lifted his light eyebrows.

"She *trusts* him. More than she trusts me. I told her I could handle the running of the ranch. Lordy, Albert, it's been me and Mama for so long, how could she think of bringing a stranger on the ranch to oversee things? It's not fair and I won't have it." Although she knew the man her mother had hired wasn't really a stranger, Letty Sue wouldn't abide that notion. For all purposes, he was a stranger—*to her.*

"Seems to me your mama's mind is set."

"Well, I'm not letting anyone run roughshod over me at the ranch my father lost his very life trying to protect. They shot him right before Mama's eyes, Albert. And you know what she did? She picked up her Winchester without so much as a skip of her heartbeat and chased those cattle rustlers right off our property."

"Your mama's as brave a woman as I've ever known, Letty Sue. Everyone in town respects her."

"Yes, I know." Letty Sue's ire plummeted. She took a deep breath of air, sighing. "Mama's wonderful and all, but sometimes it's just plain hard being her daughter. It's time I proved that I'm a capable woman, just like her. "

"Why?" Albert asked, a curious expression on his face.

"Why?"

"Yes, why all of a sudden do you want to prove your worth?"

She shook her head slowly, contemplating her answer. It had dawned on her recently that she wanted the same respect her mama had attained. Joellen Withers had lost a husband. That in itself might have done in a weaker woman, but Joellen had brought the Double J to prosperity and raised a daughter at the same time. She had struggled through the years, made lifelong friends and survived in a business that was essentially managed by men.

"I'm approaching twenty-one years old and Mama still treats me like a child. She's been so overprotective since…well, since the Indian attack. If only she'd give me a chance, Albert. That's all I ask."

Letty Sue glanced out at the land her father had worked from sunrise to sunset. Grazing cattle roamed over the rugged terrain, finding sources of food nature provided by way of rain and sunshine. Letty Sue had been just a little girl when her father died. Then had come the Indian attack. She didn't blame her mother for her protective ways, but it was time for Letty Sue to set things to right. "I want to travel some, Albert. Once Mama returns with her new husband, I plan to strike out on my own. I want to see something of the world. It's been a dream of mine…forever."

"I can't imagine Joellen letting you go off."

"She will, I'm certain of it," Letty Sue answered, nearly willing it so in her mind. "I just have to prove I can handle myself." She put a hand to her abdomen. "All this unpleasant talk is just too unsettling." With a little groan, she added, "My stomach's churning inside."

Albert took her hand and brushed a kiss along her knuckles. "I sure am glad you trusted me enough to share your troubles, Letty Sue. It means a great deal."

Letty Sue removed her hand from his. She was just letting loose some frustration, and Albert seemed willing to listen. She wasn't at all sure how much she trusted him. "Can we speak of more agreeable subjects now? Please?"

Letty Sue cast him a sweet smile, hoping he was capable of making her forget any unpleasantness for a few hours. But her mama's words kept pounding in her ears.

I trust Chase Wheeler with my life, and yours, too, Letty Sue.

Chase Wheeler, part Cheyenne Indian, a stranger. Letty Sue shivered, then shook her head, breaking free of thoughts so perplexing they clouded her mind. She wouldn't think about it. She'd keep her mind set on having a pleasing picnic lunch with Albert and forget about her fate for the moment.

"Are you cold, Letty Sue?" Albert asked, witnessing her slight tremble.

"No, not at all, Albert."

"Well, uh, sure is a nice day for a picnic. I'm glad you suggested it."

She grabbed onto him to steady herself when the buggy hit a bump in the road. Her breast brushed against his coat sleeve. Albert's face flushed with color.

"Yes, I am, too, but Mama says there's a storm brewing. Why, the sky's as blue as my new sapphire necklace, and the air is warm as anything. 'Course, Mama's seldom wrong. She's got good instincts predicting the weather."

"I promised her I wouldn't keep you out too long," he said, then added, "You sure do look pretty today, Letty Sue."

"Why, thank you, Albert. How very nice of you to say so. Do you like my new necklace?" She fingered the blue gem delicately. "Robbie Nichols gifted it to me on my birthday. Wasn't that nice of him?"

Albert studied the necklace, a frown bringing down the corners of his mouth. "Uh, why yes, Letty Sue. Be sure to tell me when your birthday comes up again. I wouldn't want to miss such a special occasion."

"Oh, I certainly will, Albert."

He drove the buggy a far distance, to a clearing near the creek that separated the Double J from Kincaide land. Helping her down, he braced his hands on her waist. Letty Sue lingered in his arms a bit, before swinging away to stroll by the creek, which was high from recent rains. Water rushed by, splashing against a large boulder before the creek took a turn south. A sparrow flitted in the trees, stirring the leaves, then settling on a branch to chirp in rhythm with Letty Sue's wistful heartbeats.

After a minute, Albert called to her. "Letty Sue, are you hungry?"

She turned to find that he had laid a thick quilt on

the switchgrass under a mesquite tree. He'd emptied the basket Mama had packed onto one corner of the quilt. Foodstuffs were spread out, along with a jug of lemonade.

"Not particularly, Albert, but you go ahead if you're hungry."

"No, I'll wait. Come and sit down with me."

Letty Sue hesitated, wondering if she should continue the touching game Albert had initiated on their very first date. Albert would kiss her, and each time he'd become just a little bit more bold. It had started out with his stroking her arms when they kissed. The next time he'd caressed her leg—through her dress, of course. The last time they'd been together, his fingers had worked their way to her ribs, urgently moving over the material of her dress, pressing her for more. She'd stopped him quickly, noting the hot look in his eyes. Today, she questioned if she liked him enough to allow more.

She came to stand by him. He took her hands and gently guided her down to the blanket. They sat facing each other, his light brown eyes twinkling.

"I don't believe I've ever met a more beautiful woman, Letty Sue. You have the bluest eyes I've ever seen. Spring-sky blue, and your hair is like the finest silk. You're smart and clever and..."

She smiled at that as his lips came down on hers. It was a pleasing kiss, she thought, as he lowered her down to the blanket. She kissed him back softly, experimenting with his mouth. He groaned aloud and probed her with his tongue until she gasped. Somehow his body seemed to be surrounding hers, lying half on top of her. She tried to shift away, but his legs held her firm.

His hands moved frantically over her stomach now, rising higher, up over her ribs. She slapped them down.

"No, Albert."

"C'mon, Letty Sue. I won't tell a soul, I promise."

"I said no." She tried to pry herself up, shoving at him, to no avail.

"With your mama gone, we can spend more time together," he said, kissing her lips again. "And get to know each other much better." He rubbed his body against hers, frightening her with his boldness. "We both know that was what you were hinting at before. I'll help with the ranch, I swear."

She twisted in his arms, a swell of panic rising. "No, Albert. Let me up. Now."

He didn't budge, and though she wiggled, she couldn't get out of his grasp.

"You've made me crazy with want, Letty Sue. Letting me touch you, just enough to stir my blood. Brushing your sweet body against mine every chance you get. You've teased me unmercifully for weeks. This is what you want." He spoke low in her ear. "What we both want. Relax now, you're gonna like it."

She shook her head briskly. Foodstuffs scattered across the ground as she struggled. "I won't like it. Don't touch me!"

Her attempts to pull away were futile. His hot

breath and the dangerous gleam in his eyes alarmed her like nothing else ever had. "Please, Albert! Let me up."

"Do as the lady says."

The husky command came from just beyond the edge of the blanket.

A man, tall and broad of shoulder, stood above them, pointing his gun. Albert immediately froze while eyeing the stranger. And when he finally lifted his weight from her, Letty Sue breathed a quick sigh of relief.

"Good. Now get yourself on out of here."

Albert stood, lifting his arms in the air. The gun was trained on him. "B-But I have t-to see her home."

The stranger laughed—a derisive, cold sound. "Don't think so."

"B-But I can't leave her h-here with a stranger."

Albert was being noble *now?* What had happened to his gentlemanly nature just a few minutes ago? Letty Sue wondered.

She stood and straightened, shaking out the creases in her dress and mustering as much pride as she could under the circumstances. When she looked up, the stranger's silver eyes were on her, perusing her with intense interest from the top of her mussed sable hair down to her delicately encased toes.

"I'm no stranger," the man with the gun stated.

Realization dawned quickly. Those eyes... She'd never forget them. Flashes of faded memory came bursting forth. She'd been just a child, but the sight of those gray eyes, the color of cold hard steel, had been stowed away permanently in her mind.

Silver Wolf.

"Remember me?" he asked, lowering his gun but directing his razor sharp gaze toward her.

Speechless, she nodded. She remembered the boy, barely, and his Cheyenne name. But he was a man now, tall in frame, with strong features—dangerous eyes, aquiline nose, a rigid jaw. And she sensed he was a powerfully competitive opponent to any who crossed him.

He'd saved her life, and Mama's, too, when Letty Sue was just a child, coming to their rescue when Dog Soldiers had both females pinned down. The young Cheyenne brave of twelve had surprised the renegade Indians and fought them off, saving both Witherses' lives.

The gloomy images had faded in a little girl's mind, but they resurfaced today—clouded and perhaps distorted, but they were there just the same. A bleak reminder of the terror they'd all been through.

The half-breed was dressed in white man's clothes, a plaid work shirt, chaps over his trousers and a black Stetson that seemed to cover up rather long ink-black hair.

He was known as Chase Wheeler, but to Letty Sue, he would always be Silver Wolf.

He turned his attention back to Albert. "Get going, *Albert.* No harm will come to her. I'm the new foreman on the Double J. Now hop into your buggy."

Letty Sue watched Albert until he was well on his

way down the road. Humiliation set in then. How much had this man seen? Heard? He'd certainly heard enough to call Albert by his name.

Oh Lordy, Letty Sue.

"I suppose I should thank you," she said lamely.

Silver Wolf began gathering up the food and putting it back into the basket. He rolled up the quilt and stood again, facing her.

She spoke once more, louder this time. "I said thank you."

He drew in a deep breath, his eyes once again raking her. A cold shiver ran down her spine. "If you play games with boys, you have to suffer the consequences." He shoved the quilt into her arms.

Outraged, she tossed the quilt to the ground. "I wasn't playing games!" It wasn't entirely the truth. Although Albert had startled her with his boldness, she'd never thought for a moment that he would force his attentions on her that way.

And somehow Letty Sue knew if she let the half-breed get the upper hand today, she'd be in for the longest, most insufferable three months of her life.

He stared at the blanket she'd just tossed down. Expressionless, he bent and rolled it up again. Standing tall, inches away from her, he shoved it into her arms once more. "You try tempting a *real* man like that and you'd lose your highly prized virtue within a matter of seconds."

"Ha! A lot you know."

He grabbed her wrists, firmly, without causing her any pain. He came near, the quilt the only thing separating their bodies. She backed up as he pressed forward. "I know what I saw. A beautiful woman enticing a man without an ounce of regard as to what she was about. You little fool. You're a handful of woman *any* man would want to bed—without all that teasing. But don't go thinking that bedding relates to wedding. You're more trouble than you're worth. You'd be left out in the cold, darlin'."

A thick tree trunk stopped her from backing away any farther. She was pinned between two thick bodies, one just as immovable as the other.

"Do I make myself clear?" he asked, as if she were a child being given a stern talking to.

Letty Sue's blood boiled. Her heart pounded in her chest. How dare he treat her this way? There was a sudden chill in the air—or was it Silver Wolf's eyes penetrating her with calculated coldness?

She smiled sweetly, glancing at the firm set of his mouth. She licked her lips slowly, making sure she had his attention. "Yes, perfectly clear. You think I'm beautiful, and you want to bed me. Did I get that right, *Silver Wolf?*"

His eyes went coal-black and wide with astonishment. He cursed profusely and released his grip on her. "Start walking. It's a long way back to the ranch."

"You're not leaving me out here!" She clutched the quilt tightly and raced after him.

"Watch me." With a movement she could describe only as fluid grace, he mounted his horse, then tipped his hat to her. "See you back at the ranch." His bay mare trotted off, pretty as you please.

Letty Sue slammed her eyes shut. She let out a few vile curses, which though unladylike, sure sounded good to her ears.

The air became increasingly cooler, causing her to glance up. Clouds crowded the sky, bringing a vast, gloomy gray covering to the once blue heavens. A loud boom made her jump, then the sky twitched with brightness. Within seconds, rain pelted down, soaking her to the bone.

She covered herself with the quilt and, with head bent, began her long trek home. She'd walked only a short distance when she came upon horse's hooves. Uncovering her head, she peered up.

Silver Wolf sat on his horse, his expression grim. He leaned over and put out his hand. "Get on, before lightning strikes us both down."

The rain poured down in buckets, a Texas thunderstorm so powerful it could knock branches off the most sturdy of trees. Chase Wheeler grimaced, realizing he'd have to find a place to hole up until the storm eased some. Besides, the bay mare he'd ridden today wasn't going to last much longer with the added weight of the woman and the chore of stomping through the heavily pitted, muddy road.

He remembered seeing a supply shack not far from here. He reined his horse in that direction, hoping his recollection would serve him well. He'd been on his way to Joellen's ranch earlier, stopping by the creek to water his horse. That's when he'd come upon this bundle of trouble he'd seated in front of him on the saddle.

Letty Sue.

Damnation, she was a beauty. 'Course, right about now, she wasn't at her best, with her long dark hair matted like a drowned cat and her clothes drenched.

Her fancy dress molded to her petite body, clinging to all her curves. She had many, he noted, then tightened the quilt around her more snugly when he saw her trembling.

He hadn't bargained on her when he'd made the agreement with Joellen. Hell, he hadn't given Joellen's daughter a single thought. In his mind, the little girl he'd saved all those years ago hadn't grown up. He'd thought of her only as a child.

But Chase hadn't been in her company longer than three minutes before realizing that Letty Sue Withers, with her sky-blue eyes and buxom body, was a barrelful of trouble. Hell, he'd just left one tempting woman behind…a woman who'd caused him nothing but grief and a haystack of hurt. She'd deceived and betrayed him, playing him for the biggest kind of fool.

Never again.

And to think he'd have to play nursemaid to this troublesome woman for the next three months. For Joellen, he'd oblige. But for no other reason.

"Th-this isn't the w-way b-back to the r-ranch," Letty Sue said, her teeth chattering.

"Lightning's getting too close. It's dangerous to head back now."

"Th-then w-where are we g-going?" She shifted in the saddle to look at him, her almond-shaped eyes blinking away the rain.

"There's a supply shack not far from here. We'll hole up there for a spell."

Within minutes Chase reined his horse in. Fortunately for his mare, the shack had an overhang. He tied her up where the majority of rain wouldn't pelt down on her. He reached for the woman, noting her state of saturation as he pulled her down into his arms. She was quiet, cold to the core and exhausted. Chase carried her into the small shack, hoping he'd made the right decision. The shack had no fireplace, no place to sit, and was almost as cold inside as the stormy day had become outside. Fencing supplies lined the walls, as well as several sacks of oats for the horses.

"Well, here we are," he said, carefully setting the woman down on her feet. She clung to him, not as a ploy, he believed, but from sheer fatigue.

Her body trembled uncontrollably. "I h-hate the c-cold."

"You're gonna hate this even more," he said evenly. "Take off your dress."

Her head shot up, her blue eyes sparking with indignation. "No."

"Fine then. Sit down on that sack of oats and freeze. Ever see a body die from pneumonia? They cough so fiercely, blood spurts out, their chest feels like it's being crushed by a half-ton longhorn and then, after days of suffering, they feel nothing at all.''

Chase turned his back on her and removed his rain-soaked shirt. He twisted it into one long length and wrung out about a pint of water, then hung it up on a peg on the wall.

"How w-will taking my d-dress off keep me w-warm?" she asked. He noticed her lips had changed color, going from rosy pink to pale, icy blue.

"It won't. I will. Body heat."

She sucked in a breath, then bit down on her blue lip. "You mean, me and you?"

He wasn't going to think about her naked in his arms. Thankfully for both of them the shack was in short supply of daylight. There were no windows and only a dim light worked its way in through the slats of the rough plank walls.

The cold wasn't so bad for him; he'd endured much worse. But she was a delicate woman who'd probably freeze to death without his help. "That's what I mean. Unless you can think of another way to get warm?"

She looked helplessly around the small supply shack. Already, puddles were developing under their feet from their dripping clothes. "D-do I h-have your word…" She lifted wary eyes his way.

He nodded. "Nothing's gonna happen, except you'll get warm."

An idea struck him, and he quickly turned around, noting the size of the large grain sacks. Taking a knife out of his boot, he sliced through one sack and poured the oats into the only bucket he found until it overflowed onto the floor. "Don't suppose Joellen is gonna mind the waste, being as I'm saving your modesty."

He was left with a rough, but dry rectangle of cloth. He worked his knife through it, cutting a few holes, then, once satisfied with his creation, handed the garment to her. "Here. It's dry. Now, you'd best get out of those wet clothes and into this."

She grabbed the empty sack, realizing his obvious intent, and nodded. "Turn around."

He turned his back on her to arrange the rest of the sacks of grain as a makeshift bed. Then he lay down, waiting. She came to stand before him.

He groaned inwardly, cursing his bad luck. At any other time, with any other woman, he'd relish the situation he was in. A woman wearing nothing but a flimsy piece of material cinched in at the waist by a length of rope and barely covering her female essentials—a woman needing his body warmth for survival—wasn't a bad place to be.

But this woman was too beautiful, too much trouble, and worst of all, she was Joellen's daughter. He'd never do a thing to dishonor Joellen Withers Brody.

"Lie down here." He patted a spot in front of him.

"Which way?" Letty Sue asked timidly.

Either way would cause him havoc. If he faced her, their bodies would press intimately from the front, and the other alternative didn't make for a better selection. He'd be rubbing against her backside.

Hell.

"Your choice. Just get down here. Your skin's turning to gooseflesh."

She lay down and turned away from him. He brought his body close, meshing his chest with her back, and began rubbing her cold arms. She trembled under his fingertips.

"You'll be warm in a few minutes. Close your eyes."

"Why are you doing this?" she asked, her voice barely above a whisper.

"Can't have you freezing to death."

"I...I didn't think you liked me."

He let out a wry chuckle. "I don't."

"Oh," she said, sounding sincerely hurt by his admission. Something unraveled in his gut from that one small word.

For years he'd thought kindly of the woman and child he'd rescued from the two renegade Cheyenne who'd struck down white settlers in retaliation for Lean Bear's untimely and unjust death. Chase, too, had been appalled that Lean Bear, who'd fought for peace and had worn a medal given to him by the white man's leader, had been brutally slain. Lean Bear had died holding a written letter of peace given to him by President Lincoln.

But even then, more boy than man, Silver Wolf had realized murder wasn't the answer.

The brave white woman and child he'd rescued had stayed with him in his heart, filling it with a sense of peace. Somehow, in his mind, he'd remained their protector, feeling a kinship, a special bond to those whose lives he'd saved.

Hurting Letty Sue now hadn't been planned or calculated. He'd only spoken the truth. He didn't know her, but he'd known her kind before, having firsthand knowledge of women who played one man against another. Still, the need to protect and keep her safe warred with the contempt he'd felt for her when he'd watched her tempt that young man the way she had earlier today.

She shifted restlessly, wedging herself closer to him.

"Try to rest." He lifted up slightly, stroking life back into her shoulders and neck, warming her, but attempting to relax the stiffness, too.

"Do you think the storm will last long?"

"With the way it's thundering, we might be here for a time." A booming thunderclap seemed to prove his point.

There was silence inside the shack while the rain pummeled the roof above, and Chase thought she had finally fallen asleep. He closed his eyes.

"You don't speak like an Indian," she whispered softly, minutes later.

"My mother was Cheyenne. I never knew my white father. But after Snow Cloud died, I lived with the white man. Got a job breaking horses on a big spread in Abilene."

"Is that when you changed your name?"

"I'll always be Silver Wolf to the Cheyenne. But

I took a white name when I started at Seth Johnston's ranch. Been Chase Wheeler for ten years."

"Mama thinks the sun sets on your shoulders."

There was resentment in her tone. It was something he was accustomed to, the price he paid for his mixed heritage. He would never quite measure up, and no matter how much good he might do in the world, a single questionable deed would see him hanging high from the rafters.

Or maybe he was mistaken. Perhaps it was the woman's own inadequacies that caused her resentful tone. Could it be that Joellen, with her kind and generous heart, had spoiled her daughter overly much, and high praise came on a short rope where she was concerned?

"Are you going to tell her about today?" she asked with trepidation.

He began working the chill out of her legs. Stroking gently, massaging up and down, he heard a small moan escape her throat. Damn. He'd never felt softer skin. His hands slid over the smooth contours, bringing an unwanted surge of pleasure. He closed his eyes and concentrated hard on her question, the distraction of her body more than taking up all the space in his addled brain. "Haven't decided."

"W-will you tell her about before, with Albert?"

"I should," he said, in a warning tone.

"Please, I don't need another lecture right now." She twisted around to face him, her eyes bright, the blue orbs capturing his gaze with determination.

"Damn well deserve a lecture." But it wouldn't be

coming from him. He'd learned a hard lesson from getting involved with a beautiful, spoiled woman once before. He'd not be a fool again.

Snow Cloud's dying words were always with him. He'd made the mistake of not taking heed of his mother's wisdom, and the pain had wounded his heart, turned it cold, unyielding.

Do not make the life mistake I made with your father, Silver Wolf. When you find a spirit who will reside forever in your heart, walk as one with her. Stand together and you will find happiness.

Walk as one. Stand together. Chase wondered if there was such a woman for him.

He glanced down at Letty Sue. Certainly, the woman who lay quietly in his arms—the stillness before the storm—wasn't such a woman. Inwardly he scoffed at the notion. Letty Sue was a responsibility he'd rather not have.

She broke the silence with a softly spoken question. "What will you tell Mama about this?"

This? The fact that he was holding the most beautiful woman in the entire territory in his arms and both of them were nearly buck naked? "She doesn't have to know the particulars. We got caught in the storm and waited it out in this supply shack."

Letty Sue let out a compressed breath. "Thank you." Her voice was soft and sweet. She didn't seem the spoiled temptress at the moment, only a cold and exhausted young woman.

He wove his fingers through the long waves of her hair, fanning it out to keep her as dry as possible.

Bringing her closer, he wrapped both arms around her and spoke into her ear. "Don't thank me. I'm not doing it for you. Your mother would be real upset if she found out about this. Might even change her travel plans."

Angry sparks lit Letty Sue's blue eyes like a match to kindling. When she opened her mouth, he muffled any protests she would make with his hand. "Quiet now. It's time we both got some sleep."

She wrestled free and scooted inches away, turning her back on him. Fine by him, he thought. Holding her soft body brought too many unwelcome notions.

Once again, Chase cursed his bad luck.

This woman was trouble. No doubt about it.

It would serve him well to keep his distance. Jo-ellen's daughter was strictly hands-off.

He had a job to do and he wouldn't let Joellen down.

The slightest hint of jasmine, diluted by the scents of earth and of rain, invaded his senses. Letty Sue wiggled deeper into the grain sack, but kept close enough to feel his heat.

And he, hers.

Chase gritted his teeth.

All of a sudden, three months at the Double J sounded like a long stretch of time.

Hell, this was only the first day.

Chapter Two

Joellen set a plate of hot chili in front of him. The spicy aroma made his mouth water. "This is hardly the welcome I'd anticipated for you, Chase."

"It's all right. Nothing like a Texas storm to thwart your plans." He stirred the chili slowly, letting the steam rise up. Glancing at Jasper, then at Joellen, both of whom were watching him intently, he took a spoonful in his mouth. "This sure is good."

"Thank you." Joellen said, facing him across the kitchen table. "It's one of Jasper's favorites. And Letty Sue's. Too bad she isn't joining us for dinner. Appears she's had a tough time today. Good thing you came along when you did, rescuing her from the storm."

He shrugged. The less said the better. He hated lying to Joellen. "Glad to help out."

"You know, Chase, my daughter is…well, at times you might find her…difficult to deal with. I've made it clear to her that your word is gold. She's to abide by your rules while we're gone."

Jasper added, ''I've become quite fond of her myself, but on occasion, and I'm sure my wife won't
mind me saying, Letty Sue can be…well, impetuous.''

Chase hid a smile. ''You don't say?''

''She's a good girl, but she's also headstrong and,
well, you've seen her. I don't think I'm bragging to
say my daughter's a beauty,'' Joellen added.

Chase nodded, not wanting to add that her skin was
soft as silk, her body was created for pleasure and her
sky-blue eyes could render a weaker man completely
helpless.

''That's part of the reason I summoned you here,''
Joellen said.

Chase stopped eating, his spoon in the air. ''I don't
understand.''

''Jasper and I have sold off the majority of our
cattle. It's always been my husband's dream to breed
horses. We're converting the ranch to that end. I knew
you'd be the best one for the job. You have a way
with horses, Chase. Your mother would often boast
to me about your abilities. Not that she had to, since
I've seen them firsthand, but it gave her great joy to
speak of her son so highly. I know we have you only
for the three months we're away. Do you plan to head
back to Seth Johnston's spread when we return?''

''Don't know yet. I left for personal reasons.'' In
truth, Joellen's request for him to work temporarily
at the Double J couldn't have come at a better time.
Marabella's deceit had left him cold inside. He didn't
want to be in the same town as her, much less on the

same ranch. "Johnston understood why I had to leave when I did. He's given me the time off I needed to come here. After that, he expects me to return."

"Then we should be grateful to him. He's letting go a talented man," Jasper said.

"He's a fair man. I've been with him since Snow Cloud died."

Joellen sighed. "I miss your mother, Chase. She and I had become close friends." She turned to Jasper, explaining, "I'd visit her on the reservation whenever I had the opportunity."

"She valued the visits, too," Chase added.

With softness in her eyes, Joellen continued explaining to her husband, "I enjoyed watching this fine man grow up. And later, after his mother was gone, I looked him up whenever I was near Abilene. It was a promise I made to Snow Cloud."

Jasper patted her hand. "And you kept that promise, didn't you?"

"She did," Chase said. "And I, too, valued your friendship."

He didn't say it, but he'd come to think of Joellen Withers as family. She'd been the only white woman who'd cared about him, keeping in touch through letters and rare visits.

Jasper turned to him. "Your horse knowledge was one reason we asked you here. But Joellen had another reason. Want to explain, darling?" Jasper's loving gaze fell on his wife.

Joellen smiled, then drew in a breath. "I'm afraid Letty Sue's too strong-willed for most of the ranch hands here, Chase. She can easily persuade them to do her bidding. That's the other reason I wanted you as foreman—to look after my daughter. I needed someone I could trust, someone a bit older than the boys she's used to.''

''I believe I can handle her.'' Chase had no doubts in that regard. He'd seen Letty Sue in action, had figured her out, and had known her kind before. He wasn't some besotted suitor, willing to allow the woman her way just because she turned her blue eyes in his direction.

''I know you can, Chase, because I can trust you. I'm asking you to watch out for Letty Sue.''

Chase cleared his throat and straightened in his seat. ''You don't have to worry. I'll do my best with the ranch, and with your daughter.''

''I know you will.'' Joellen's smile was wide with relief. ''Well, thank heavens. I feel so much better about leaving her now.''

''Mama?'' Letty Sue stood in the doorway, her eyes darting from her mother's to Jasper's, then settling on Chase. She'd cleaned up and looked well rested. Had it only been a few hours since he'd brought her back to the ranch?

''Letty Sue, I'm glad you decided to join us. Are you feeling better?''

''I am. I, uh, just needed some rest.'' She glanced at Chase, her blue eyes searching his in question. He would just let her stew a bit. She must be dying to know what he'd told Joellen about their encounter this afternoon.

"Are you hungry for dinner now? Come and have a seat. I made your favorite," Joellen said.

Letty Sue sat down next to Chase, in the only available chair. "No, Mama, I'm not at all hungry."

"Poor dear. I guess it was fortunate for you that Chase came along when he did today. I understand Albert's buggy broke a wheel. You would have had to walk all that way back to the ranch in the pouring rain. Whatever did happen to Albert?"

Letty Sue's face flushed ruby-red. She swallowed hard and found her lap real interesting. "Uh, Mama, I, um—"

"He was determined to fix that broken wheel, Joellen. Couldn't talk him out of it," Chase explained.

Letty Sue fixed her startled gaze on him. "Yes. Yes, that's right, Mama."

"Oh, well, I suppose he made it back to town all right then."

"I don't expect we'll be seeing much of him for a while," Chase added, rubbing his jaw.

"Really? Why is that?" Joellen asked.

"Uh," he began, capturing Letty Sue's wide-eyed, fearful expression. "I imagine the man's caught himself one heck of a chill." He raised his eyebrows at Letty Sue. She froze, sending him a stony look. Chase cleared his throat. "What with trudging all the way back to town in the downpour."

"Oh, dear. Maybe we'd better check on him before we leave, Jasper," Joellen said, deeply concerned.

"No!" Letty Sue exclaimed, shaking her head. "I

mean…I think Albert's going to be just fine, Mama. Really, there's no need.''

Chase kept his expression blank. ''I agree. Men don't usually like to be coddled. He'll be fine. You and Jasper have more important matters to tend to. You're leaving day after tomorrow, isn't that right?''

''Yes, that's right. We're almost all packed. And Jasper and I have some details to go over with you about the running of the ranch. Tonight you'll bed down in our sparc room, but I'm afraid, once we're gone, you're going to have to sleep in the bunkhouse.''

Chase glanced at Letty Sue. The ruby-red color singed her cheeks once again. She was a beauty who could tempt a man to distraction, so how on earth was it possible the woman was still as innocent as a newborn foal? Yet he'd bet his bottom dollar that she was. ''Wouldn't have it any other way.''

Jasper stood and slapped him gently on the back. ''Good, then let's retire to the parlor and have us a smoke. We'll go over those details Joellen was referring to.''

Chase raised up from his chair, but not before casting one more glance Letty Sue's way. ''Night, Letty Sue.''

In a haughty tone, Letty Sue replied, ''Good night, Mr. Wheeler.''

Letty Sue bristled in her bed. Oh, that man, she thought scornfully, he'd loved making her squirm tonight at the supper table. For one frantic moment, she thought he'd told her mother the truth about what had happened with Albert.

That would have been disastrous.

But in the end, Chase had concealed the truth, making up that story about the buggy breaking down.

Still and all, she didn't trust him. He was too sure of himself, a bit too confident.

Letty Sue had been reduced to receiving his aid in a most undignified manner this afternoon—wearing that scratchy grain sack and having his hands on her, rubbing her limbs back to life. She'd shivered so fiercely from the cold, her brains had nearly rattled inside her head.

Yet he'd been kind to her and he had warmed her. His touch was gentle and sure and, Letty Sue admitted grudgingly, better than anything she'd ever experienced with Albert.

Chase Wheeler's hands, filled with strength and tenderness, had made her tingle with warmth almost from the first moment they'd caressed her skin. She closed her eyes now, recalling how he'd made her feel—soft, feminine, womanly.

A thought filtered in: he'd be a wonderful lover....

Letty Sue! Your brains must be rattled today. He's a half-breed, this side of savage, and not at all the man for you!

She punched her pillow and shifted in bed. Besides, she thought bitterly, he doesn't even like you.

And she certainly didn't like him, either.

* * *

The next two days sped by faster than stampeding cattle. With Jasper and Joellen's chest packed, all details taken care of on the ranch and Chase Wheeler firmly in place as foreman, Letty Sue said a tearful goodbye to her mother. They stood on the sidewalk in Sweet Springs in front of the stagecoach that would deliver the newlyweds to the railroad station in Fort Worth. There, the journey would truly begin, and her mother would return East for the first time since she was a small child.

"Oh, Mama. I do hope you'll have a great experience, but I'm going to miss you so much." Letty Sue hugged her tightly, reluctant to end the embrace.

"Letty Sue, darling, I'm going to miss you, too."

Letty Sue tugged her lower lip in, contemplating. "Maybe one day soon you'll see fit to let me do some traveling on my own, Mama. I've dreamed of it thousands of times."

Joellen chuckled. "Letty Sue, you do exaggerate. I'm going to miss that, and so much more." Her mother's expression changed then, and taking Letty Sue's hands, she said, "We'll see. But darling, you're in the best of hands with Chase Wheeler. I want you to honor the promise you made me…that you'll not give that man one ounce of trouble. He's a fine man, admirable and trustworthy. He deserves your respect."

Letty Sue flinched, hearing her mother speak more highly of Chase than she ever had of her. "Mama, please. Let's not go over this again. I made the promise. Now, you have to promise me something—that you'll wire me whenever you have the opportunity. I want to hear about everything you do, everywhere you go.''

"I promise, darling. You'll be hearing from me often.'' She glanced down the street. "Well, then, I guess this is goodbye. Looks like Jasper is heading over here with Chase. The driver is ready to go.''

"Oh Mama, you do look lovely in your new blue traveling suit.'' Suppressing the tears threatening to flow, Letty Sue watched as her mother climbed into the stagecoach. She managed a big smile for Joellen's sake, but her mind whirled, contemplating the day she'd be getting on that stage herself.

Jasper reached her then, gave her a big bear hug and wished her well. She returned his embrace and sighed. "Take care of my mother. Please.''

Jasper's eyes met hers as he cast her the fatherly smile, warm and loving, she was becoming accustomed to. At times Letty Sue believed the man actually cared for her. "I shall, Letty Sue. You know how much your mother means to me. You take care, too, and listen to Chase, here.'' His gaze fell on Chase, who was talking with the stage driver. "Three months won't seem like any time at all, I'm sure.''

Letty Sue ignored that statement, turning once again to her mother. "Bye, Mother. I love you.''

Joellen blew her a kiss from inside the stage. "I love you, too, Leticia Suzanne.''

Chase came up to stand beside her. Letty Sue felt his presence—the quiet, calm, commanding man who would now run the Double J. "Enjoy your trip,'' he said to Jasper, shaking his hand. "And Joellen," Chase said with a sly wink, "don't you worry about a thing."

Joellen smiled widely, deepening the fine crinkles around her eyes. "Thank you, Chase." She waved to them both as the stagecoach pulled away.

Letty Sue and Chase stood there watching until the dust settled and the stagecoach was completely out of sight. "Leticia Suzanne?" he finally asked, rubbing his jaw in a pitiful attempt to hide a grin.

"Yes, that's my formal name. Is something wrong with it?" She lifted her chin.

"No, no. It's a fine name, I suppose. 'Course, if you were Cheyenne, you'd have a much different name."

"I'm sure I would," she said, feeling forlorn, as if she'd just been abandoned by her mother. But she had to admit Chase had her curiosity sparked. "What... would it be?"

Chase took her arm and guided her toward the buckboard wagon they'd come to town in. "Brave Spirited Raven."

"Brave Spirited Raven," she repeated, testing the name on her lips. She wasn't sure she liked it. She'd thought a name such as White Dove might have been more appropriate, or Graceful Doe. Silly of her to even be thinking of Cheyenne names, anyway. "Why?"

Chase stopped and turned to her. He lifted a lock of her hair, studying it with his smoky silver eyes. "Your hair is the color of a raven's, you've just done your darnedest to be brave, and you have a child's spirit.''

''Oh, is that a compliment?''

''Depends.''

''What does it depend on?''

''On whether the child's spirit is noble or spoiled and selfish.''

She stood in the street utterly at a loss for words. She watched him press forward, noting *his* noble gait, the strength of his broad back, and hoping for the oddest reason, one she couldn't at all name, that he didn't view her as a young, spoiled child.

When he reached the wagon, he turned to her, putting out his hand. A crooked smile graced his face. ''You coming, Miss Leticia Suzanne?''

She allowed him to help her up, feeling the heat of his touch on her waist. A touch that elicited a sharp memory of being in that supply shack with him three days ago, his hands roaming over her near naked body, warming her to the very bone.

Once seated as far from him as possible on the buckboard, she tossed back her hair and huffed, ''It's Letty Sue to you, Mr. Wheeler.''

The man reared his head back and laughed.

Chapter Three

Letty Sue ran out of her house the minute she saw her best friend climb down from her buggy. "Sally Henderson, you're a sight for my blistered eyes! I'm so glad you came to visit. It's been dreadfully lonely out here."

Sally grinned and the two hugged. "Your mother's been gone one week, Letty Sue. How lonely can you be with all these men around to keep you company?" Sally was forever teasing Letty Sue about her string of suitors.

"I need female company, Sally. I need my best friend. Oh, I'm so glad you came." She slipped her arm through Sally's and headed toward the house.

"I'm sorry I didn't come sooner, but little Elias took sick and I had to nurse him to health. I think he was part faking it. He hates going to school, and sometimes I think he'll do anything not to go."

"Your little brother sure is a devil. I caught him one time down by the creek, fishing. When I asked him why he wasn't in school, he lied to me flat out and said Miss Wheaton gave them all the day off. I *know* Miss Wheaton would never have done that, as dedicated as she is to her students' education.''

''Elias sure did get a whipping for that one, Letty Sue, when Father found out about it. Elias was too darn proud of the dozen fish he'd caught, and boasted to the entire family.''

''Oh, sometimes I envy your big family, Sally. I can't imagine having seven brothers and sisters.''

Sally agreed. ''Yes, sometimes it's real nice. I won't speak of the times it isn't so wonderful.''

Loud whoops and hurrahs coming from the corral caught their attention. Both women stopped and turned to see what was causing the commotion. Double J ranch hands lined the fence, waving their hats and cheering, commending a rider for taming the stallion known as Tornado.

Chase Wheeler rode the horse with smooth agility, murmuring soft words of encouragement and patting his mane. Once he'd brought the stallion to a dead halt, he slid down to the ground and slowly handed the rope to Sam Fowler. The stallion shied away from Sam, looking toward Chase, who stroked the horse once again, with a skillfulness and calm that could only be due to his Cheyenne heritage. Within minutes, Chase had earned Tornado's trust and brought Sam into the circle of trust, as well. Sam led the horse away, and Chase dusted off his chaps.

Sally let out a deep sigh. ''Oh my, so that's the new foreman the whole town's been talking about. He's absolutely divine, Letty Sue.''

Letty Sue flinched. "He's not divine, Sally. Why he's downright...difficult."

Sally kept her eyes focused on the man across the yard. "Don't you dare tell me you haven't noticed how positively handsome he is."

"Handsome? Sally, are you blind? Why, he's... he's nearly a savage."

Sally inhaled deeply. "Why yes, my friend. He's all man. Not like those dapper gents with the three-piece suits and bowler hats you seem to prefer."

"So I like a man of refinement. When I marry, I'd like my husband to be cultured. You know—someone uncomfortable with mud on his boots."

"Letty Sue, you can have just about any man in Sweet Springs you want. Isn't that good enough for you?"

Letty Sue sighed. "I want to see something of the world, Sally."

"Oh, I bet your new foreman could take you places you've never ever been before."

"Sally!"

Her friend chuckled, lifting her hand to her mouth. "That was completely sinful of me, wasn't it?"

"Yes, it was," Letty Sue answered, giggling. "But that's why you're my best friend."

"So, did you invite him to the church social next week?"

"Heavens no. Chase Wheeler isn't the type for church socials. Believe me, he wouldn't go."

Sally watched Chase close the corral gate. "Oh my, looks like he's heading this way. I'm going to ask

him, Letty Sue. I swear, I'm going to ask him.''
Sally's voice nearly squeaked with eagerness.

"Don't you dare," Letty Sue cautioned. But it was
too late. Sally had that determined look in her eye.
Letty Sue didn't want Sally to be turned down
harshly, but at least she had tried to warn her.

Chase took off his black hat, swiped at his forehead
and smiled at Sally when he approached. "Afternoon,
ladies."

Letty Sue was forced to make introductions.
"Chase Wheeler, I'd like you to meet my friend Sally
Henderson. Sally, Chase is the *temporary* foreman of
the Double J while Mama is gone."

Chase didn't let her comment bother him. At least,
his expression didn't change, she noted. He continued
to smile at Sally. "Pleased to meet you, Miss Henderson."

"It's just Sally," she gushed.

"Sally," he repeated with a smile and a nod.

"I came out to visit Letty Sue. I'm teaching her
how to bake a pecan pie this afternoon. She's got to
put together a basket for the church social next week.
You are going, aren't you?"

"Wasn't planning on it," he answered, his silvery
eyes meeting Letty Sue's. "Didn't know a thing
about it."

"Oh, well, consider yourself invited, Mr. Wheeler.
The whole town usually comes out. We have games,
music, and we auction off the lunch baskets. Whoever
wins the bid for a particular basket lunches with the

woman who made it up. I always tie a big red-and-white ribbon on my basket, and set a flower on top.''

''Sounds real pretty.'' He smiled at Sally before returning his gaze to Letty Sue. ''And how do you prepare your basket?''

''I, uh, Mama usually ties bows all along the handle.''

''They call it the rainbow basket,'' Sally interjected, '''cause Joellen uses ribbons from all the colors of the rainbow. Everybody in town knows it's Letty Sue's basket. You can't miss it. It goes for the highest price.''

''I see,'' he said. ''Well, I'll have to think about going. Got a whole lot of work to do here. Don't know if I can spare the time.''

''Oh, you have to come!'' Sally's face flushed a rosy hue.

Chase grinned, his dark eyes gleaming. ''Maybe I will.''

Sally returned his smile and stared at him.

Letty Sue twisted her mouth. She wasn't going to stand there while Chase Wheeler flirted shamelessly with Sally. And Sally...why, Letty Sue had never seen her act so bold.

''Mr. Wheeler, did you have a reason for coming over here?'' Even to her ears, she sounded rather shrewish.

Chase continued to smile. Nothing seemed to daunt that man, she thought with annoyance. How often she'd tried. ''I came over to tell you I'll be late getting in this evening. I have to ride out to a ranch on the other side of the county to check out their stock. I'll see you when I get back.''

Letty Sue felt Sally's eyes on her. She still couldn't tamp down her irritation. And heaven only knew what Sally was thinking right now. "All right. Is that all?"

He shot her a wide grin. "Yes, ma'am. That's all.''

When he turned to leave, Sally chirped, "Don't forget the church social, Mr. Wheeler.''

He spun around and nodded. "You know, I think I just might find the time. Pleasure meeting you, Miss Sally.''

"Nice meeting you, too, Mr. Wheeler.''

"Call me Chase,'' he said, shooting a quick glance at Letty Sue. She returned his glance with a frown and watched him saunter back to the corral.

"Oh, my, Letty Sue,'' Sally said, taking her arm and leading her into the house. "My heart's never going to be the same.''

Letty Sue rolled her eyes. Sally was forever falling for the wrong man. "Never mind your heart, Sally. Chase Wheeler can only do it damage.''

"I'd be willing to chance it, Letty Sue. Why, he's the most appealing man that's come to Sweet Springs since I can remember.''

"You know what's more appealing to me, Sally? Your baking skills. I'm relying on you to show me which end of a fry pan is up.''

That evening, Sam Fowler sat next to Letty Sue on the porch swing, sipping coffee. Luminous bright stars filled the sky and the Texas night air was delightfully warm. "You're getting better at brewing this stuff, Letty Sue. Doesn't have a bitter edge to it this time." Sam glanced into his cup.

"Oh, Sam," Letty Sue began, "I should let you believe that my culinary skills are improving, but the truth is, Sally brewed that coffee just before she left an hour ago. She tried her best to teach me how to bake a pecan pie, but my crust flopped."

Sam chuckled, bringing out a dimple at each corner of his mouth. His boyish charm and friendly manner were like a soothing balm to her woes. Aside from Sally, Sam was her best friend, and he knew her just about as well as anybody ever could. "So, your crust flopped. How does that happen?"

"I don't know exactly, Sam." Letty Sue recalled carefully watching everything Sally did, while half listening to her instructions. How difficult could baking a pie be, after all? But while Sally's flaky crust took on a fine golden color, hers resembled a hard-shelled armadillo. Sally said she'd overworked the dough—that making a crust was tricky and you had to have just the right touch.

"But when I was all through," Letty Sue lamented, "my dress was a mess, my hair was dusted with flour, making me appear about as old as ancient Rowena Eldridge, and worst of all, my pie tasted like mush. Brittle crust, soft center." She threw her hands up in despair. "I don't think I was created for such things, Sam. I'm not good in the kitchen."

Once again, Sam laughed lightly and set his coffee

mug down. He took her hands in his. "Letty Sue, I think you can do whatever you set your mind to do."

She pursed her lips, still feeling a bit like a failure. "I have to learn, Sam. All the other girls know these things, and Mama just won't take me seriously. She still thinks of me as a child."

Sam's brown eyes softened, going about as mushy as Letty Sue's pecan pie filling. "Ah, Letty Sue. It'll come to you. Just be patient."

She smiled then, feeling a surge of newfound confidence. "You know I treasure your friendship, Sam. You're my best friend here at the ranch. I'm so lonely with Mama gone. Thank goodness I have you." She kissed his cheek.

He patted her hand. "It's just hard being friends with such a lovely woman, Letty Sue. Kinda makes a man wonder 'what if'."

She shifted in her seat to look him square in the eyes. "One day soon, Sam, we'll both find what we're looking for."

"I hope so, Letty Sue. Sure wouldn't like to see you disappointed. Sometimes what we go hunting for is right before our eyes. Kinda jumps up at you faster than a rattler looking for his next meal. And to think your mama didn't have to go far to find Jasper Brody. He came to her. He's a fine man."

"I suppose," Letty Sue allowed, "but that was different. He was searching for his long-lost niece. When he found Lily here in Sweet Springs, he decided to stay on."

"A lucky day for him. Your mama makes him mighty happy."

"Mama is a wonderful woman. Don't remind me or I'll start missing her all over again."

With their coffee finished, they sat in companionable silence, a soft spring breeze blowing by as the porch swing swayed gently. Letty Sue let her mind drift off to all the cities she planned to visit, all the new exciting things waiting for her.

"Evening, Sam, Letty Sue." An all-too-familiar deep voice interrupted her pleasing thoughts.

"Evening, Chase," Sam said, straightening a bit in the swing.

Letty Sue nodded.

"I came by to check on Letty Sue," he said, focusing his attention on Sam.

"Yes, sir."

"I'm fine, as you can see. Visiting with my good friend Sam," Letty Sue offered airily.

Chase leaned on the porch rail and said sternly, "It's late, Letty Sue. Best you get inside."

Anger jolted through her instantly. The audacity of the man, she thought heatedly, treating her no better than a disobedient child. She was bone-tired of being treated that way. Especially from him! She jumped up from the swing. "Don't you dare issue me an order, Chase Wheeler. I won't have it."

Sam stood then and turned to her. "He's right, Letty Sue. It's a bit late and sun up will come mighty quick if I don't hit the sack soon. Thanks for the coffee."

"But Sam—"

"Good night." He cast a quick, indulgent smile her way, then headed down the porch steps and past Chase, wishing him a pleasant evening as well. Oh, Letty Sue was ready to bash her frying pan over Chase Wheeler's obstinate head! Or better yet, an armadillo pie to his face would do nicely!

"Lock the door behind you now." He waited, his patient stance more irritating than the calm in his eyes, telling her he fully expected her to obey.

"You're not my keeper, Chase," she said, folding her arms across her middle. Chase's gaze dropped to her chest, puffed out now in righteous indignation. There was a flicker of awareness in those smoky depths that gave Letty Sue a measure of satisfaction.

"Until Joellen returns, I'm afraid I am. Now get yourself inside."

Letty Sue inhaled deeply, her eyes on his, locked in a stubborn battle. Finally, Letty Sue relented. She was tired, mostly of his commanding ways, so she entered the house, slamming the door behind her.

Anger roiled in the pit of her stomach. She put a hand there to stop the commotion. Being bullied by the ranch foreman, a virtual stranger, didn't set well. It just wasn't fair.

As she made her way to the parlor, she glanced into the kitchen, noting the mess from this afternoon. Flour speckled the floor, the counter and the chairs. The utensils she'd used today were still soaking in a tub of water, and there on the table, looking quite pitiful, sat her pecan pie of stone.

She groaned aloud. This evening couldn't get much worse. Her stomach clenched once again and she knew she'd not get a wink of sleep tonight, not until she made some sort of truce with Chase Wheeler.

But in her heart of hearts, she knew she'd most likely have better luck making a pact with the devil himself.

The stallion was in a feisty mood tonight, Chase surmised, taking a brush briskly to Tornado's coat. He murmured soft words, earning the animal's trust once again. "No hoof pick for you this evening," Chase offered soothingly to the chestnut stallion. "I wouldn't enjoy taking a swift kick to the ribs. You're a bit too jittery for my liking. Sort of like me tonight, right, big fella?"

By the time Tornado gleamed from his ministrations, Chase had worked up a sweat. He tossed off his shirt, letting the cool air hit his chest. He needed cooling down, he thought wryly, but not from the work he'd done currying the fine animal. Hell, Chase was always honest with himself.

He needed to cool off more from seeing Letty Sue tonight than from any brushing he'd done to Tornado. It had bothered him to catch her sitting so cozily on the porch swing with Sam Fowler earlier. More than he liked to admit.

The woman was completely female, with a body that practically begged for a man's touch and a face so damn near perfection it muddled the mind. Chase didn't like her; she was spoiled and selfish and completely useless on the ranch. It'd be best to remember that.

He closed the gate to Tornado's stall and hung up the grooming brushes on a peg inside the tack room. The musty barn smells of leather, earth and animals suddenly took on a pleasing hint of fragrant jasmine. Chase whirled around instantly and saw her.

Letty Sue stood in the doorway to the small tack room, wearing a lacy blue dress and a tentative smile.

The dress hugged every curve the woman possessed and matched the brilliant hue of her bright, sky-blue eyes. Her smile, though, was less than bright and her lips trembled. "Hello again, Chase." Her voice held a note of trepidation.

"Letty Sue," he said warily, attempting to figure out what plan the woman was devising. Women like Letty Sue always had a plan. He'd learned that hard lesson not long ago. Marabella had used him for her own gain, then tossed him aside once he'd served his purpose. He'd been a fool for hooking up with the boss's relation to begin with, and actually believing he might have a future with the woman. He'd not make that mistake again.

No more tangling with beautiful, tempting, deceitful women. It was a vow he intended to keep.

"Can we talk?" Letty Sue asked.

"It's late."

"I don't think I can sleep."

His jaw clenched and he was about to refuse when she added, "It won't take but a minute of your time."

He gestured to a bench along the wall. "Come in."

The small room was darker than most, since there were no windows to let in the moonlight. He brought a lantern over to hang above them. "Have a seat."

"Thank you." She sat down, adjusting the folds of her dress. Her eyes sparkled like blue diamonds as the lantern light caressed her face. And her scent, of fresh jasmine, filled the air.

Chase sat down, too. He still didn't know what she was up to.

She gasped, glancing at his bare chest. The light hit his scars in such a way that made them stand out even more harshly. He'd forgotten how frightening they must look to a woman with delicate sensibilities.

"H-how did you get those?"

Her gaze traveled up to his and for the very first time since he'd known her, he saw undeniable compassion in her eyes. "In a Cheyenne ritual."

Surprise registered on her face, immediately marking their inherent differences. "But—"

"As I said, Letty Sue, it's late, so say what you came here to say."

She concealed her anger, but Chase sensed it. "I don't like you giving me orders. This is my ranch, not yours. And you don't have to tuck me in every night."

Chase hid his grin by rubbing the stubble on his face. "Tuck you in? Honey, if I tucked you in every night, you'd not be in here complaining."

She blinked, then comprehended his meaning. "Oh! You know that's not what I meant. You don't have to make sure I'm locked in the house at night."

"Interrupted something with Sam tonight, did I?"

"No, of course not. Sam's my friend. It's just that, well, I'm not a child, Chase. I can take care of myself."

He didn't think so, but wasn't going to argue the point. "I promised your mother I'd watch out for you."

"I know. Mama's always been overprotective. Ever since father was murdered, and, uh, the other attack."

"You were both very brave." He braced his elbows on his knees and leaned forward, shaking his head. "That must have left you with some bad memories."

She became thoughtful, tilting her head, heaving a heavy sigh. Her voice was soft, sweet. "I was very young. I don't remember much. Mama was the brave one."

"She's a special woman."

"I never thanked you properly."

"No need, Letty Sue." He straightened to look into her eyes. "I'd do it again if I had to."

"You went against your own kind."

"Dog Soldiers weren't my kind. They were ruthless renegades out for revenge. Both white men and Indians have been brutal at times, but my Cheyenne mother always taught me that violence wasn't the answer. She'd hoped for peace, had trusted in the Cheyenne and white leaders to come to terms. But that really never happened, did it?"

Letty Sue shook her head. "I don't know."

"I do," he said adamantly. "There are Indians dying of starvation and disease on the reservations."

"Oh Chase...your mother?"

"She didn't suffer long. For that I'm grateful."

"I'm sorry. If anything happened to Mama I don't know what I'd do."

"And she feels the same way. You're her only daughter, her only child. I'm here to see to your safety."

"Can't we come to a truce of some kind?"

"A truce?"

"Yes. I'm tired of all the fighting. I want you to treat me like the woman I am, and not as a child."

He took a leisurely tour of her body with his eyes, and thought of dozens of ways to treat her as a woman. But that was out of the question. Letty Sue Withers with the bright blue eyes and pretty face was completely off-limits.

"Okay."

"Okay?" She sounded astonished.

"If you behave like a grown-up, then I'll treat you that way. I won't *tuck* you in at night, but I will check your doors. Just be sure to lock up carefully before you turn in. If you go into town or to a neighboring ranch, let someone know, if I'm not around. And no more *Albert* incidences."

Letty Sue blushed, but held her head high. "That was not entirely my fault."

"Humph."

"Do we have a truce?" she asked quickly, obviously not intending to rehash the day they'd met.

"We have a truce." He stood up and put a hand out to help her up.

"A truce," she repeated, taking the hand offered and rising up to stand close to him. He released her hand slowly, their eyes meeting.

"Will you tell me about the scars now?" Her gaze fastened on his chest, softening as she looked at his wounds.

"They're from the sun dance. It's believed that performing the ritual will bring revitalization to the earth around us. The tribe builds a sun dance lodge with a tall pole in the center, topped with buffalo robes celebrating our most respected warriors. After the lodge is blessed and prayers are offered to the Great Spirit, the dance begins."

Letty Sue reached out and touched a scar on the right side of his chest. Her delicate fingers slid over its length, her gaze focused on the place her fingers traveled. She said softly, "But that doesn't explain these."

Immediate heat shot through him and his body tightened. Her innocent touch created an unwelcome stirring in his blood, a potent flame he could only name as fierce desire. He should back away, tell her to leave, anything that would take her hand away. Yet he didn't. Instead he endured the torture of having her caress him. "After four days, young Cheyenne men engage in a ceremony thought to arouse the pity of the spirits. Sharpened skewers are hooked under the skin on different parts of the body. It's a display proving Cheyenne bravery and endurance."

"It sounds very painful." She outlined each scar, staring at them intently.

"It's meant to be."

"I didn't notice them the day of the storm, when we were in the supply shack."

Chase closed his eyes briefly, trying to block out vivid, arousing images of lying with her and holding her in his arms. But he could almost feel her skin under his palms now, and the recollection became stronger each time Letty Sue fingered one of his scars. "In the shadows, they blend in with my skin."

"Hmm," she said, lifting her sparkling blue gaze to his. Her eyes filled with passion, a hunger he was sure she wouldn't really want satisfied, innocent as she was.

He grabbed her wrist, meaning to shove her away, but instead flattened her hand to his chest. The jolt sent his senses flying, and blazing hot fire flamed from under her palm.

She whispered his name so softly, he barely heard her. "Chase."

Chapter Four

Letty Sue had never felt such power, such strength in a man before. His bronzed chest, smooth and sleek, exuded pure natural masculinity. She brought her other hand up to touch his skin, hot now, matching the blazing warmth in his eyes.

"Don't play games, Letty Sue," he whispered harshly.

Her hands seemed to move of their own accord, slowly and tentatively, over the muscles of his chest. And when her finger slid over one smooth, flattened disk, Chase inhaled sharply.

She couldn't fathom what was happening inside her head or her body. Every fiber of her being wanted him. And a deep, low burn of longing settled in her belly. She shook her head. "That's just it...I don't think this is a game."

She was inexplicably drawn to him, rather like a moth to a flame. And like the moth, if she got too close, she'd surely get burned. Yet she'd never known another man like him, so confident, so impossibly virile and strong. And he'd been right that day at the creek when he'd first arrived, saying she hadn't known a real man, not until now. She stood there, wanting his touch, wanting so much for him to kiss her, yet knowing all the while nothing good could come of it.

"Easing the lust of our bodies won't change a thing."

Stunned by his boldness, Letty Sue asked tentatively, "L-lust?"

"That's all it is. I could take you, right now, in this room, but in the end we'd both be sorry."

"But I—"

"You'd best get back to the house," he commanded sharply.

She yanked her hands off his chest and nodded, dropping her gaze to the ground. She couldn't look at him—her pride wouldn't allow it. He was turning her away. A rush of humiliating heat coursed through her. She hoped it wasn't evident on her face.

She brushed by him, heading for the door, but his hand snaked out and grabbed her wrist gently. His eyes, hard as gunmetal now, pierced hers intently. "Letty Sue," he said almost too calmly, "you and I barely tolerate each other. We come from different worlds, want different things. I made a promise to your mother and I don't intend to…"

"What, Chase? What don't you intend?"

His long silence unnerved her. She made a move to remove her wrist from his grasp. He held firm and his gaze roamed over every inch of her, appreciation evident as his eyes caressed each curve of her body. Small consolation, she thought.

Chase released a breath. "Truce or no truce, it'd be best if we kept our distance."

"I see," she said quietly. She tilted her head to one side and attempted to smile. She meant nothing to him. But then, why should she? She was a thorn in his side. He had a ranch to run and didn't need a troublesome woman around, causing havoc. He didn't like her, and now she understood just how much. This time, when she yanked, he released her arm. "You're right, of course. We are worlds apart." She hoisted up her chin, recovering her pride. "And I'm suddenly very tired. I'm going to bed, and I suggest you do the same. But don't forget about our truce, Chase Wheeler. From now on, you treat me like an adult, the woman that I am."

Chase scratched his head and cast her a look that said he'd just treated her like a woman and look where that had got them. There was a hint of sympathy in his eyes, and another emotion as well. It was something she never thought she'd elicit from him. Pity.

"Letty Sue."

"Good night, Chase," she said, and with head held high, walked out of the tack room.

Chase rode Tornado hard, testing the stallion's strength, his endurance. There wasn't a better horse on the ranch, and Tornado appeared more than willing to prove it. After riding out quite a ways, Chase brought the horse to a slow trot, giving them both a respite. He checked the line fences on the southern end of the property, looking for damage—a section down or an area where the barbed wire wasn't fastened properly.

He found Sam Fowler working on a broken fence. Chase dismounted, ground tethering Tornado. When the horse didn't take flight, Chase felt immense pride. Taming the stallion hadn't been as hard as he'd thought.

But taming one wayward woman had Chase warring with emotions so perplexing he couldn't piece together two consistent thoughts. Conflicting battles waged inside his head. Letty Sue made it clear she wanted to be treated as a woman, and Chase knew dozens of ways to satisfy her in that regard.

But he'd made a pledge to Joellen, and one thing Chase Wheeler had never done was go back on his word. And as womanly as Letty Sue was on the outside, with her enticing body and beckoning blue eyes, Chase feared she really didn't know her own mind. She was a true child at heart, playing at being a woman.

"Howdy, Chase," Sam called out.

"Sam." Chase walked over and inspected the downed fence. "Need some help here?"

"Sure wouldn't refuse a hand." Sam struggled to lift the heavy fence post. Chase braced the post from below, and the two managed to ease it upright. "Got it," Sam announced.

Chase held it firm.

Sam took a large hammer and pounded it in, until the post was steady. "Much obliged." He removed his gloves, using them to wipe the sweat from his forehead. "Got three more broken sections down the line a piece."

"Well, let's get to them."

Sam smiled and nodded. "Appreciate it."

They mounted up and slowly ambled along the fence line. The blazing sun beat down hard, the way everything seemed to happen here in this rugged land. Nothing subtle about Texas, Chase thought. The majority of the land was wild, free and formidable, just the way he liked it. He lowered the brim of his hat, fighting off sunlight.

"Heard you met Sally Henderson the other day," Sam said, twisting a long strand of switchgrass in his mouth.

"Sure did."

"She invite you to the church social?"

"She did. I'm thinking about going," Chase said.

"Sally's great. Got loads of brothers and sisters. One of her brothers married a sweet young gal. She's part Indian. Family embraced her like a cowboy throwing his best loop. They sorta roped her right in. Know what I mean? "

Chase slanted him a look.

"And well, I know Sally…she'd take to you right fine. You gonna bid on her lunch basket?"

"Sam," Chase said evenly, "you been skirting around something worse than a saloon girl doing a jig. Say it outright or don't say it at all."

Sam tossed his reed of switchgrass away and eyed Chase. "All right. I'm bidding on Letty Sue's basket. I outbid everyone for the past five years. Just thought I'd warn you."

Chase chuckled. "How'd you stomach her food?"

A wry grin crossed over Sam's face. "You know about her cooking?"

"Word gets around."

Sam's lips twitched. "Joellen usually does up the basket for the church social. But it don't matter. I'd bid on Letty Sue's basket if there was nothing in it."

"Might be a safer choice for your gut."

"Yeah," he agreed. "But still, it's been my honor for as long as I've known her, and I'd like it to stay that way."

Chase nodded. "Won't get an argument from me. Letty Sue know how you feel?"

Sam's eyebrows lifted, nearly meeting his hairline, as he met Chase's gaze head-on. "And how's that?"

Chase shrugged. "Man's willing to risk his stomach for a lady. Means something, I'd say."

"We're friends. Good friends."

Chase nodded.

"Fact is, she thinks she's going to find happiness traveling the world."

"And you know better?"

"Yeah, I know Letty Sue. She doesn't know it, but she's a Texan, through and through. She'd never be happy off the ranch. It was her and her Mama for so long. Letty Sue's only dreaming, but it ain't real."

"And you aim to prove it to her?"

"I hope to rid her of all them fancy notions. Yeah."

"I wish you luck."

He let out a self-chastising chuckle. "That woman curls her finger and I come running. I'd say I'd need more luck than a gambler holding four aces."

Chase's smile was quick. "She's got that effect on a corralful of men."

"You included?" Sam asked with genuine interest.

Chase shook his head. "I'm foreman, Sam. It wouldn't set kindly with Joellen for me to tangle with her daughter, now would it?"

"Don't suppose, but Letty Sue has a way about her."

Chase reined in Tornado when they reached the next downed fence post. "She does at that, Sam. But you're the one bidding on her lunch basket, remember?"

"I remember. Just hope the rest of the male population of Sweet Springs doesn't forget it, you included."

Chase twisted his lips, battling off a grin. "Not me, Sam. I have a great memory."

Letty Sue mopped her forehead with her sleeve. The kitchen was hot from all the smoke filling the air, created by her last attempt at making a pie. She'd tried three times, and each time something different went wrong.

Either the crust burned or the filling did. The last time, as she was pulling the pie out of the cookstove, the whole thing slid out of her hands and made a giant pecan mess on the floor. It took her the better part of an hour to clean it up.

She wasn't cut out for household chores, but

darned if she wasn't determined to change that. Her mind drifted to Jasper and Joellen having a grand old time in New York. Her mother had sent a wire just yesterday saying that very thing.

Letty Sue dreamed of the day she'd be allowed to travel, to see new sights, enjoy citified life and know something of culture and refinement. She'd been too long on the ranch, and now that Mama had remarried, it would be her turn.

Soon, she thought, she would have her chance.

And she'd not have to dwell on the likes of Chase Wheeler.

Her rational mind knew he'd been right to cast her off last night. She'd been swept up in the moment, her heart overriding her good sense. Seeing those scars on his chest and feeling his massive strength had done something to her, affecting her in a way she'd never been before.

A river of compassion had flooded her senses as she'd realized what Chase had endured, how he'd lived, how his mother had died. She'd let herself become immersed in him, in the intimacy of the quiet small room, in the way he'd spoken to her. But then he'd turned her away.

Letty Sue hadn't had much experience with rejection. It was new to her. She'd not met a man like Chase Wheeler before. It would be better for both if they kept their distance.

Let Sally have him.

The thought brought a jolt to her insides—a powerful jolt.

She shook her head and banished all thought of Chase Wheeler. He perplexed her overly much. Right now she had to concentrate on cooking. Sally had suggested she start with something easy.

Biscuits.

How hard could it be to make sour milk biscuits?

Letty Sue arranged all the ingredients on the counter: flour, salt, baking powder and soda, sugar and sweet milk soured by a few drops of lemon juice. After measuring carefully, she dumped everything into a large bowl and began to stir. The dough began to take shape, and Letty Sue smiled for the first time today.

She pulled the dough out onto a floured board and kneaded it, pounding with her fists, then rolled it to a one-inch thickness, just like Sally's recipe called for. Once satisfied, Letty Sue took a coffee cup and inverted it onto the dough to cut circles. Yes, they actually looked liked biscuits.

With a contented sigh, Letty Sue opened the cookstove door, ready to bake the biscuits. Intense heat and smoke came rushing out, choking her. She blinked and coughed, but before she could back away, licking flames from the overly hot oven swirled up and caught her apron.

Letty Sue flung the biscuit pan up in the air, letting out a horrified scream.

She was on fire!

Chapter Five

Chase heard Letty Sue's screams as he stepped outside the barn. He whirled around quickly, seeing a flaming flash whiz by the parlor window. He blinked, adjusting to the sunlight, not truly believing his eyes. Then he took off running.

Hell and damnation! Letty Sue was on fire!

Chase raced to the front door within seconds, yanking hard. The door wouldn't budge. It was bolted from the inside. With no time to spare, he picked up a twisted vine chair on the porch and tossed it through the window, shattering glass everywhere. He dove in headfirst, somehow managing to land on his feet. She let out another boisterous scream right before he tackled her, knocking her to the floor.

He grabbed her tightly, unmindful of the penetrating heat, and rolled her over and over. Their bodies hit the wall, then the fireplace hearth, then the wall again. He spun her until the fiery flames died, leaving the scent of scorched clothing in their wake.

He wound up with Letty Sue beneath him on the

floor. Her breaths came rapidly, her chest heaving. He held her close, trying to quell her trembling. Fear filled her eyes, and amazement.

Smoke fumes billowed up from her clothes, but as Chase looked her over carefully, he didn't believe the flames had touched her skin. While most men hated all the undergarments, petticoats and doodads women wore in the name of modesty, today they just might have saved Letty Sue's life. For that, he was grateful.

"Letty Sue," he said, brushing aside the hair that fell wildly onto her face, "are you all right?"

She burst into tears then, a flood that diluted the sky-blue of her astonished eyes. Her arms wrapped around his neck frantically, pulling him down on her.

"Shh," he whispered, "don't cry. It's going to be okay. You didn't get burned. Did you?"

He pried himself up enough to gauge the look in her eyes. She shook her head. "Nooooo."

Her arms latched onto his neck again. The length of him more than covered her entire petite body. He stroked her hair and let her cry it out. He knew he should sit her up and make sure she wasn't hurt, but she seemed to need this more.

"Y-you s-saved my l-life, again," she said, and little sobs escaped her throat.

"I helped," he whispered in her ear. "But I think the layers of clothes you're wearing saved you this time."

Her wide eyes met his as her head moved up and down very slightly. "You think so?"

"I do."

She wiggled underneath him and Chase's body went rigid. She had her arms wound tightly around his neck, her breasts crushing into his chest. With pouty lips and red, swollen eyes, Letty Sue appeared like a small child, but Chase knew without a doubt she was all-woman. His body told him so, as well as the clear look of longing on her face.

Their lips were close, so close that they shared the same air. Her sweet breath caressed his face softly. He stroked her cheek with the backside of his hand, removing a bit of blackened soot. She squirmed under him again, and a shot of intense desire speared through him.

Her eyes stayed on his, and he felt the rapid beating of her heart. Chase lowered his mouth to hers, noting how she closed her eyes, ready to respond.

His whole body churned with need of her. Every male instinct he possessed hungered to show her how a man could pleasure a woman and take them both to ecstasy. His need was more than elemental. It went further than that, he realized solemnly. When he'd seen Letty Sue in flames, raw emotion had roiled within him and he couldn't get to her fast enough.

Walk as one. Stand together. His mother's words played in his mind like the string on a tightened bow.

But Joellen's words of trust echoed a moment later.

Abruptly, Chase stood, leaving the heat of her body and turning away from her. He raked both hands through his hair, drawing in a deep breath. Glancing at the broken glass on the carpeted floor, he shook his head. "Damn it, Letty Sue, you should be more careful!"

She gasped in surprise then, and Chase felt a measure of guilt. It was better this way, he told himself, better to be at odds with her. He couldn't afford tender feelings.

"Chase?"

He closed his eyes at the pleading note in her voice. "Did you wake up this morning and think today was a good day to die?"

"No, I, uh—"

He turned to see her puzzled expression. Slowly she rose on shaking legs, but managed to straighten to her full height. Her apron was charred, and a few tendrils of smoke still curled upward. He was tempted to reach over and untie her apron, but stood his ground.

"Well, you almost got yourself killed today." The words came out with a bitter edge.

Her wounded expression changed to anger instantly. She glared at him. "Wouldn't make you look good in Mama's eyes if I got hurt, would it, Chase? That's the only reason you're upset. Well, I'm just fine, as you can see."

The prideful tilt of her chin made Chase's blood boil. He reached for her, grabbing her arms. "Don't be a fool, Letty Sue. Next time, you might not be so lucky. Why in hell don't you know…things?"

"I'm trying, Chase Wheeler." She yanked free of his grasp, rubbing her wrists where he'd held her. He glanced down. "I never wanted to know before.

Mama tried teaching me, many times. But I put up such a fuss, only half listened to her instructions. I guess it just became easier for Mama to do everything herself.''

She'd given her mother a difficult time of it. That didn't surprise him. His assessment of Letty Sue's qualities hit the mark dead on: she was spoiled and selfish. "And you aim to change that?"

"Yes, I do," she said resolutely.

"Just be sure all your learning doesn't blow up the house."

She folded her arms across her chest, her blue eyes sparking more flames than the fire he'd just put out. "It won't happen again."

When Chase let out a vile curse, Letty Sue only raised an eyebrow. He bent down to pick up his hat, brushing away glass particles that coated it like a fine layer of winter snow. "I've got to see about replacing this window."

She nodded. "I would appreciate that."

Chase jammed his hat on his head. "And toss that apron in the hearth before another fire breaks out."

He slammed out the door. A crashing sound from behind made him jump. He nearly tripped down the porch steps.

Damn woman. She'd thrown something!

Ah hell, he thought. He should march back in there and turn her over his knee.

But well-honed instincts told him that if he marched back into the house, turning Letty Sue over his knee to discipline her wouldn't give him the necessary results.

Lust-filled images immediately came to mind of her body atop his.

He shook them off quickly, but somehow he knew that tonight, when he closed his eyes, that mental picture would plague his sleep.

Letty Sue didn't try to hide the disgust on her face when she picked up the bloody bird she was about to cook and slapped it down on the tabletop.

"Lordy, Letty Sue, today, one way or another, you're going to have yourself a delicious meal," she muttered in the empty kitchen.

Each night she'd watched the ranch hands sit down to a meal cooked by Earl, the oldest of the bunch, under the thatched roof by the outdoor cooking pit. She'd been invited many times to join them—not by Chase, she mused, but by Sam and the others. Stubbornly, she refused. She wouldn't give Chase Wheeler the satisfaction of knowing how hungry she'd been or how many more meals she'd ruined.

With great care, she cut the bird into pieces, wrinkling her nose at such a detestable chore. Good thing the ranch hands had plucked the feathers for her. She doubted she'd be able to do that by herself. Next, she coated one piece of chicken in flour and herbs and flung it into the pan. Grease splattered up, just missing her cheek. She jumped back and watched the grease settle.

She was more careful after that, rolling two chicken

legs around in the flour and setting them into the pan. So far, all she'd done was ruin meals, not injure herself. Of course, she had almost gone up in smoke the other day, along with the ranch house. She'd never be that careless again.

Loud voices from outside startled her. She glanced out the kitchen window. The ranch hands had circled around two men, and were cheering them on. Curious, she dashed out the kitchen door and lingered on the steps, watching. In a friendly wood-chopping race, Chase Wheeler and another ranch hand were busy slashing their axes with precision, splitting logs in two.

Letty Sue chuckled. The ritual, instituted by her mother, made a game of a chore most of the hands abhorred. The winner had the privilege of carving his name in the last bundle of firewood, and received a half dozen of Joellen's fruit pies.

They're going to have to wait on those pies until Mama gets home, Letty Sue thought with a smile. She hadn't mastered pie baking techniques as yet. Heavens, she hadn't mastered much of anything, and she was running out of clean clothes.

Soon she'd have to do the washing.

Lordy.

But her thoughts were interrupted when she saw Chase Wheeler stop his chopping for a moment, yank off his sweat-stained shirt and toss it onto the fence.

Sunlight caressed his broad shoulders, coating his bronzed skin like dark honey. Finely honed muscles rippled and bunched with each swing of the ax.

"Oh my," she whispered, breathless. She'd never seen him like this, with the setting sun on his shoulders. His dark hair was tied back and his body flowed gracefully as he lifted and lowered his arms to make each cutting blow, his eyes keen on the target.

Virile. Strong. *Savage.*

Mesmerized, she watched the race continue. Her gaze rested solely on one man. Chase Wheeler.

But then the scent of something all too familiar wafted to her nose. She sniffed once more and took off running. "Oh no!" She dashed inside the kitchen to the cookstove.

Burned offerings awaited her.

She wrapped several cloths around the handle and quickly pulled the fry pan off the burner, staring blankly at the shriveled pieces of chicken, singed and scarred beyond recognition.

"Ruined," Letty Sue said forlornly. She grimaced when her stomach grumbled. "I don't believe my stomach can take another slab of stale bread and cheese."

Then a thought struck. She didn't have to eat goat cheese and bread again. No, tonight she'd have herself a fine meal.

After cleaning up the kitchen, she glanced out the window. The wood-chopping race had ended and the men had dispersed. Most importantly, Chase was nowhere to be seen.

Good. She'd just wash herself up a bit and change her clothes. She did have a few clean dresses left.

Tonight, Letty Sue would eat in style.

* * *

Chase Wheeler bedded down the horses, giving his favorite, Tornado, one last handful of oats. He slapped the stallion affectionately on the back and closed the stall door.

"I'm turning in early myself," he said to the horse. Tornado snorted in reply and Chase smiled. He wasn't sure winning the wood-chopping race was worth the trouble. He stretched out his stiff back and sighed. He'd probably not be around long enough to get a chance at the winnings—Joellen's pies.

The men had teased that he could always have Letty Sue bake them. Chase had scoffed at that, shaking his head. Letty Sue had been spending a good deal of time in the kitchen. He wondered if she was making progress with her cooking skills. He'd hadn't heard or seen much of her in days.

But in the evening, he'd made sure she was "tucked in." It was a promise he'd made to himself—to see that all was well inside the house before he turned in for the night. She didn't have to know about it. He stayed in the shadows and waited for lights out before checking on her.

Only then could he sleep peacefully.

Chase made his way to the house and climbed the porch steps. He tugged gently on the front door and was gratified to find the door bolted. He glanced into the windows he passed on his way to the back door and puzzled over why he couldn't see any lantern light in any of the rooms. Had Letty Sue turned in especially early tonight?

And a sense of dread washed over him like a bucketful of rainwater when he yanked open the back door. It, too, should have been bolted shut.

"Letty Sue," he called out to the darkened rooms. Silence.

"I'm coming in," he said, "so get yourself decent."

Silence.

Chase made his way through the house, calling out for Letty Sue a dozen times. She didn't answer. Chase pretty much knew from the moment he'd pulled open the back door that Letty Sue wasn't home.

So where the hell was she?

With long strides, he rushed to the bunkhouse, and finding Sam sitting on his bunk, ready to turn in, Chase questioned him.

"Nope, I haven't seen her tonight. But if she took off, she'd be riding Starlight."

"Riding? Letty Sue rides?" Now, this was news. Chase hadn't believed she possessed any ranching abilities.

"Since she was big enough to peer over this here bunk. Yep, she rides. Darn good, too."

Chase scratched his head. "Wouldn't have laid down a bet on that one."

Sam chuckled. "Surprisin', I know. But Letty Sue's real intelligent, and when she sets her mind to something, there's usually no stopping her."

"Damn. I'd better see if her horse is missing."

"I'll go along with you."

Chase and Sam made a quick inspection of the corral that housed the mares. It only took a minute to determine Starlight wasn't among them.

"Where would Letty Sue go at this hour?" Chase asked.

Sam shrugged. "Don't rightly know. But I do know Starlight's got on special shoes. Seems one of Letty Sue's beaus made them up, trying to impress her. Shod the horse right on the property just a few weeks back. And they leave a different mark on the ground. If you're good, you can pick up on it. Here, I'll show you."

Sam lifted a kerosene lamp off the post and turned up the flame. Searching the dirt near the corral, he called Chase over when he spotted what he was looking for. Pointing, he said, "This one here belongs to Starlight, all right."

Chase inspected the hoofprint on the ground. "I see it. Can't be too hard to track."

"You going after her?"

"Do I have a choice? She's out there somewhere, alone, in the dark. She didn't tell anyone where she was going, did she?"

"Don't suppose, but I'll check with the men anyway while you're saddling up."

A few minutes later, Sam met Chase just as he was mounting Tornado. "Earl thinks he saw her kick up some dust just before sunset, heading toward town."

"Well, that's a start."

Sam handed the lantern up to Chase. "Want some help?"

"No. It'd be best if you stayed here, just in case

she comes back. Tie her up if you have to, but keep her locked inside the house until I get back.''

Sam rubbed his jaw, contemplating. ''Letty Sue don't like taking orders, so I might just have to.''

''Do you have any idea who'd she go visiting at night? Any special *friend?*''

Sam's eyebrows lifted. He clearly didn't like the implication Chase was making. He shook his head slowly, showing his displeasure with a frown. ''Letty Sue's not the type of woman—''

''I wouldn't be too sure. Women are full of surprises. That's the one thing I do know about them.'' Chase slapped his hat on his head and rode out, leaving Sam to ponder that notion.

Starlight's tracks left no room for doubt; Letty Sue had headed for town. Chase had picked up her trail immediately. He kept wondering whom she was meeting. Why had she left the ranch so late, without telling anyone where she was going? Perhaps he'd misjudged her altogether. She might not be the innocent woman she claimed to be. Or she just might be heading for more trouble than she could handle. Chase pressed Tornado hard, riding with agility, hoping to stop a disaster before it happened.

He made it to town in less than an hour. Except for the boisterous noise from the saloon, the main street of town was quiet. Chase rode along, his gaze darting from one building to another. He was past the middle of town when he spotted Letty Sue's horse. Starlight was tethered to a hitching post outside the diner.

Chase dismounted quickly and strode to the diner's front window. Pressing his face to the glass, he was able to see into the dark dining area. The chairs were upended onto the tables and the whole place appeared deserted.

Now that didn't make sense.

Where was Letty Sue? And who was she with?

But then a flicker of light caught his eye. He heard laughter, female laughter. He pressed his face close again, noting shadows casting images against the back room wall.

Faintly, he peered in, and what he saw twisted something in his gut. Two shapes in the shadows— one male, one female—were standing close, intimately close.

"Letty Sue," he whispered. Damn woman. What was she up to? And didn't she know not to go meeting men in dark, deserted places in the dead of night?

He'd warned her before.

Hell, they'd had a truce.

He had a mind to turn around, mount his horse and leave her there. Let her get out of this one on her own, he thought. Again he heard her laugh, the sweet sound grating in his ears.

Hell. That's just what he'd do. Turn around and head home. If she wanted to be treated like an adult, well, he'd oblige. "You're on your own, darlin'." He spun around quickly, ready to hit the road.

Then he heard her shriek.

The sound jolted him into action.

He threw his weight against the door. It opened

easily, since it wasn't bolted, and he found himself off balance, halfway into the dining room. He righted himself, drew his gun and entered the back room.

"Hold it right there," he announced with authority.

Both the guilty parties stopped what they were doing and froze. Stunned expressions greeted him.

But no one was more startled than he was.

Letty Sue stood over a pot of stew, with ladle in midair. A boy, no older than fifteen and wearing an apron, stopped cutting up vegetables.

"What the—" Chase lowered his gun. A hundred muddied notions entered his head, but then one clear thought filtered through. The clandestine meeting he'd imagined in his mind had come to pass. Chase had caught them in the act, all right.

He'd caught them, with guilt-ridden faces...cooking!

Chapter Six

Letty Sue's mouth dropped open. Astonished, she gazed into the equally astonished, confounded face of Chase Wheeler. He stood there, eyes blinking rapidly, taking in the whole scene.

With his gun drawn and those silver eyes narrowed, he'd looked like a man ready to pull the trigger, a man who'd likely down his opponent, a man who wouldn't miss his target.

But now, as he holstered his gun with a befuddled expression, he simply looked…foolish.

Letty Sue set down her ladle. A full measure of anger swelled within her, matching the heat of the beef and vegetable stew bubbling over the flames. "Chase, what are you doing here?"

His dark brows lifted. "A better question is what are you doing here?" He regained his composure quickly. Chase wasn't one to let down his guard too long.

"Isn't it obvious?"

"No," he said stubbornly, "it isn't obvious." He crossed his arms over his chest and glared at her.

"Petey is giving me a cooking lesson."

Chase glanced at the boy, then returned his gaze to her. Out of respect to Petey, who'd been so obliging this evening, and to the Mayfields in general, Letty Sue offered introductions.

"Petey Mayfield, I'd like you to meet Chase Wheeler, temporary foreman at the Double J."

Petey hesitated, setting aside a batch of carrots he'd been ready to dice up, then came forward and offered Chase his hand. Chase blew out a breath, then shook it.

"Nice meetin' ya," Petey murmured.

Chase nodded. "Same here." He turned to her. "I heard a scream."

"Chase, were you spying on us?"

Letty Sue's initial anger dissolved when she noticed Chase shift his stance, clearly uncomfortable. Was that color rising on his cheeks?

He *had* been spying on them. The fact not only amused her, but also gave her the upper hand for once.

"Listen up, Letty Sue. You know darn well we had a truce. You didn't tell a soul on the ranch where you were heading or who you planned on meeting." His gaze rested on Petey, obviously sizing him up.

"I didn't want anyone knowing," she said simply. The truth was, she didn't want *him* knowing she'd ruined yet another meal. She didn't want him to find out how inept she was at cooking, a task most women took to easily. For the first time in her life, Letty Sue felt inadequate as a female.

And it was all Chase Wheeler's doing.

"I know my way to town, Chase. Besides, a woman's got a right to a little privacy."

"Privacy?" Chase's voice rose. "You want...privacy?" He looked fit to be tied. "Damn it, woman, I'm responsible for you."

"You keep saying that. But I *can* take care of myself."

"Is that so? So why'd you scream? And don't deny it, because I heard it plain as day."

"You mean, when you were spying?"

"Letty Sue," he began and there was enough warning in his tone that she rushed to answer.

"All right, it was the stew. I screamed when I tasted it."

Chase's mouth twisted, hiding what she knew to be a smug grin. "That bad?"

"That good!" Her joy wiped that all-knowing expression off his face. "I couldn't believe it. It tastes just like Mama's, even better. And I cooked it myself. Petey watched, but I did all the cooking. Isn't that right, Petey?"

Petey nodded. "She's done real good for her first lesson, Mr. Wheeler."

Letty Sue smiled, feeling great pride at her first real accomplishment. Coming to the diner had been a smart notion. At first she'd thought she'd just pay for a good meal and be done with it, but on the ride to town she'd realized nothing would get settled that way. Asking Emma Mayfield or one of the other ladies working at the diner would have been humiliating, but then she noticed Petey in the back, cooking, and the idea struck. She'd waited until all the patrons left the diner and then approached him. Petey had been more than happy to help. "And not even seeing you here tonight is going to spoil my good mood, Chase."

"Well, then, your stew's a success." Chase scratched his head and angled his chin toward the door. "Now it's time to head back."

"Oh, no you don't, Chase. You're not going to order me home, not now. Petey and I are going to dine on this delicious meal. And even though you're most disagreeable, I'm happy to ask you to join us."

Chase glanced at her, then at the pot of stew simmering, lending off the most deliciously fragrant aroma. He shot Petey one quick look, then answered, "No, thank you kindly though. You two enjoy your meal. I'll be waiting out front."

"But Chase, you don't have to wait for me. Petey said he'd be glad to escort me home."

Chase turned and headed out the door. "Like I said, Letty Sue, I'll be waiting out front."

Privacy? The woman wanted privacy and all else be damned. Just like a woman. Just like Letty Sue. Nothing they'd agreed upon had sunk in. She'd deliberately taken off without telling him where she was going. She'd gone out at night, mindless of her own safety. She'd made him chase after her, nearly humiliate himself in that kitchen, and *she'd* gotten angry with *him!*

It was clear now she planned on obeying the rules of the truce only when it was convenient for her.

Only more reason for Chase to keep his eye on her.

Chase let a solid oak post of the diner's porch hold his weight as he leaned back and puffed on a cheroot. The night air was crisp, a gentle breeze blowing away the dust of the warm dry day.

His mind still on Letty Sue, he found a smile surfacing. She was something, if not a handful of trouble. But her happiness tonight over cooking that simple meal took most of the starch out of his fight. He simply didn't have the heart to argue much over her leaving the ranch, not when she positively beamed with joy over bits of browned meat mingling with a batch of vegetables. Hell, even he could conjure up son-of-a-gun stew.

And he had to admit a wave of relief had swept over him when he'd barged into that kitchen, expecting the worst only to find Letty Sue innocent of any wrongdoing. There'd been no clandestine meeting, no private affair, no planned rendezvous.

Still, he'd eyed the boy closely. Petey was clearly smitten with Letty Sue. There was no mistaking that puppy-dog look of longing in the boy's clear brown eyes. Letty Sue had that affect on most men, young ones included. It made Chase itchy, nervous because it was completely out of his control. He liked to be in control. He hadn't bent to temptation often, but when he had, back in Abilene, he'd been burned, badly.

Giggles, soft and feminine, had him turning his head. Letty Sue and the boy sat at one of the tables in the far corner of the diner. One candle flickered over their meal and paraded over the walls, allowing him to view them sharing the meal.

A knot of remorse niggled at him.

He could be dining with her.

Enjoying her company.

Listening to her bursts of joyous laughter.

Chase puffed on his cheroot one last time, dropped it to the ground and stomped it out.

It was a hell of a good thing he'd refused her offer.

Yep, hell of a good thing.

Ten minutes later, they were headed back to the Double J. "How the devil do you ride wearing a dress?" he asked.

Letty Sue turned to view him sitting tall in the saddle. The slight light of the moon and stars above painted his face in shadows. Handsome, nearly savagely so, she thought, studying his profile.

"Easy, I don't wear any petticoats when I ride."

His head snapped around and his gaze flowed over her with so much apparent heat she'd have sworn she felt the warmth of it melting her bones. There was something sinful in that smoky gaze, like she was a ripe peach and he was a starving man.

Lordy, Letty Sue.

He cleared his throat noisily. "I didn't know you could ride."

"I grew up on a ranch," she said, her chin lifting defiantly. Did he believe she possessed no skills whatsoever? "I've been riding since I was a tot. That's one thing Mama did manage to teach me."

"You do it well, even with wearing those clothes."

"Or rather, lack of them," she said, then realized how entirely wicked that sounded. Chase didn't appear shocked, but a deep, low groan emerged from his chest. "Thank you," she hurried to add before he could say more. That was the first genuine compliment she'd ever received from Chase Wheeler.

They rode in silence for a time, then Chase said quietly, "You know, you didn't give a thought about the truce we'd made. I suppose white folks only pretend to honor their word, to get their way."

"Chase, I had good reason."

"There is no good reason to break your word."

Letty Sue's long sigh filled the silent night. Chase wasn't arguing or lecturing, but rather speaking conversationally. It surprised her. She'd had enough of his overbearing ways, but when he spoke to her like this, on equal terms, she felt more willing to open up. "I just couldn't face another ruined meal."

She wouldn't add that he'd been the cause of it tonight. He'd been a distraction since the moment they'd met, but this evening, watching him best his opponent in the wood-cutting contest, well, Letty Sue hadn't a mind for anything but him.

"What'd you ruin this time?"

"Fried chicken."

"My favorite," he said, then smiled. Her heart flipped at that rare, quick smile. "Maybe you'll try that one on your next lesson."

That he allowed there would be another lesson caused Letty Sue to feel a moment of sheer joy. "Maybe I will," she said softly.

"Long as you tell me where you're headed, and don't go out at night."

"I think I can do that."

"See that you do," he said.

A short while later they reached the Double J and led their mounts toward the barn. Chase dismounted just outside, holding tight to the reins. Tornado snorted, sidestepped, then reared his head. Chase soothed his stallion with soft, murmured words.

"What's wrong with him?" Letty Sue asked.

"Your mare's got him excited. Best you dismount now, before Tornado gets too close."

Chase turned to her and raised his arms. She dismounted quickly, his hands finding her waist, helping lower her to the ground. She felt his strength, his heat as his splayed fingers grazed the soft underside of her breasts. She sucked in air, but thankfully her gasp was silent. "Maybe Starlight wouldn't mind his attentions," she said gently.

"Maybe," he replied, his gaze moving over her face, resting finally on her lips. "When the time is right."

"And when will that be?" She lifted her eyes to meet his.

"Not...now," he answered cautiously.

The ranch was quiet except for an occasional owl hoot and the muted snorting and rustling of horses in the corral. All the ranch hands had most likely bedded down for the night. Letty Sue's heart pounded in her chest and she wondered if Chase felt the turmoil he was creating with his hands still on her.

Tornado snorted loudly once again, bumping Chase with his flank. It brought Chase up against Letty Sue and he wound his arms about her protectively. "You okay?"

"Mmm...fine," she answered, still wrapped in his arms.

He released her quickly. "I'd best put Tornado in the stall tonight. With the mood he's in, no telling what might happen."

Letty Sue stared into his silvery eyes, hoping to read his thoughts.

He stared back, but then Tornado let out one more agitated, impatient snort and stomped his front hoof. Chase backed away and took his stallion's reins. "I'll be back to put Starlight in the corral. It'd be wise to keep him away from her."

Letty Sue dug her teeth into her bottom lip as she watched Chase lead his horse into the barn. She had something on her mind, something she had to ask him. She knew she'd be better off not stirring up trouble, but then, that particular notion had never stopped her before. Chase Wheeler had some explaining to do.

She tethered her mare to a corral post and followed Chase inside the barn. A golden ray of lantern light brightened the area where Chase worked on Tornado, rubbing him down. The rest of the big barn was cast in elusive shadows. She stood there hesitantly, watching and wondering if she had the nerve to confront him. Then Chase's voice broke the silence. He spoke in low tones, commiserating with his horse.

"Females make you do crazy things, huh, big fella? Like chasing after them in the dark, smelling their scent, wanting what you can't have."

He stroked Tornado's long snout affectionately, then began combing the stallion down. Tornado relaxed, and Letty Sue watched man with animal, noting how very alike they were. How untamed they could be one moment, then tender. How high-strung and temperamental in one instant, then so at peace, so calm the next.

"Letty Sue?"

She froze. How had he known she was there, standing in the dark shadows as she was? She'd been spying on him—the very thing she'd accused him of doing at the diner. "I just came for a currycomb. Starlight needs a good combing." She lifted up the bristled brush to show him her intent.

He came out of the stall, latching it and headed her way. Taking the comb from her hand, he said, "You don't have to do that. I'll take care of her tonight."

"All right," she said.

"'Night, Letty Sue." He turned away, ready to leave the barn.

"Uh, good night. Chase?"

He stopped and spun around. "Yeah?"

"Why'd you come after me tonight?"

Chase lifted a neckerchief from his rear pocket and rubbed the back of his neck. He blew breath out, a sound much like Tornado's impatient snort. "You know why and I won't be repeating myself."

She wouldn't let the subject drop. "Because I left and you didn't know where I was?"

He nodded.

"So then, when you found me at the diner, why'd you come barging in, ready to shoot?"

He didn't respond, except for the smallest shake of his head.

"What'd you think I was doing in there?"

Chase closed his eyes briefly, then shot her a hard look. "A woman goes off in the dead of night to meet up with a man...what'd you suppose I was thinking?"

Letty Sue rolled her eyes. "Petey's hardly a man and *I was cooking.*"

He took a step toward her. "I didn't know that."

Letty Sue smiled. "But you thought I'd be meeting a man for...for—"

"That's right, damn it, that's what I thought."

Letty Sue lowered her voice, in sharp contrast to Chase's thundering one. "And you didn't like it, did you?"

"Hell no, I didn't like it one bit." He took another step toward her, pointing his finger. "I'm responsible for your doings, woman. Get that through your head. I can't have you running off whenever you fancy, and I sure as hell can't be chasing you down every night."

Letty Sue approached him. She stopped when her boots met his. ''Or just maybe there's another reason you came toting that gun tonight, Chase.''

He looked down at her. ''Doubtful.''

She tilted her chin up. ''Is it?''

''Just what in blazes are you getting at?''

She met his eyes directly and spoke ever so softly. ''How'd you know I was in the barn just now?''

Chase flinched as though she surprised him with her sudden change of conversation.

''Well?'' she asked.

He cast her a solemn look of resignation. ''You smell…pretty,'' he said, ''better than anything in this here barn.''

She smiled. ''Thank you.''

He grunted in reply. ''I've gotta bed down Starlight. You coming?'' he asked as he headed for the barn door.

Letty Sue matched his strides, but just as he was about to throw open the wide door, her boot tangled with a coiled rope on the ground. She struggled to stay upright, to no avail. She felt herself falling.

Chase caught her just in time, bringing her up against him. This was the second time tonight they'd been thrust together. This time, he didn't let her go. He held her close, his powerful chest crushing her bosom, her head tucked under his chin.

Chase huffed out air. ''Sometimes I wish you'd just stay the hell away from me.''

Letty Sue wound her arms about his waist, but pulled away enough to look up into his eyes. They were black as coal now and just as hot. "Is that really true, Chase?"

Tension ripped through the air in the stuffy barn. Letty Sue felt the evidence of his desire, crushed to him like she was. It should have shocked her, it should have sent her running home, it should have jostled good sense into her. It did none of those things. She stayed in his arms, their bodies both humming.

He bent his head. She licked her lips. He cupped her chin. She lifted her face.

Tornado bucked in the stall, snorting wildly, clearly agitated.

Chase raised his head, blinked, looked down at her and unfolded his arms. "What the devil am I doing?"

Letty Sue wouldn't let her disappointment show. "I believe you were about to kiss me."

He dragged his hands through his hair and glanced at her mouth. There was the slightest hint of regret in his expression, a certain flicker of remorse in his eyes. "Go on to bed, Letty Sue."

She smiled then, a smile meant just for him. "I'm going, right now." She sashayed out the barn door, then turned to him. "Oh, and it appears Tornado isn't the only one who wants what he can't have."

Hearing Chase's muttered curses from behind, she lifted her skirts and dashed to the house, only finding safety once she was behind the thick, bolted door.

Oh Lordy, Letty Sue.

Chapter Seven

"Let him bid on Sally's basket. It's no concern of mine." Letty Sue forked the fried chicken over hastily, a splash of fat nearly jumping up to take a bite of her cheek. She stepped away from the fry pan until the sizzling died down. "I don't give a hoot. Not a one. I have chicken to fry up, and heaven above, I don't plan on burning one bit of it."

Sam Fowler had come by earlier to see if Letty Sue needed any supplies from town. During their pleasant conversation, Sam had announced that not only was Chase Wheeler going to the church social, but Sam was pretty darn sure he would be bidding on Sally's basket. He'd inquired about the color of it again, having forgotten what Sally had told him the day they'd met.

Sam thought they'd make a good match, Sally being so even-tempered and all. Letty Sue hadn't disagreed, pretending to Sam that it didn't matter. But inside the hurt ran deep. Why did the thought make her suffer so?

And oh, Sally would be thrilled. She thought Chase the most appealing man in Sweet Springs.

Lately, the man consumed her thoughts, but Letty Sue didn't understand the why of it. They certainly weren't suited for each other. Chase had made his position very clear to her.

She flipped the chicken over one last time, then took the fry pan off the stove. She still had biscuits and potatoes to cook, and a pie to bake, but at least she'd managed all right with the chicken. It wasn't burned.

"I need a break from this heat," she said much later, after finishing up her cooking. She removed her apron, then wiped her forehead with her sleeve. It was an unusually warm spring day, the bright sun pouring in through the kitchen window.

She wandered into the parlor, noting how the heavy, jade-green velvet drapes kept out much of the day's heat. Enjoying the refreshing coolness, she sank down onto the sofa, closing her eyes. She'd rest here for just a few minutes, she thought wearily, before dosing off into oblivion.

Hours later, Letty Sue opened her eyes to darkness. She blinked. Dazed, she shifted, realizing it was evening and she wasn't in bed. Then she remembered. She'd fallen asleep on the sofa earlier in the afternoon.

Now the sun was setting.

Oh Lordy. She still had the decorating of the basket to do!

She went searching for ribbons. Her mama always

kept fabric and sewing supplies in a small storage room just off the kitchen. Letty Sue shuffled through all the cabinets and shelves, coming up with one strand of yellow ribbon tucked under some cotton batting. The strand was less than twelve inches long. She lifted it up and stared at it. "This will never do. Where does Mama keep all of her pretty bows and ribbons?"

Frowning, she entered her mama's bedroom. An odd feeling swept over her as she saw some of Jasper Brody's things about. She was too young to remember her father, really. For her, his presence in the house was only a fleeting childhood memory. But she'd known he'd been there. Mama had kept his memory alive for many years. It wasn't until Joellen met Jasper that she'd begun slowly to put Jacob Withers to rest.

It was good thing, Letty Sue supposed, for her mother. She did seem happy with her new husband. Letty Sue doubted she'd find that kind of happiness with anyone in Sweet Springs. She planned to travel, see something of this big, exciting world before settling down. Maybe in her travels, she'd meet the right man. One could only hope.

With a deep sigh, she continued looking for ribbons. With each drawer opened, each shelf checked, Letty Sue became more frantic.

"Now, where are they?" She raced through the house, yanking open cabinets and tossing supplies aside in a panic. For her endeavors all she found were old, threadbare black, moss-green and dirt-brown ribbons.

The basket was in no better shape. The only one she located, under a small table on the porch, was weathered and misshapen.

"Oh no!" she cried.

It was too late to ask Sally for help. It was too late to go to town; none of the shops would be open. Why hadn't she given the basket a thought before now? She could have sent Sam for the items she needed earlier today. But now she feared it was far too late for her "rainbow" basket.

She slumped down on the porch swing and stared out into the night. No one could save her from this. It was her own fault. She should have made sure she had all the supplies needed. She should have bought new ribbons when she was in town the other day. She should not have fallen asleep this afternoon.

Lordy, she was in trouble.

Chase Wheeler rode into the yard, his stallion prancing with high spirits. The foreman reined his horse in and dismounted just outside the barn.

Oh, she'd bet he'd have a good laugh over this one. Chase would probably come up with a new Cheyenne name for her. His black Stetson rode low on his forehead so she couldn't see his eyes when he turned to glance her way. She wished she could vanish like a puff of smoke, into the night.

She did the next best thing.

She ignored him completely, rising and leaving the night's breeze to stir the unoccupied porch swing. She slammed the front door shut and locked herself in, good and tight.

Tonight, Chase Wheeler was the last man on God's green earth she wanted to see.

Chase knocked on the kitchen door. He rubbed tension from the back of his neck and waited. Not for long. He knocked again. It was a mistake coming to her in the middle of the night. The third knock was louder than the first two, rattling the door on its hinges. "Letty Sue."

Damn, he knew she was awake. He hadn't imagined seeing her all alone on the porch swing when he rode up, looking like she'd lost her best friend.

Unless his mind was playing tricks.

Wouldn't be the first time a man lost his head over a woman, only to find out she'd been nothing more than a mirage, a vision conjured up by an addled brain. And in his case, caused from three stiff shots of whiskey and the blows to his head and ribs he'd taken tonight.

Damn, his head hurt. Pounded. Throbbed.

He wasn't even going to think about his ribs.

Why the hell was he thumping on Letty Sue's door, again?

He couldn't remember, but he needed to see her.

Mistake! his muddied mind kept screaming. He knocked again. "Letty Sue, I know you're in there. Open up!"

He heard footsteps padding to the back door, and cracked a smile, finally recalling why he needed to see her. He was grateful to have a real reason, because something in his gut said he'd be pounding on her door tonight just as hard, even if he didn't.

"Go away."

"No."

"I'm not in the mood to see you, Chase."

"Too bad, now open the door."

"No."

"I have something here you'll want to see."

"Liar."

"That ain't nice, Letty Sue." He raised his voice and commanded, "Open up."

She let out a sound that wasn't a bit ladylike and yanked the door open. "Hush up, Chase Wheeler. You'll wake the dead," she ordered in a hasty whisper. Then her gaze met with his.

She gasped and her face paled, making the blue in her eyes even more brilliant.

Mistake to be here.

"What happened to you?"

She wore a white cotton nightdress, simple in design, with buttons that rose to her delicate neck. Buttons he'd have no trouble undoing. And the moonlight streaming in cast just enough light to illuminate what was underneath.

Chase's mouth went dry.

It took all his balance to stay upright, not so much from whiskey consumed, or from the pain shooting along his ribs, or from Letty Sue's unnerving beauty. No, it was a combination of the three that hit him hard and had him swaying against the opened door.

Letty Sue grabbed for him.

"Ouch!" he barked. She'd caught him just under the ribs.

"Chase, what's wrong? Come and sit down. You're bleeding."

"My chin's going to be just fine. It's higher and lower that's got me woozy."

He staggered, trying to keep most of his weight off of her. She guided him to the parlor, toward a cushioned wing chair. He slumped into it.

"What happened?" Her voice lost its edgy tone. She spoke softly as she kneeled down to look up into his face. "Tell me."

She put her hands on his knees for balance. Heat shot straight through him. His head spun in circles. Having her kneeling at his feet, looking up at him with those almond-shaped eyes gone wide with shock, was enough to make a man lose all his good intentions. He closed his eyes and the spinning slowed to a near stop. "Ran into some drifters at the saloon that don't take kindly to Cheyenne."

"What'd they do?"

He looked down at her and shrugged. "Pretty much caused a scene with the woman serving me drinks. I had to defend her honor. And mine."

Letty Sue inhaled sharply. She blinked several times. "How many were there?"

"Three. But don't you worry. Each one of them looks a hell of a lot worse than me. Sheriff took their guns and made them hightail it out of town."

Letty Sue rose to dampen a cloth. Chase watched

her enter the kitchen, his eyes following her every move. He shouldn't be here, he told himself again. His feet weren't moving, though, and neither was his humming body.

When she returned and bent down to dab the cloth against his chin, the scent of jasmine filled his nostrils, and soon just about everything that ached hurt a bit less.

He let his gaze wander over her face: eyes the color of a spring sky; slightly turned up delicate nose; a mouth made for kissing. Then his gaze dropped to those buttons at her throat, and lower, witnessing perfection in two rounded globes straining against the thin cotton gown. The pink of her nipples formed circular shadows against the material.

Another ache developed, one he was familiar with. This one, he didn't want to fight anymore.

He swallowed hard.

"There," she said, dabbing at his chin. "Where else does it hurt?"

"Took a hit to the ribs, and I think I've got a good lump on my head."

Gently, Letty Sue removed his hat. "I don't see anything, Chase."

"Maybe the lump's on the inside."

"What?"

"Nothing, Letty Sue. I'd better get going." He had to get out of there. But when he made a move to lift himself up from the chair, her hands were on him, easing him back down.

"No you don't. Close your eyes and rest awhile. I'll make you a cup of tea."

He arched a brow her way. "Tea?"

"Yes, for heaven's sake, Chase. I know how to make a cup of tea. It has healing qualities. Now wait for me here. Close your eyes."

"Yes, ma'am." He closed his eyes, but as she left, her fragrant scent wafted to his nostrils, filling his senses.

"Here we go," she said minutes later, bringing in a tea tray. "Honey, sugar? How do you like your tea?"

Honey? Sugar? If only those words were used on him, as endearments. He half-smiled, chuckling to himself. He couldn't imagine Letty Sue calling to him that way.

And suddenly, it was exactly what he wanted. "Any way is fine. I'm not much for tea."

She put a drop of honey and a spoonful of sugar in both cups, stirring gently, then handed one to him. She sat down on the sofa across from him with her cup. He sipped the tea slowly, then set it down.

"Don't you like it?" she asked.

"It's fine tea. Thank you." He flinched when a sharp pain slashed across his ribs.

"Your ribs hurt." She was up from her spot on the sofa, rushing over to him. "What can I do?"

Chase's body ached all over, some from the earlier altercation at the saloon, but most from having Letty Sue standing there, in her nearly transparent nightdress, tending to him. Without thought, he grabbed her wrist and gave a gentle tug.

"Chase!"

She landed on his lap, just as he intended. "Well, you asked what you could do."

"I meant, to make you feel better."

He snaked his hand around her neck and pulled her face close to his. "This is going to make me feel a whole lot better." His lips met hers with blistering heat. He tasted her once, then twice, and when a tiny moan escaped her throat, Chase parted her lips and drove his tongue into her mouth.

Heaven wasn't any better, he was sure. After her initial shock, she met him thrust for thrust, boldly, and Chase's body went from solid to hard as stone in just one second. He was on dangerous ground, but hadn't the power to stop.

Not now. It would have to come from her.

He drove a hand into her hair, pulling out the one pin that held that glorious mane up. Dark silky tresses spilled onto his fingers and floated down to graze his cheek.

She wiggled her bottom, getting comfortable, and destroying his own comfort completely. "Ah, Letty Sue."

He removed his mouth from hers to suckle the straining fabric over her breast. He crushed his head to her chest and felt her give up her body to him. Her pleasured gasp was all he needed to hear. She arched and he moved to the other breast, suckling again, moistening the fabric until the full rounded globe appeared, pert and ready for him.

Chase's heart pumped faster and faster. Stop me, Letty Sue, his mind screamed, because he knew he couldn't stop on his own accord. Nothing but little pleasured moans escaped her lips.

He cupped her breast in his hand and, with his thumb, rubbed over and over the soft nub until it was pebble hard. She whimpered in pleasure, giving him great satisfaction. He claimed her mouth again, thrusting his tongue inside. His hand burned from where he caressed her, the soft, giving globe contrasting sharply with the diamond-tipped peak. His body was on fire, like dry brush igniting on an arid prairie.

"Oh Chase," she whispered frantically, squirming against him, seeming to want more, asking for him to deliver what she craved. "I've never..."

"Tell me to stop, Letty Sue. Now."

"But I've never felt this way before," she exclaimed. "I'm trembling inside, Chase."

"I know."

"It's a good trembling. Isn't it?"

Chase groaned, kissing her one last time. He shouldn't have let it go so far. His need for her tonight overwhelmed him, taking with it all common sense. "It's a good trembling when it's with the right person."

He'd done his share of trembling, too. Gently, he lifted her off him. She looked up with fearful eyes as they stood facing one another. He had to tread carefully or he'd hurt her again, and they both knew it.

"I'm not that person, Letty Sue."

"But, Chase, you made me feel…that maybe you were."

"No." He shook his head, and finally some sense entered into it. He slipped his hand into his pocket. "This is what you really want, darlin'." He handed her the telegram. "It's from your mother. It's the reason I stopped by tonight." The words rang false. He knew it now. He hadn't come to her because of the telegram, he'd come to her because…he couldn't stay away.

She took the paper and turned it to the lantern light so that she could make out the words. After staring down at it for several minutes, she lifted her eyes to his. "Mama wants me to meet them in St. Louis in a few weeks. She misses me. She said they'd both love to have me join them for the last months of their trip."

Letty Sue's gaze probed his, as if asking something from him. It wasn't his permission, he knew—she would never ask for that, being far too obstinate. No, this was something more, something he couldn't give. "It's your decision."

She closed her eyes. "I thought it's what I wanted." She searched his eyes once again. "Now I'm not sure of anything."

"Letty Sue, don't let what just happened between us change your mind. You've always dreamed of traveling East. It's what you want."

"Are you saying you want me to go?"

No. Dammit. He wanted to take her to the floor

and make love to her, right there in front of the fireplace, until the sun came up. Drawing in a deep
breath, he rubbed the back of his neck. "It's not what
I want that matters. It's what *you* want. Go, Letty Sue.
You might regret it if you don't."

"I might regret it if I do," she said very softly,
dropping her head to peer at the telegram once again.

He cursed quietly when he noted her hands quiv-
ering. "I'd better leave now. You have some thinking
to do."

Because of the late hour, Chase chose to depart the
same way he'd come, through the kitchen door. No
sense stirring up any gossip, even though he'd been
sure the whole bunkhouse was asleep when he'd
knocked on her door earlier.

Letty Sue followed him out. "Will I see you tomorrow at the picnic?" she asked, her blue eyes filled
with sudden sadness.

"I'll be there."

Chase took several steps out the door, but her soft
voice stopped him. "Chase?"

He didn't turn around. "Yeah?"

"Are you bidding on Sally's basket tomorrow?"

He put his head down for a moment. Then he
turned to her, meeting her eyes. "It's best that way,
Letty Sue." He swallowed hard. "Lock your doors."

And lock me out.

She pulled her lower lip in, bruised now from his
kisses, swollen from his desperate passion. She nodded.

Chase turned around and continued to walk. He

didn't dare look back, not into the face that could make him change his mind.

Wildflowers dotted the hilly rise just beyond the church grounds. Intermittent hues of pink, yellow and blue mingled amid the verdant green, proclaiming that spring was most definitely upon them.

Letty Sue took a deep breath and sighed.

She was glad to be off the ranch today. There were just too many perplexing problems at home, Chase Wheeler being first and foremost. She would put aside all thoughts of him and of her decision whether or not to make the trip East to join up with her mother.

Today was too glorious a day to spend time worrying.

She'd not concern herself about her picnic basket, either. She'd done her best with the drab colors she'd had to work with, and that was all she could do.

She greeted her friends and watched a baseball game in the yard behind the church. The new game was fun to watch, completely absorbing all the male players. She applauded their efforts each time they managed to hit the ball with that stick, called a "bat."

"Morning, Letty Sue." Tyler Kincaide walked up with his wife, Lily. He was holding his daughter, Bethann, by the hand. Lily had their new baby papoose-wrapped in a blanket in her arms.

"Morning. Isn't it a wonderful day?" Letty Sue always had a soft spot for the handsome rancher, but Lillian Brody, Jasper's niece, had managed to corral him into a wedding.

"Yes, it is," he answered.

"How's the baby?" She peered at the tiny infant, a shudder working its way done her spine. She knew nothing about children, much less babies. They looked so fragile and tiny, as though if you held them the wrong way, they'd just about break.

Lily smiled and shifted her son into a more visible position in her arms. "See, Letty Sue? He's just fine. Little Ty's got a sweet temperament."

"Like his mother," Tyler added, kissing Lily's cheek.

"But he's got his father's handsome looks." Lily smiled at her husband.

"And I'm goin' ta get a chance to watch him, all by myself, when I gets older," Bethann said proudly.

"My, that's quite a responsibility, Bethann. Good for you."

"How are you doing, out on the ranch these days?" Tyler asked.

Letty Sue knew Tyler was just being polite by inquiring, and that Joellen had probably asked him to keep an eye on her. "I'm fine. Really. I do miss Mama. She wired me and asked me to join them in St. Louis."

"Uncle Jasper sent us a wire, too, last week. Sounds as though they're having a splendid time. Are you planning on joining them soon?" Lily snuggled the baby to her chest and began rocking him in her arms when he fussed. "There, there, now Ty."

"I, uh, I haven't decided yet."

"Well, let us know when you decide, Letty Sue,

and if there's any way we might help you." Lily placed an adoring kiss on her baby's forehead.

"Thank you. I will."

"Sorry to say, it's time for us to head home. This is little Ty's first trip to town. I think he's tuckered out. Send word if you need anything, Letty Sue," Tyler said with sincerity.

"I will. Goodbye." Letty Sue watched Tyler and his family walk off. They were a true family now. And all of them were as happy as could be.

Letty Sue had doubts as to what it would take to make her truly happy. But she shuffled them aside when little Elias Henderson came up and announced excitedly, "Time for the kissing booth, Miss Letty Sue. And I want to be first in line. Sally ain't here yet. She stayed behind to help Sam Fowler."

Letty Sue drew her eyebrows together and asked Sally's younger brother, "Help Sam? Why would Sam need her help?"

"We found him on the road. His horse spooked at a snake crossing its path and threw Sam a mile into the air. Hit his shoulder hard when he came down. Sally took him back home to patch him up."

"Oh dear. I wonder if I should go and check on him."

"Nah, it ain't that bad. Sally said they'd both be up at the picnic later. 'Sides, who's going to do all the kissing in the kissing booth if you go?"

"Sally was supposed to share the time with me."

"Looks like it's gonna be just you now, Miss Letty Sue."

"Well, I guess I'd better get to my booth."

They walked to the makeshift booth, consisting of two tall poles set in the ground and a plank table. A banner attached to the poles and waving in the breeze announced:

Kissing Booth—2 Bits Each
Limit 5 to a Customer

Letty Sue chuckled. "Who made up that sign?"

"Me and a bunch of my schoolmates at Sunday school."

"Well, it is for a good cause." The money donated today would go to building new benches in the church and fixing the roof. The whole congregation had got flooded out when the last thunderstorm hit during Sunday services, leaving the church in a shambles.

Letty Sue took her place in the booth, behind the table. A line formed that stretched across the yard and out the church gate.

Oh Lordy.

Kisses to the cheek only, she decided.

No matter what.

Chase leaned against a mesquite tree, watching the festivities from a distance. He took one last heady puff on a cheroot, then tossed it aside. A tick in his cheek worked overtime, pulling the skin taut with undue tension. He scrubbed his jaw, then clasped his hand into a fist.

What in blazes was wrong with him?

He refused to believe it was the overly long line forming for Letty Sue's kisses. Though from this distance, it looked innocent enough. She'd plant a quick kiss on a man's cheek and he'd walk off with a satisfied smile.

Chase hated that he noted which of the men took all five kisses at once. He hated that she smiled at the men in line with that innocent-seductive smile of hers. And he hated that she was the prettiest woman on the church grounds today in her sunflower-yellow dress and white bonnet.

It was a dress fit for a Sunday afternoon picnic, with just a touch of lace, and modest lines. But on Letty Sue's body, there'd be no mistaking the curves and swells, the dips and hollows or the feminine shuffle of petticoats as she sashayed by.

Last night, he could have had her. She'd been willing, but her damn innocence had kept him at bay. She didn't know what she'd done to him, how the yielding arch of her body had told him in an unwritten law of lovemaking what she'd offered him.

But, she'd have paid a sorry price in the morning for his sexual cravings.

And she would never have forgiven him.

He wasn't forgetting his promise to Joellen, but hell, last night Letty Sue had nearly made him forget how to breathe, much less his trusted obligation to her family.

Chase pushed himself away from the tree. He needed to get away for a spell. Watching nearly the entire male population of Sweet Springs put their hands on Letty Sue made his blood boil.

And he hated that, as well.

Letty Sue stood on the sidelines. Eight baskets had been auctioned off already, the creator of each one anonymous. Blue, yellow or red checkered clothes covered each one. The auctioneer, Elvin Monahan, lifted a cover to reveal a lovely vine basket covered with an array of dried flowers. He called for a beginning bid, and the unattached males of Sweet Springs began to holler out. The colorful basket brought a decent price of four dollars. Applause broke out when the gentleman met the lady responsible for the basket. Timothy Higgins, a ranch hand, took up the basket, then met the shy brown eyes of Ellie Singleton, the sheriff's daughter. Together they entered the eating area, set up with benches and tables under tall, shady mesquite trees.

Elvin Monahan uncovered the next basket in line. As the red checkered cloth was removed, Letty Sue held her breath. It was hers.

Compared to the others, this basket looked as though it had been through a stampede. A hush settled over the crowd. The auctioneer stumbled with his words. "Well, now, uh, look what we have here. Certainly, a worthy prize for anyone with a hankering for good food. Smells awfully delicious." He lifted the basket up high. "We'll start the bidding. Who'll give one dollar? One dollar, I say, who'll bid one dollar for this basket? C'mon now, gents, loosen up your pockets.''

Silence.

Letty Sue's heart nearly stopped. Heat enveloped her as humiliation coursed through her veins. She'd die of mortification if no one bid on her basket.

She'd tried her best, but the Withers's traditional ''rainbow'' basket was a complete failure with the most dismal colors. Even the small purple wildflower she'd picked to place on the very top had shriveled up, matching the rest of the gloomy creation.

''Let's hear one dollar,'' the auctioneer coaxed, ''one dollar for a good cause here.''

Murmurs went through the crowd.

Letty Sue waited, ramrod stiff, with head held high, ingrained family pride keeping her from bolting. She refused the tears welling up. No. She wouldn't cry.

She looked out over the crowd, her eyes scanning desperately. Where was Sam? she wondered. Hadn't he made it to town yet?

Oh Lordy, Letty Sue.

Oh Lordy, Lordy, Lordy.

Chapter Eight

Chase stood back from the auction, watching. He didn't notice the basket Sally Henderson had described to him. As a matter of fact, he hadn't seen the girl all day.

But he was determined to have himself a fine lunch with Sally. She'd be a pleasant distraction, just the diversion he needed to keep his mind off last night and Letty Sue. Yes, having a companionable afternoon with Sally Henderson would serve two purposes.

She'd keep him occupied with her friendly manner and artless ways. And secondly, Letty Sue would know for certain he'd meant what he said to her last night.

It'd be best for both if she took off to St. Louis to meet up with her folks.

When the auctioneer called the last bid for a god-awful basket, Chase's mind spun out, recalling this morning, when he'd spied Letty Sue out among a patch of wildflowers. She'd picked one, purple in color, and walked back to the house.

The very same wildflower sat rather limply atop the basket the auctioneer was holding up.

A sense of impending dread settled in his gut.

That hideous basket was Letty Sue's.

"Two bits!" a craggy-faced old dough puncher spat out. Chase recognized him from one the ranches he'd done business with a while back.

Chuckles went through the crowd.

Letty Sue's eyes went wide with shock. Her face contorted in a way Chase had never seen it do.

No doubt about it, that basket was hers.

Where the hell was Sam? Chase scanned the grounds quickly. Sam had warned him off about bidding for Letty Sue's basket. Said he'd always had the privilege and wanted to keep it that way.

Fine by Chase.

He didn't want to interfere.

He needed to stay the hell away from Letty Sue.

He'd made himself that promise last night.

So where the hell was Sam?

"Last call for this, uh, fine basket," the auctioneer called. "I've got two bits. Going once, going twice—"

"Ten dollars!" Chase called out.

All eyes turned to him and a hush settled over the crowd.

Chase ground his teeth, holding back a curse.

And quick as you please, the auctioneer finalized the sale.

Chase glanced at Letty Sue. Relief registered on her face, erasing the worry lines and contorted expression. Then the relief was replaced by a look much more frightening; her sky-blue eyes glowed with something akin to hero worship.

Ah, hell.

Chase made his way to the front where the auctioneer stood holding out the basket. He paid for it, doling out the bills slowly while the crowd watched.

Then he turned to Letty Sue with basket in hand. She joined him, her eyes bright, filled with gratitude.

Chase led her away from the curious onlookers.

A knot of dread twisted in his gut.

He wasn't looking forward to this lunch.

"Delicious chicken, Letty Sue," Chase said, offering her a compliment. "And the biscuits are real fluffy."

"Uh, thank you." Letty Sue couldn't meet Chase's eyes at the moment. She wiggled uncomfortably on the picnic bench. Chase had chosen a table far away from the crowd, much to Letty Sue's surprise. From the look on his face when he'd guided her away from the auction, she didn't think he'd want to spend any time alone with her. He wouldn't accept her gratitude, wouldn't allow her thanks. He simply sat down and began eating.

"Can't wait to dig into this pie. Cherry?" His steely eyes gleamed, taking in the perfectly browned crust.

"Uh, yes. It's cherry."

"You did real good with cooking this food, Letty Sue."

"My basket was a flop, a failure." She dipped her head.

"Ah, but I'm sure getting my money's worth with this meal."

Letty Sue snapped her head up. "Why'd you bid ten dollars?"

He shrugged. "Doesn't matter."

It did matter. She wanted to know. "After last night, I...I didn't think you'd... You said you were bidding on Sally's basket."

"Sally's not around. And where the devil is Sam today?" His head up, Chase searched the church grounds.

"Sally's brother said Sam's horse got spooked. Sam hurt his shoulder and Sally stayed behind to tend him."

Chase rubbed his jaw, his hand working over the area that had been bruised last night. "Too bad. He missed a fine meal." Chase picked up his fork and dived into the cherry pie.

"Is that all you care about? The food? Why, with the way you're eating, you'll be as stout as Mama's prize heifer in a matter of days!"

Chase lowered his fork, obviously startled at her outburst. "Letty Sue, calm down. What's got into you?"

"You like the food, don't you? But you won't admit the real reason you bid on my basket. You won't admit that last night—"

"Was a big mistake." Chase steeled his voice, exhibiting that ever-present calm that Letty Sue found most annoying. "It was my fault. I had too much to drink, Letty Sue. I take full responsibility. It's best we both forget it ever happened."

Angered and hurt by his rejection, Letty Sue inhaled sharply. A deep pain lodged in her chest, burning low like glowing embers. Chase Wheeler was the most infuriating man she'd ever known. He confused and perplexed her time and again. Last night he *had* felt something, she was sure, just as she had. He'd come to her when he was hurt and bleeding. He'd needed her.

No man had ever needed her before. They'd wanted her, she believed, but Chase had needed her. He'd kissed and caressed her, making her body sing with passion before denying her more. And then today, he'd come to her rescue yet again, spending far too much money on a miserable picnic basket.

"You bid ten dollars on a basket you knew darn well wouldn't be fit for consumption, Chase Wheeler."

He finished off the last bite of pie. "But it *was* fit for consumption. It's one of the best meals I've ever eaten, Letty Sue." His smug expression was her undoing.

She stood, tossing her checkered napkin across the table. "Well, you can just thank Emma Mayfield for that! I paid a visit to the diner after the stupid wagon hit a rough spot on the road. The basket fell off and everything spilled out! I had to beg her to cook up her very best for my disastrous basket!''

Shock registered on Chase's face. His eyes went wide with astonishment and his gaze roamed over the plate of food he'd just eaten. Letty Sue stood there with hands on hips, happy to have finally rattled the man.

He stood then, unfolding to his full height, taking her in, his smoky eyes penetrating hers.

Then he burst out laughing.

Chase made his way to a tall mesquite tree. The meal had filled his belly and he was ready to sit for a while, maybe close his eyes and rest. He sat down, then sprawled out, bracing his head against the tree trunk. Overhead, leaves rustled and the thick lacy branches shaded him from the day's heat.

Lifting the brim of his hat, he scanned the area. Angry with him, Letty Sue had taken off a minute ago, but now he spotted her talking with Sam and Sally. The two had lunched together after the bidding was over. Sam's shoulder was wrapped, but from all appearances, the man seemed fine. It didn't appear that he minded Sally's attentions, either.

Chase closed his eyes, ready for a short respite, but Letty Sue's image, furious and indignant, popped into his head. He knew the woman had spent the entire day cooking yesterday. She'd probably worked harder in one day than she had in her entire young life. Then, by accident, all her hard work had been dumped off the wagon when it hit a bump in the pitted road.

But he did admire her resourcefulness. Her dismal failures would have bested a weaker woman. Letty Sue hadn't given up. She'd been determined to show up here today with a basket filled with food. She'd done it, too.

Chase grinned. It was plain as day that Letty Sue wasn't cut out for domestic skills. Any man who wound up with her would have to know that from the start. Yet that man probably wouldn't care, given her other female attributes.

She could make a man forget his own name.

She'd had that very same effect on him last night.

Chase had regrets about their encounter, but the memory of her pliant body in his arms, the soft, creamy smoothness of her skin, the giving way her mouth pressed his would be forever etched in his mind.

He yanked his hat down low on his forehead and closed his eyes. Nothing like a good nap to clear a man's head.

The all-too-familiar scent of jasmine wafted in the air, bringing Chase out of his slumber. He turned his head in the direction of the pleasing fragrance and opened his eyes slowly. Raising up slightly, he made sure not to disturb the silence.

Letty Sue lay curled up next to him on a thin quilt she'd brought to the picnic. Her pinned-up hair had come half-loose in a wild tangle. Dark strands framed her lovely face, creating a vision so darn enticing Chase could only stare, watching her sleep peacefully.

"Brave Spirited Raven," he whispered. He longed to run his fingers through the dark silk, but he didn't want to disturb her peace, or his own. Touching her again would only bring forth images he'd best wipe clean from his mind.

He still couldn't believe she'd come anywhere near him again. Her anger had matched her exasperation when he'd laughed in her face today. He hadn't meant to hurt her and he hadn't been laughing over her carelessness with the basket, as she believed. It was her clever and inventive way of dealing with a dilemma that surprised him.

But the woman would never believe his claims of innocence on that matter. They were too different, though both were more than a bit stubborn, and they tended to lock horns more than they ever agreed on a subject.

Walk as one, stand together.

With his gaze fastened on Letty Sue, so pretty in her saffron-yellow dress, her ample chest rising and falling serenely in her slumber, Chase could only shake his head.

Letty Sue, the temptress with the near perfect face and brilliant azure eyes, would never be his.

He knew that as sure as he knew that the blazing sun would most certainly vanish below the horizon tonight.

Letty Sue opened her eyes to find herself lying next to Chase Wheeler under a tall mesquite tree, away from the festivities. His gaze was on the potato-sack race happening in the clearing just beyond the picnic tables. She sat up quickly, fidgeted with the hair that had come undone and straightened out creases in her dress. It hadn't been her intent to fall asleep next to him. She'd come to speak with him, and while she patiently waited for him to awaken, she must have fallen asleep as well.

He turned to her and smiled. Why did his smiles mean so much to her? And why were her feelings all jumbled up? Up until now, she'd been a woman who knew her own mind. She'd always known what she wanted from life, had always known how to get it.

But it was Sally who'd coerced her earlier into coming back here. She'd said that Letty Sue didn't really know Chase, and that to better understand him, she should try talking with him. Simply talking. They'd never really done that.

It seemed all they managed to do was get angry with each other.

"Didn't think you'd come back." He spoke softly. She felt the heat of his dark gaze.

Turning to him, she shrugged. "I thought we could talk."

"Talk?" Chase's expression revealed his outright confusion.

"Yes, Chase. Talk. Like two grown-ups."

He raised his brows. "About what?"

"Anything you want."

"I'm not much for talking, Letty Sue, but I will say this, you're a remarkable woman. Not too many women would have done what you did today."

She didn't agree. She'd felt inadequate, and then humiliated until Chase had once again saved her pride. "Because I hired someone to cook a meal for me?"

Seeming admiration sparked in his eyes. "Well, yeah."

A hint of a smile began surfacing, curving her lips. "I do what has to get done, Chase."

"Resourceful."

"When I have to be."

"It's an admirable trait, Letty Sue. You don't give up and you hold your head high."

"At least I got something from Mama."

Chase leaned back, stretching out his long legs, bracing himself with his elbows. Letty Sue did the same. The strong sweet Southern sun peeked through the branches, warming her cheeks.

She glanced over at Chase. His rugged jaw was set, and his ink-black hair curled slightly at the nape, lifting in the soft breeze. A white shirt fit snugly on broad shoulders, the color setting off his deeply bronzed skin.

Letty Sue recalled his potent kisses last night, his tender yet tough way of making her yield to his passion. He'd touched her as no other man ever had. She wanted more—she'd wanted it all. She should feel shamed at the wanton way she'd behaved, but instead, she felt contentment such as she'd never known before. The recollections of last night heated her body and warmed her heart. No other man had ever evoked in her such intimate and heady responses.

Only Chase.

"Is it because of Mama, Chase?"

He caught her meaning immediately and didn't hesitate to answer. For that, she was grateful. He glanced at her quickly before lifting his face to the sun. "There was a woman once that caused me nothing but grief, Letty Sue." He brought his head down and leveled a gaze at her. His eyes were bright with honesty, his voice earnest. "Spoiled, selfish, beautiful." He stared at Letty Sue then, and added, "The boss's stepdaughter."

The similarities couldn't be missed. And by the way Chase was looking at her, she knew he, too, believed her to be all of those things. A lump lodged in her throat. To deny those similarities would serve no purpose. Chase had stated his case, more than once, letting her know exactly what he thought of her. The insult felt like a harsh slap to her cheek.

"She hurt you. You wanted her and she hurt you."

Chase didn't deny it. Unwelcome emotion roiled within her as she thought of Chase and his desire for another woman.

"What we want and what we can have are two different notions, Letty Sue."

"I've heard that said before. But I never understood the meaning. I always thought you should go after what you want, as long as no one gets hurt."

"Snow Cloud once told me that sometimes you can't help the hurt, even when you do the right thing."

"What did your mother mean by that?"

"I think she was speaking of my father. She said she loved him fiercely, but knew when the time came for him to leave, she wouldn't go with him."

"What happened?" Letty Sue turned to face him fully, eager to hear about Chase's family, his past.

"She often spoke of my father, but never with much detail, really. She'd tell me I had his honor and strength. She found him near dead in Indian Territory one winter. He'd been bushwhacked and left to die. She brought him home and nursed him in her lodge. They fell in love and were married in the eyes of the Cheyenne. When he fully recovered, he had to head back to his own life. His white life. Snow Cloud knew she could never live in the white world. She loved the tribe and her heritage too much and knew she'd never fit in anywhere but with the Cheyenne. He pleaded with her for months, delayed his leaving, but finally she made it clear it was for the best. I know it cost my mother her heart to let him go, but she knew it was the only way. He couldn't stay and she couldn't leave."

"What about you?"

"He didn't know about me. He'd left long before I was born."

"You never had a father, then?"

"No, but my grandfather and I were very close. At night, I'd visit him. He was a master storyteller. I learned all the Cheyenne legends from him. He and Snow Cloud were enough for me."

"We both grew up without fathers," she said sadly.

"We had strong mothers."

They seemed to have that in common, but their differences more than made up for what they mutually shared.

Yet Letty Sue felt a kinship with him now, grateful he'd shared this part of his past with her. He'd been hurt in many ways, had lost ones closest to him. Impulsively, she reached out to touch his arm. "Chase…"

"Come on, Letty Sue," he said, standing abruptly. He leaned over to help her up. "We should get back."

Letty Sue sighed wearily and took the hand he offered. She knew he'd not be offering anything more.

Chapter Nine

Chase stood on the sidelines with Sam, watching the children's relay races. Both Letty Sue and Sally were on the front lines, cheering their assigned teams on. Both women had volunteered to help with the games and hand out the ribbons to the winners.

"How's the shoulder, Sam?"

Sam rubbed his left shoulder. "Better after Sally tended to it. She rubbed some liniment on and patched me up real good."

"I heard a snake crossed your path."

"Yeah, usually I'm watching out, but I was anxious to get to the festivities. I guess my mind wasn't much on where I was going. That old diamondback put a fright into Willy. Never saw that cow pony get so doggone jiggled. It caught me off guard, and when Willy jolted, I flew off and landed flat out on my shoulder. It's gonna be stiff for a while, I imagine."

"You might just have to get Sally to rub that liniment on it again," Chase said, teasing.

Sam peered over at the young woman with the

blond curls. He chuckled. "Now that ain't a half-bad idea."

Chase grinned and his gaze followed the women, but the one that caught his eye, the one who always seemed to get into his sights, the one who regularly captured his attention, was Letty Sue. Both women were pretty, Sally with her wheat-colored hair, expressive eyes and slender frame, but dammit if Letty Sue didn't outshine her and every other woman here.

"You know, you missed a real fine meal."

"I apologized to Letty Sue," Sam said. "I guess she sort of expected me to be there."

Chase nodded, taking his eyes off Letty Sue. Instead, he concentrated on the races. "She did."

"But I heard some ranch foreman bid the highest ever for her basket. Geez, Chase. Ten dollars? That's gonna bust me next year. What got into your head? Not that Letty Sue ain't worth it, but *ten dollars?*"

Chase took off his hat to scratch his head. "Yeah, I know. Damn fool thing to do. But this old dough puncher insulted her with a two-bit bid."

"And you laid down a week's wage because of it?"

Chase shook his head. "At least it was the best meal I've had in a while."

"That's something," Sam agreed, then his mouth split into a grin. "I heard Emma Mayfield cooked it. Letty Sue said her lunch flew off the wagon when it hit a hole in the road. The whole thing dumped onto the ground. Guess that was sorta lucky on your part."

"Guess so. Letty Sue was mad about it."

"Mad at you, you mean."

"That's nothing new, Sam. That woman and me, we don't see eye to eye on anything." Chase slapped Sam on the back, making sure not to injure his sore side. "Now that you're here, you can spend the rest of the day with her."

Sam's gaze darted directly to Sally, who was busy pinning red ribbons on the winners of a three-man relay race. "Uh, Chase...I was sorta gonna spend some time with Sally, if you don't mind. I was hoping you'd see Letty Sue home tonight. I promised Sally I'd escort her home later, you know, as a thank-you for her helping me today."

"That so?"

"Do you mind?"

It meant spending more time with Letty Sue. Something he didn't want to do, especially not after that talk he'd had with her earlier. Being honest with himself, he admitted it had been nice sharing bits of his Cheyenne life with her. He'd not spoken about his mother and father to anyone, really, and Letty Sue seemed to understand. She hadn't made judgments, but simply listened, seeming truly interested. He'd begun to feel something akin to friendship with her, but he wouldn't fool himself into believing they could be friends.

Chase had never had a woman friend, much less one as beautiful and tempting as Letty Sue.

He'd best just stick to his original plan of keeping his distance. But he wouldn't refuse Sam the favor, even if that favor meant having to spend the rest of the day with Letty Sue. "Sally's a nice girl, Sam."

"I'm just now learning that," Sam said. "She's real sweet."

Chase agreed, keeping his reluctance to himself. "I'll see Letty Sue home tonight. You go on and court Sally."

"Court her?" Sam's forehead wrinkled.

Chase laughed. "Sam, that's what you're doing, isn't it?"

"Well, I suppose. She is nice…and real pretty."

"Sweet, too," Chase said, repeating Sam's words. "Go on and have fun."

Sam took one more look at Sally. "Appreciate it, Chase. Hope you and Letty Sue manage to have a pleasant evening."

Doubtful, Chase thought. Every time he thought about her, it was as if he was pushing her away with one hand and pulling her in with the other. "I think we can manage that," he answered tightly.

"Chase told you he had a woman in Abilene?" Sally asked, her interest piqued. They sat on a picnic bench folding napkins. The festivities had died down some. Most of the younger children had been taken home; now just the dance was left. Letty Sue didn't feel much like kicking up her heels.

And she wished she hadn't spoken about Chase to Sally. Letty Sue wanted to put thoughts of him aside. And now Sally had nothing but questions. "She hurt him real bad. He didn't have kind words to say about her.'' She didn't add, ''And he thinks I'm just like her.'' The pain of his silent comparison was still with her. Chase didn't hold her in high regard. He probably didn't much like her at all. But he had to be civil to her because of Joellen and his job at the Double J.

Sally's green eyes gleamed. ''Any man who'd bid ten dollars on your basket can't still be hankering for another woman. Letty Sue, why, nearly the entire town's talking about how he bid so high for you. It means something. You and him, out on the ranch. No chaperons.''

''*He's* my chaperon. He's forever telling me where I can go, whom I can see, what to do, what not to do. I swear, he treats me like a child, Sally.'' Except when he took her into his arms and showed her his passion—Letty Sue hadn't felt like a child then. Chase made her feel like a real woman.

''I think there's more to it than that, Letty Sue.'' With the napkins folded, they stood and went to different ends of the picnic table. Lifting the tablecloth easily, they brought the points together. Letty Sue dropped her end and Sally finished squaring off the folds.

''I really don't want to think about him anymore today.''

Sally chuckled then and peered over Letty Sue's shoulder. ''Well, doesn't look like you're going to have much choice. Here he comes now, with Sam.''

Letty Sue watched Sam twirl Sally around the dance area. The picnic tables had been moved to form a large circle, much like a wagon train, so that the center arena could be used as a prairie grass dance floor. Nobody minded. It was far too lovely an evening to be indoors, anyway. In an hour, dusk would settle on the land.

A fiddler played a lively tune, and Sally, with skirts swishing, laughed at something Sam had said. They looked good together, happy. Letty Sue smiled, glad that her friend was having a good time.

"Care to dance, Miss Letty Sue?" Toby asked.

Letty Sue had to let the ranch hand down gently. She cast him a sweet smile. "I'm so tired, Toby, my feet refuse to move. I'm sorry."

"That's all right. Maybe next time, then." Double J's youngest employee sauntered off.

"You really don't feel like dancing, do you, Letty Sue?" Chase came up to stand next to her. He handed her a glass of punch. "That's about the fifth man you refused."

"Normally, I love dancing. Just not tonight," she said, taking a small sip of the punch. Chase hadn't asked for a dance. Not that she'd have danced with him, but he didn't even have the courtesy to ask her. "We can leave anytime you're ready."

He nodded. "I've got the wagon all packed up." He took her cup and placed it on the table. "Let's go."

Letty Sue waved her goodbyes to Sam and Sally, and had turned to leave with Chase when she nearly collided into the chest of Sheriff Singleton. He made a quick apology, then turned his attention to Chase.

His face was solemn, as were the faces of two other men, lawmen, whom she didn't recognize.

"Chase Wheeler, I believe you know Sheriff Mercer from Abilene, and this is Deputy Bodine. They, uh, they came here to speak with you."

The three men encircled Chase, leaving her out. She stood there listening, a sense of dread creeping up her spine.

"What's this all about?" Chase asked, looking each man straight in the eye.

Sheriff Mercer stepped forward. "I've got some questions for you. We can do it here or back at the jail."

"Here is fine," Chase said.

"Okay," he said, "did you work for Seth Johnston over the past years?"

"You know I did, Sheriff. You've been to his ranch. You've seen me. I worked there for ten years."

"And were you involved with his stepdaughter, Marabella Donat?"

Chase's lips thinned to one grim line. "Now, that you're going to have to ask her yourself."

"We did, Chase. She said you and she, well, you were nearly engaged."

Letty Sue gasped. Engaged? She didn't know it had been that serious with Chase and the woman.

Chase slanted her a quick sideways glance, then focused all his attention back on the sheriff. "I'm sure you didn't travel all this way to Sweet Springs to ask about my love life, Mercer. What's this all about?"

A small crowd began to gather. They stood back,

but were close enough to hear the goings-on. Letty Sue pushed forward, wedging herself between Chase and Sheriff Singleton.

"A man's dead, Mr. Wheeler, murdered. That's what this is all about. Did you know a Mr. Pierce Mainwarring from Georgia?"

Chase flinched. His body went rigid. "I met him…once."

"And when he showed up at the ranch, did you and he argue?"

Chase nodded. "We did."

"Over Miss Donat?"

Chase nodded again.

"He shows up and next thing you know, Marabella Donat is engaged to him. Would make just about any man angry enough—"

"To kill?" Chase interrupted. "I didn't kill Pierce Mainwarring, Sheriff, if that's what you're getting at."

"It is, exactly, what I'm getting at. Man's body was found halfway between here and Abilene. A long night's ride would be just about enough time for someone bent on revenge. He'd been tied up and shot, dumped down a ravine. Where were you three nights ago, on the fifteenth?"

"Where I always am, on the Double J Ranch."

"Did you see anybody, talk to anybody late that night?"

"No, I went to bed."

Sheriff Singleton came forward then. "Chase, I got no quarrel with you. Lord knows, Joellen Withers thinks mighty highly of you, and aside from last night at the saloon, you've had no trouble in this town. I already explained to Sheriff Mercer that last night wasn't your fault. But to be truthful, I've asked around and none of the Double J ranch hands laid eyes on you that night.''

''Doesn't mean I killed a man.''

''No, but this might.'' Sheriff Mercer turned to his deputy. The man handed the sheriff a hemp rope. ''We found this on the dead man. The boys at Johnston's place said it was yours. They recognized the different way you braid it up and tie it off—the *Cheyenne* way. Is this your lariat?''

Chase glanced at the rope and nodded. ''It could be. I left more than few things behind when I came here. Anybody could have used that rope.''

Mercer took his hat off and scratched his head. ''But seems you're the only one with no alibi, and good cause to want to get rid of the man. Jealousy and revenge make darn good motives.''

Chase's face went hard as stone, an unyielding mask of anger and indignation. ''You arresting me, Sheriff?''

''I'm afraid I am.'' He lifted his gun from his holster. ''Josh, get the rope and tie his hands. Chase Wheeler, I'm placing you under arrest for the murder of Pierce Mainwarring.''

Up until that point, Letty Sue had stood ramrod stiff, taking in all that was happening. She couldn't believe her eyes or her ears. They were arresting Chase for murder!

"Stop!" She set herself between Chase and the deputy. "You can't do this."

"Letty Sue, what are you doing?" Chase asked harshly.

"Back away, Letty Sue." Sheriff Singleton kept his voice calm, but his gaze warned her off.

She didn't care that she was obstructing so-called justice; she had to put a stop to this ridiculous claim.

"Not until you listen to me. Chase Wheeler is *not* a murderer. He didn't commit this crime. You can't haul him off to jail. It's not right."

The deputy sidestepped Letty Sue, put both of Chase's arms behind his back and began tying him up.

"Stop this," she pleaded with Sheriff Singleton. "You can't let them arrest him. Do something!"

"Nothing I can do, Letty Sue. Now, move aside and let these men do their job."

Letty Sue didn't hesitate. She knew what she had to do. Chase wasn't a murderer. He couldn't be. There was too much honor in him to shoot a man, then dump him down a ravine. Chase would never do such a thing. He'd saved her life countless times, and her virtue, too. Her heart spoke and she listened, all else be damned.

"He was with me that night and every night since!"

Murmurs went through the crowd as nearly the entire church congregation witnessed the scene. The fiddler quit playing, and she was sure everyone on the dance floor stopped and turned to listen. Letty Sue held her head high and fixed her gaze on John Singleton.

The sheriff stared at her in disbelief, his patience nearly tried. "Now, Letty Sue, you know that ain't true."

"You've known me since I was a tot, John. Do you honestly think I'd admit that in front of the whole town if it weren't true?"

"Don't, Letty Sue," Chase warned.

She ignored Chase's admonition. "We spend our nights together. He's trying to protect me, but it's the truth, Sheriff, I swear."

"She's lying, Sheriff. Don't believe her," Chase declared rigidly, his silver eyes now burning black with anger. And he turned those black eyes on her. There was dire warning in his voice. "Don't do this, Letty Sue. Tell them you're lying."

Letty Sue stood her ground. She couldn't let them take Chase to jail for murder. If it meant losing her pride, then that was the sacrifice she'd have to make. "Chase Wheeler and I spend all our nights together, that's how I know for sure. He *was* with me three nights ago. The entire night."

She didn't dare look at Chase. She could almost feel his anger scorching her skin. Instead, she shot Sheriff Singleton a look of indignation. "Well?"

"Uh, just a minute." Sheriff Singleton took Mercer aside, while the deputy trained his gun on Chase. They spoke in hushed tones and finally, after several minutes, Sheriff Mercer approached.

"Let him go, Josh. Sheriff Singleton vouches for

her word." He turned away from his deputy and shot her a sharp, cautioning look. "But if I find out you're lying, miss, I'll be back. And Mr. Wheeler won't be the only one getting arrested."

She held her breath and nodded. No words would come. At least now she'd repaid Chase for all the times he'd come to her rescue. With a glance, she noted the deputy removing the ropes. Chase rubbed at his wrists and marched over to her. She cast him a tentative smile.

He grabbed her arm and yanked her off to the side, away from the curious onlookers. "You little fool. You don't know what in the hell you've done!"

"I do know what I've done, Chase. I kept you out of jail. Or do you want those ropes that were on your wrists a bit higher—say, around your neck?"

"I'm innocent. I could've proved it."

"I don't see how. Seems Sheriff Mercer's mind was made up before he spoke with you."

"Letty Sue, damn you! I'm not going to let you ruin your reputation."

She cringed then, acknowledging that her reputation was, in fact, ruined. The whole town had heard her admit to spending nights with Chase, sharing his bed. "It's too late for that. Besides, all I truly care about is our own friends on the ranch. And they all know it's not true."

A dubious look crossed Chase's face, replacing the anger. "And how's that?"

"Why, because they all know you sleep in the

bunkhouse with them. They know you don't come to me at night.''

His mouth twisted and his dark look frightened her. ''That's where you're dead wrong, woman. I haven't spent one night in the bunkhouse. Not one. I sleep way out back beyond the barn.''

Letty Sue flinched as though she'd been slapped. ''Oh.''

''And now not only the whole town, but all the men at the ranch believe I've been bedding you all this time.''

Heat flushed her cheeks, the implications of what she'd done coming full circle now. Her heart pounded wildly, frantically. She'd gotten herself in trouble before, but nothing compared to this.

Chase's lips twitched angrily. He spat out, ''You've given me no choice. I'm going to have to marry you.''

Chapter Ten

"M-marry m-me?" Letty Sue's eyes widened in shock. He couldn't be serious. Her racing heart speeded up even more. "Y-you don't w-want to do that."

"No, I don't. But I will."

"Chase, it's not necessary. I'll...I'll find a way out of this mess. You—"

His face went hard like granite and his dark gaze bored into her with such powerful intensity she thought she'd split in two right on the spot. "You'll marry me and that's the end of it."

"The end of it?" She raised her voice. "I'm sorry, but when I marry, the joining won't be the end of anything...but the beginning of something grand. My answer is no."

He took her arms and shook her gently but thoroughly. She felt his restraint, what it cost him not to shake the dickens out of her. "You *will* marry me. Tonight. *Now.*"

"But—"

"Letty Sue." Sam came forward, interrupting. "He's doing right by you. It's the only thing a man can do. I'd do the same if I were in his place."

She stomped her foot. "Sam, you're my friend."

Sam shook his head. "I'm telling you like it is, Letty Sue. It's best you get married. The sooner the better."

"Oh," she said, bewildered. She hadn't thought Sam would side with Chase. Letty Sue wasn't ready for marriage. She didn't want a man who felt obliged to marry her. Chase would never love her. He hardly tolerated her. What kind of marriage would that make?

"Let me have a minute with her." Sally took Letty Sue by the arm, away from Chase's scrutiny. She spoke softly, calmly, once they were out of earshot of the men. The crowd stood back, but watched curiously, most likely wondering about the outcome to the most scandalous occurrence Sweet Springs had ever seen. "Letty Sue, my friend, I'm afraid this is one fix you can't get out of on your own. You helped Chase, and I understand why you did it, but honey, he's trying to help you now."

"He's furious. I'm to marry a man who's not at all happy about the marriage? How can I do that, Sally?"

"Simple. You just do, my friend. Your reputation is at stake. Think of your mother and how the town respects her, Letty Sue. Do it for her, if not yourself. Besides, you and Chase, you're like two rushing streams flowing alongside one another, each one on its own path. But honey, once you two merge, the currents will unite like the waters filling a river full up, and make for a beautiful union.''

Letty Sue was skeptical. Doubts gnawed at her, yet she couldn't see any other way out of her predicament.

Sally continued to beseech her. ''Chase is handsome, intelligent, and Letty Sue, his eyes burn with desire when he looks at you.''

Letty Sue stole a quick glance at Chase, then shivered. ''They're burning now, Sally, but it's not desire I see in his eyes.''

Sally's blond brows lifted and she spoke low in her ear. ''I know there's something between you two. Marry him, Letty Sue. Find out what it all means.''

''I guess I don't have a choice,'' she said, attempting a smile. She glanced back at Chase, who was staring directly at her, pinning her with a gaze filled with rigid determination. Her legs weakened and her whole body trembled.

''Cheer up, Letty Sue. You're marrying a good man.''

But would he make a good husband? And she a good wife? Marriage had been the farthest thing from her mind. She planned to travel, to see new things. Now she'd have obligations, wifely obligations. Again, her body shook with trepidation.

Sally laced their arms together, giving Letty Sue courage as they walked over to the men. ''You have yourself a bride, Chase,'' Sally said with pride in her voice. Dear Sally, she truly was a good friend.

He grunted in acknowledgment, yet his eyes stayed

fastened on Letty Sue. Her breath caught in her throat. She swallowed hard and prayed she was making the right decision.

Sam called for the preacher, who'd been observing the entire scene from the steps of the church. He rushed over and spoke with them, making sure there was mutual consent. Then he invited everyone inside the church. "Please stay for the service," he said. "There's going to be a wedding."

"Tonight, Reverend Davidson?" Letty Sue asked.

The robust, balding man smiled warmly and took her hand. "Tonight, Miss Withers. There's no time like the present."

Letty Sue felt the eyes of the entire congregation on her back. She stood stiff and straight next to Chase, listening to the vows Reverend Davidson read out. He made fast work of getting them married, the ceremony taking scant minutes. She could almost hear the preacher's silent sigh of relief once the vows had been spoken.

Chase turned to her and placed a chaste kiss on her lips. Still and all, with nearly the whole town watching, Letty Sue felt heat singe her cheeks. She was astounded at how one lie could manifest such dire consequences.

She was a married woman.

Chase Wheeler was her husband.

She was Letty Sue Wheeler now.

The magnitude of her actions just hitting her, she turned in a daze and allowed Chase to lead her out of the church. There were congratulations, hand-shakes, kisses to the cheek, and as quickly as they were wed, Chase whisked her away from the well-wishers surrounding them.

Just before the ceremony, Sally had quickly rounded up flowers blooming outside the church gates and made up a small bouquet. She'd also insisted on repinning Letty Sue's hair and tucking in bright yellow buttercups along her crown.

Chase said little to her, but had taken her hand and walked her down the aisle automatically, as though this ceremony was an everyday occurrence. He'd said his vows, yet never once did he look at her face or into her eyes. Tears had welled up then, but her stubborn pride wouldn't allow them to fall.

Letty Sue had imagined her wedding day, when the proper time came, to be much, much different.

And Mama wasn't even here.

Letty Sue gasped inwardly. What would she tell her mother? And when?

Oh, she'd put that dilemma aside for now. Right now, she had enough to contend with—namely, one deceivingly calm, handsome, headstrong husband.

"Where are we going?" Letty Sue ventured to ask, noting they weren't heading toward the livery where the horses were stabled.

"To the hotel."

She stopped walking, pulling her hand free from Chase's. "The hotel?"

He turned a scornful gaze on her. "It's late, I'm

tired and it's best we show the town this marriage is real.''

Her body stiffened with shock. She asked quietly, "Real?"

His lips puckered and his tone mocked. He took her hand and continued down the street. "Don't worry, Letty Sue. Only you and I will know the truth of it.''

Letty Sue wasn't sure of his meaning. Was he protecting her by making sure everyone believed her claims earlier? Was he being noble once again, to insure Sheriff Mercer would not return to arrest her as well as him?

Is that what he meant by *real?*

Or did he mean to bed her tonight, to consummate the marriage?

They entered the hotel amid curious eyes. The clerk stared inquisitively, then, upon witnessing Chase's seething look, quickly busied himself with the ledgers.

"We'll take your best room. Nothing's too good for my bride,'' Chase said out of the corner of his mouth.

"Uh, why certainly, Mr. Wheeler.'' Chase signed in and the clerk handed him the key. "Room 214. It's the nicest one we've got. Up the stairs, three doors to your right.''

Chase slipped a gold coin into the clerk's hand. "And see that your finest bottle of whiskey is delivered to our room.''

"Yes, sir.'' The clerk dared a glance at Letty Sue

and smiled timidly. She turned her head away. This was all so humiliating.

"It's our wedding night," Chase said unnecessarily.

The hotel clerk blustered, "Uh, yes. I know. Congratulations."

Chase turned to Letty Sue and with one swift motion lifted her in his arms. Stunned into silence, she gawked at him. He didn't meet her gaze, but fixed his eyes straight ahead and proceeded up the stairs.

Mortified now, realizing his intent, Letty Sue kicked and squirmed and pounded on Chase's chest. "Put me down, Chase. Right this instant," she hissed, hoping the clerk and others in the hotel lobby weren't gaping at them.

"Don't think so. You get the full marriage treatment. Don't want anyone saying this marriage is a sham, darlin'. But you and I know different, don't we?"

She stopped wiggling. "What do you mean?"

Reaching the top of the stairs and finding the room, he put the key in the lock and opened the door. Instead of setting her down once they were over the threshold, as was traditional, he kicked the door shut with his boot heel, walked over to the bed and emptied his arms, dropping her rather unceremoniously. The bedsprings creaked and she bounced before regaining her balance. "Oh!"

"What I mean, *Mrs. Wheeler,*" he began, pointing his finger, "is that this marriage is a fraud, as fake as fool's gold. I'm saving your reputation, but that's as far as it goes. As soon as Joellen gets back from her trip, the marriage will be dissolved. Until then, you're my wife in public, but in private we'll be just as we were.''

Letty Sue sat up, straightening her clothes and mustering her dignity. Her blood simmering now, she smiled sweetly and said ever so softly, ''You mean you'll be as obstinate and bullheaded as ever.''

Chase responded to the contrast of her caustic words and her soft tone. ''If that's what it takes to put down your impulsive and foolish nature,'' he replied, his voice brittle.

Letty Sue let loose a long-suffering sigh. She didn't want to start out her marriage this way, even if it was a fraud. Emotions roiled within her, and she wasn't completely certain that disappointment wasn't the chief sensation she felt. Chase wouldn't be her husband in a real sense. She should be relieved, but instead, overwhelming melancholy set in, and it more than unnerved her. ''Chase,'' she began, then halted. What could she say? She wasn't sure a real marriage was what she wanted, yet the thought of living in a false one didn't bode too well, either.

A knock at the door brought her out of her gloomy thoughts. Chase answered it, gripping a bottle of amber liquid when he closed the door.

''Go to bed, Letty Sue,'' he said solemnly. ''I won't be disturbing you. The only one I plan on bedding down with tonight is my friend here.'' He held up the whiskey bottle to make his point.

Letty Sue closed her eyes and swallowed hard. If

the wedding hadn't been like anything she'd ever imagined, her wedding night certainly won first prize for being the worst in recent history. With the lantern light turned down, Chase slumped against the door.

A weary expression stole over his face and Letty Sue almost felt sorry for him. But then he raised the bottle to his lips and slugged down a mouthful.

With a deep, soulful breath, Letty Sue lowered herself and tried to get comfortable in the big accommodating bed.

And so began her honeymoon.

Chase cursed the whiskey that roiled around in his gut, causing turmoil, yet not the desired results. The spirits should have knocked him out by now, so he could shut his mind off for a spell and get some sleep.

Instead the alcohol did the opposite, keeping him awake and fully aware of the woman just five feet away from him, tossing and turning on the luxurious four-poster bed. Her soft moans and night sounds made him ache. He lay there watching her and, with wry deprecation, mused that he'd found a new form of self-torture, one more harmful than the Cheyenne way. His body grew taut. His teeth clenched.

And when he heard rustling, he followed the movement with narrowed eyes. Letty Sue had gotten out of bed. Centered between the parted, crimson velvet draperies, she stood by the window, gazing out. The moon fully defined the soft curves of her body, silhouetting her womanly form. The pale, glowing light caressed her, making her seem unworldly in her beauty.

Chase continued to watch her slight movements. She lifted her arms and pulled the pins from her hair. Several buttercups, nearly wilted now, fell to the floor, and her glorious curls spilled onto her shoulders. Slowly, she reached back, attempting to undo the buttons of her gown. Her fingers fumbled and he heard her mutter a soft curse. Hearing her swear put a smile on his lips. She pushed and pulled at the fabric, failing in her mission. Chase found himself standing behind her before good sense set in.

Her startled gasp was one of sheer fright, for he was certain she'd not heard him rise.

"Shh, it's just me," he murmured in her ear. She attempted to turn to face him, but he clamped his hands on her shoulders and kept her facing straight ahead. "Need some help getting out of this thing?"

She hesitated, her shoulders rigid, but finally she let the tension seep out, and nodded. "Yes, please. I'm uncomfortable sleeping in all these clothes."

He grinned, knowing she couldn't see him. He remembered her attire, or rather lack of it, the night she'd ridden her horse into town. "Wearing lots of petticoats tonight?"

"Too many, I'm afraid," she whispered. She lifted her hair, sweeping the sable waves to one side, and offered him her back.

With nimble fingers, Chase worked at the shiny pearl buttons, each one popping open to reveal the tempting flesh underneath. He breathed in her scent and wished for one small moment in time that they *were* married, in the real sense. He'd remove her clothes, then she'd turn and help to shed his, and they'd both drop to the bed in a fit of unbridled passion.

Chase drove those thoughts from his head. He could ill afford to let his lusty cravings overrule what he knew to be his obligation. He couldn't make love to Letty Sue. He couldn't take her innocence and then leave once her mother returned to the ranch.

Letty Sue had done a foolish thing. Her impetuous nature had nearly caused her ruin, but he'd rectified that tonight by marrying her. Once his anger ceased, he'd realized the price she'd been willing to pay for his freedom.

It humbled him.

But irritated him as well.

Because now he had a complication he didn't want—a wife so damn tempting he knew his willpower would be amply tested on a regular basis.

And knowing that she was *his* woman, legally, made it all the more appealing in his mind.

But his vow to protect her didn't come lightly.

And he knew for certain that Letty Sue wasn't the woman for him. He couldn't trust her. Thoughts of Marabella's deceit kept his heart cold. He'd not make the same mistake again. He would keep his judgment rational and sound, no matter how tempting his wife was.

No, Chase thought miserably, he couldn't take her

innocence, then walk away. He wouldn't dishonor either one of them that way.

"All through," he said tightly, reining in his emotions. The wedding night, the half undressed woman who was his wife, the moonlight streaming in and the big bed filling the room was just about too much for Chase.

His willpower ebbing, he pushed the material off her shoulders gently, deliberately grazing her skin with his fingers. It was creamy and soft. With a deep inhalation of breath, he stepped closer and slid his hands down her arms, following the sleeves of her gown down to her wrists.

In essence, she was trapped by the confines of her dress and completely at his mercy. He could do as he pleased with her in this position and ease the ache that seemed to consume him tonight. But her slight trembling and the little catch in her throat brought him back to his senses.

He backed off instantly, as though she was fire and he'd just been burned. He stood against the wall once again, watching.

Her back to him, she said politely, "Thank you."

She laid her petticoats and dress out across the polished oak chest and returned to the bed.

Chase had an uncanny urge to tuck her in. Hadn't he once told her that if he tucked her in, she'd have nothing to complain about?

Ah hell, he thought. The long and short of it was that if he tucked her in properly, the way he wanted to, neither one of them would be complaining in the morning.

He slid back down to the floor and lifted what was left in the whiskey bottle to his lips. It wouldn't help.

Nothing would.

Because tomorrow, Chase would be moving into the ranch house with her.

Chapter Eleven

Letty Sue glanced at the food she'd prepared, set out in lovely hand-crafted bowls on the dining room table, and foolishly hoped her husband would join her for dinner. True, he'd get a better meal with the boys under the thatched roof canopy where they ate each evening, but she'd hoped Chase wouldn't humiliate her that way. This was their first official night together on the ranch. She worried over what the ranch hands would think, how they'd react to Chase not spending time with her tonight. Chase had not spoken a word about it, leaving her to wonder.

After dropping her off this morning with a brief, polite farewell, he'd left her to her own devices. She'd tried to conjure up things to do—*wifely* things to do—but all she managed in the end was to sit in her room and contemplate her life. Self-pity not suiting her nature, Letty Sue soon had had enough, and decided to use her culinary skills, limited as they were, to cook her husband a meal.

Now the fare sat on the table on a lovely lace tablecloth, getting cold.

The back door creaked open, jolting Letty Sue from her thoughts. To her relief, Chase entered, stomping dirt from his boots at the doorway, then coming farther in to lift his hat off and hang it on a peg on the back wall.

He'd entered the kitchen first, then noted the dining table set with dishes her mother only turned out for very special occasions. His brows lifted in question.

"I—I th-thought it fitting to eat our first meal in here," Letty Sue said, loathing the trepidation she heard in her voice.

Chase gave her a quick nod. "Doesn't matter where we eat, Letty Sue."

She drew in her bottom lip. She hadn't wanted to start their marriage, sham that it was, on the wrong foot. And she'd vowed not to argue with Chase tonight. They could live in misery or they could have a decent time of it, until her mother returned.

She'd put all notions of joining her mother in the East out of her head for now. Newly married, she thought to make a proper wife for Chase, even though he wanted nothing to do with this marriage. Yet she felt an undeniable obligation to him and, admittedly, to herself. Failing as a marriage partner was not an option. Something drove her, making her want to prove to herself as well as to Chase that she could do this.

"Well, then," she said cheerily, "let's eat."

Chase sat down at the table, and she watched him

lift a bowl, staring at it as though resigning himself to eat. With a rounded spoon, he ladled some food onto his plate. Tawny misshapen objects that had sunk to the bottom of the bowl emerged onto his plate. His look of astonishment prompted her to explain.

"It's chicken…with dumplings?"

Chase's face registered no emotion. "Are you paying Petey for cooking lessons?"

"Yes, but I…only had the one," she said quietly, remembering how Chase had stormed into the diner, ready to protect her honor. She still believed jealousy was what had driven him, but he would never in this lifetime admit to that. "But I plan to have more," she hastened to add.

He picked up his spoon and ate. Whether he liked the food or not, he didn't say. They sat in silence, Letty Sue not touching a bite, but pushing the food around on her plate, hoping this wasn't the way it would always be between them. Polite silence.

"Thank you for coming in for dinner," she said. "You'd get a better meal outside tonight, I'm sure."

He put down his spoon and looked up. "This is fine, Letty Sue. And don't thank me for coming in. It's fitting a man should share a meal with his…"

Lordy, he couldn't even say the word. "Wife? It does seem strange, doesn't it? I mean, the husband-wife thing."

He let out a small laugh, but didn't smile. "It's not what I expected when I took this job, that's for damn sure."

"I know, Chase. Listen, what I did—"

"It's over and done with," he said, not allowing her to continue. "I understand why you did it."

"But you still wish I hadn't."

"Like I said, it's done. We'll just have to live with the mistake awhile."

It shouldn't have stung so much, but calling his marriage to her a mistake made her stomach clench in anguish. Was she that unappealing in his eyes? Was she that inept and undesirable as a wife? Gripping pain pierced her heart. She swallowed her pride and asked the question that burned inside her. "Where would you like to sleep tonight?"

He snapped his head up and his expression told her he'd mistaken her meaning. His eyes glittered with heat, holding her to the spot. She froze and cursed herself for choosing those words. It was clear he thought she'd offered herself, when all she wanted to know was if he planned on sleeping outside. Since he'd thought it appropriate to share the meal, she'd been wondering if he'd also deem it fitting that they share the house.

"I'm your husband now. Where do you suppose I should sleep?"

She fidgeted with her napkin and pushed her plate aside. "I only meant will you be moving into the house?"

"Yes," he answered adamantly, then just as firmly declared, "but I'll not be coming to your bed."

Her cheeks flamed, the intense heat warming her

like a wool blanket on a chilly night. "Well, I wasn't offering," she said in her own defense.

"Wouldn't matter if you were. I meant what I said last night." He rose from his seat and leaned over, bracing his palms on the table. His warm breath caressed her face. "No matter how beautiful you are or how much I want to…I won't bed you. You can sleep in peace, Letty Sue. Thank you for the meal. I've got to check on the livestock one last time and then I'll be moving my things in."

Letty Sue swallowed hard and watched him walk out the door. She stood then and began clearing away the dishes. She still hadn't touched her food. She couldn't, this turn of events being far too unsettling. Lordy, how had she gotten herself into this predicament?

She spent time washing the dishes and cleaning up, then wandered about the house, noting dust layers on the furniture. First thing tomorrow she'd attack that job. Then, of course, there was the wash to do.

Letty Sue was running out of clean clothes.

When night fell, she washed up in her room and donned her nightclothes—a thin chemise covered by a cotton robe. When she heard Chase enter the house, she tiptoed out of her room to stand in the parlor doorway.

He'd set down a pile of his clothes on the wing chair and was sitting on the sofa, removing his shirt. His sigh was long and weary, coming from the depths of his chest. One boot hit the floor, and after the second one collided with the wall, Chase laid out a blanket on the floor next to the hearth. He lowered himself down and closed his eyes. "Good night, Letty Sue."

"Oh! Uh, I was going to get a glass of milk," she said, chagrined that she'd been caught watching him. Carefully, she walked past him to the kitchen. "Good night."

He grunted something unintelligible, then rolled over and went to sleep.

Letty Sue waited until he was breathing deeply, then scurried back to her room.

Lordy, Letty Sue, can things get any worse?

Sally poured tea from a silver service and sat down next to Letty Sue on the Hendersons' fine tufted satin sofa. "So tell me, what's it like being married to Chase?" she asked.

Letty Sue couldn't begin to hide her frown. It tugged at her lips, slanting the corners down. "I don't know. I don't feel married at all."

Sally's curls bounced when she bobbed her head. "You've been married nearly a week now. How can that be?"

Letty Sue shrugged, needing terribly to confide in someone, even if her admission was humiliating. "He's not been a true husband to me. Oh, he eats my meals—I'll have to give him credit for that—but that's where it all ends. We hardly speak. When he comes in late at night, he goes right to bed."

Her green eyes round, Sally said, "And?"

"And nothing. Oh, Sally, he sleeps in the parlor."

It was as if the light went out of Sally's bright eyes.

"Oh." Her shoulders slumped and she took a moment to search Letty Sue's face. Letty Sue couldn't mask her disappointment or her frustration, but now, at least, Sally knew. Her friend reached for her hand, clasping it and squeezed gently. "And that's not exactly how you planned on starting out your marriage, was it, honey?"

Letty Sue had wondered that herself. She should be glad Chase was giving her a way out. Once the marriage was dissolved, she'd be free to do whatever she pleased. She'd still be pure of heart and body, but was that what she really wanted?

Or did she want Chase's arms about her, loving her, teaching her how to unleash her passion, showing her his?

"Oh Sally, this is all so confusing. I don't know what I expected. Chase was saving my reputation. He plans…he plans to—"

"To what," Sally asked softly.

"To end the marriage as soon as Mama comes home."

"I see," Sally said, sipping her tea, contemplating.

"I suppose I should be grateful…." Letty Sue let that thought hang in the air.

"But you're not, are you?"

"Honestly, no. I'm angry and frustrated. He's so darn noble and still thinks of me as a child. I'm real tired of being protected all the time, Sally. All of my life it was someone—first Mama, then Jasper and now my own husband."

"Sam said Chase is—"

"Oh pooh, Sally," Letty Sue interrupted with a wave of her arm. "Let's not talk about me anymore. Tell me about you and Sam. He's been coming around, hasn't he?"

Sally giggled. "Yes, I've seen him two times since the church social. My folks invited him to supper tonight."

"You like him, don't you?"

"He's such a fine man, Letty Sue. He's handsome and intelligent and so very sweet. Why, the other day, he rode up to our ranch sort of late. I didn't think my pa was going to let me see him, but Sam said he just wanted to give me something, so Pa allowed it. He'd carved a pony for me out of wood. He said he stayed up late every night until it was finished. I didn't know Sam was so talented. I keep it in my bedroom, under my pillow."

"Oh Sally, he really likes you. Sam's been doing the carvings since he was just a boy, and I don't think he ever gives them away. He keeps a collection of them over his bed in the bunkhouse. He's been offered money, but he won't part with them."

"I like him, Letty Sue," Sally said, her eyes softening. "Very much."

Letty Sue wouldn't begrudge her best friend happiness, but she wondered if she'd ever know that elation herself. Plenty of boys had courted her, but never anyone special, never someone who made her heart stop dead in its tracks, never someone like…Chase.

Her husband.

Letty Sue sighed and realized it was time to head

back to the ranch. She had a meal to cook, polite conversation to make, a lonely bed to sleep in.

And then it hit her, like a hammer to a nail, just exactly what she wanted. It frightened her silly, because she knew that where Chase Wheeler was concerned, wanting and getting were two very different notions.

Convincing Chase she wasn't a child anymore wouldn't be easy. If only he'd look upon her as a woman and place his trust in her, then maybe one day she'd have his heart.

And that, she decided with newfound certainty, was what she'd wanted all along.

Letty Sue knotted her hair at the top of her head and pinned it up haphazardly. Then she pushed up the sleeves on her finest gown. It was emerald green satin, its bodice tight, pushing up her breasts. The dress was designed for parties, for dancing and special occasions, not made for what Letty Sue had in mind.

If Mama saw her in this fancy dress, she'd bust her gut, for sure. But Letty Sue had put off the most deplorable job for last, and now not only didn't she have a clean work dress to wear, she had *nothing* else to wear.

And today, whether she wanted to or not, she simply *had* to do the wash.

She grabbed the woven basket piled high with dirty clothes and, with a grunt, lifted the heavy burden. The weighty load rocked her off balance. She righted herself, unable to see where she was going, but managed to proceed out the door.

Why hadn't she taken Mama up on her offer for temporary household help? A washwoman would come in handy just now, but Letty had stubbornly refused, convincing her mother that she could handle the chores around the house in her never-ending effort to prove her worth.

Joellen hadn't needed help. She'd run the house and the ranch perfectly, without the assistance of out-siders all these years. Letty Sue simply wanted to prove to her mother that she could do the same.

And now she was paying the price.

With the basket near to overflowing, blocking her view, Letty Sue felt her way toward the washbasin out behind the house.

She supposed if she tried hard enough, she'd get through most of the wash before sundown. But the very thought of breaking her back working over that scrub board made her wince. The cumbersome load tilted and she went along with it. She corrected her position with a twist and the load swayed recklessly. The heap of clothes leaned and pitched as she walked, but she managed to keep herself and the basket up-right.

Until her foot met a stone jutting up in her path.

She lost all sense of balance. "Whoa!" she called out, as if the laundry basket was of a mind to listen.

But it was too late. The basket soared up in the air. The clothes went flying in every direction. Letty Sue fell, landing on her bottom with a solid thump, and then, adding insult to injury, the basket flipped over and landed right on top of her head.

Muttering under her breath, she yanked the basket off, tossing it aside. Then immediately wished she hadn't, because standing right in front of her, wearing the smuggest, most unbearable grin, was Chase Wheeler, her husband.

He crouched down to her level, removing a sock from her shoulder. "That's the prettiest dress I've ever seen you wear, Letty Sue. Plan on going dancing?"

"Shut up, Chase." She folded her arms across her middle.

He tried to temper his amusement, but failed miserably. There was laughter in his tone. "What in the devil were you trying to do?"

Haughtily she replied, mimicking a Southern belle, "Why, practicing for the cotillion, Mr. Wheeler. Any fool can see that."

"Now, Letty Sue, no need to be rude. You've piled up quite a load of dirty clothes here, I see." A silky chemise on the ground nearby caught his eye. He lifted it gently, studying it.

She snatched it out of his hands. "I was trying to get the wash over to the basin." She pointed a finger in that general direction.

His laugh was good and hearty. "Sure looked like dancing to me, the way you were prancing around with that basket."

She cast him her sternest frown. "A gentleman would have come to my aid."

He stood, chuckling, and put out his hand. "And miss the fine show you put on?"

Quickly, she glanced around. Lordy, thank heavens no one else had witnessed her ridiculous display. Begrudgingly, she accepted his hand and he hoisted her up, none too gently. She bumped into his chest and almost lost her balance again.

His arms snaked around her waist, righting her and pulling her close. They stood that way for long seconds with Chase staring deeply into her eyes. Then his gaze trekked lower, to her throat, and lower still, to the tight bodice of her gown. Her breasts grew warm, scorched from his intense and blatant scrutiny.

Her ire ebbing, she read the dark, smoky look in his eyes, then boldly roped her arms around his neck. "Chase, we don't always have to be at odds with each other," she whispered, her gaze traveling over his face, to finally rest on his mouth. She wanted him to kiss her, wanted to feel once again the heady sensation of his lips on hers. She wanted to taste him, to explore what they'd started that night when he'd come to her beaten and bruised. She wanted him to touch her, to breathe her name, to take her most prized possession. The need was strong within her and she lost all sense of pride with her brazen behavior. She parted her lips.

"We don't?" he asked, seemingly fascinated and perfectly content to peruse her mouth. The pressure from his hands at her waist tightened.

Slowly she shook her head. "No," she replied in a breathy voice.

He bent his head and she anticipated the beauty of their lips joining. Then, like a bolt of lightning, he jerked back, releasing his hold on her. Blinking his eyes, he shook his head as if to break free of the spell they'd been under.

"Chase?"

With his fist, he clipped her chin gently, and winked. "Think I've dreamed up a new Cheyenne name for you, darlin'."

It was as if Chase was another person now, the guarded, arrogant, stubborn man she'd married. How rapidly he'd switched from tender to unyielding.

"Oh?"

"Twisted-foot Woman."

Twisted-foot Woman?

"Oh!" There was no mistaking his insult. He thought her clumsy, graceless, an awkward child walking in a woman's shoes.

Letty Sue's heart plummeted.

She waited for Chase to take it back, to fix it, to make everything all right, but he didn't. He stood there, perhaps with a bit of regret in his eyes, but he didn't apologize, and she knew he wouldn't. He'd meant what he said.

She turned then and briskly walked away without giving Chase a second glance, false pride spurring her on.

But it was no use. Pity the poor fool who thought she could change a man who was set in his ways.

He didn't want this marriage.

He barely tolerated her.

He would never trust her.

And she didn't think she could live this way any longer.

Not only was her pride hurt, but now the pain also involved her heart. And the sad truth remained, no matter how hard she'd tried to deny it. She was done with lying to herself.

The marriage was hopeless.

Chapter Twelve

Chase pounded the last nail into the wood plank on the barn wall. He glanced over his shoulder, as he had all afternoon long, hoping to catch another glimpse of Letty Sue. Earlier and from a distance, he'd watched her struggle with the wash, but she hadn't come out of the house since.

With the repairs done, Chase couldn't put off going in to dinner any longer. The sun was beginning to set. It was late, but he'd hoped that at least once this afternoon, Letty Sue would have come out so that he'd know she was all right.

Damn, he hadn't meant to hurt her. Well, that wasn't entirely true. He knew well and good that his comments would spark her anger, but that's exactly what he'd intended.

The woman was getting under his skin. She was breathtakingly beautiful. He had trouble looking at her at times, knowing she was his wife and that he had every right to take her to bed. The temptation tested him daily.

But when she started in with those long sultry looks and breathy whispers, when she told him with her beckoning blue eyes and delectable body that he could have her, Chase had no choice but to back off, to deny them both what they wanted.

And if that meant injuring her feelings to keep her away, well, it had to be done.

Chase slapped his leather gloves together, and sawdust powdered the air. He retired his work gloves to his back pocket, then washed up outside in a pail, splashing water on his face. The cool stream trickling from his jaw was refreshing.

He glanced at the back door, hesitant to enter. He never knew what mood his wife would be in when he came in at night. Sometimes she was talkative. He'd sit and listen, engrossed in the soothing lilt of her spirited voice. Sometimes she'd be quiet, but cordial, and they'd eat a peaceful meal, the silence often seeming more intimate, as though they were comfortable with one another.

He liked those times, too.

"Letty Sue," he called out, hoping she'd greet him at the back door as she had so many times before.

He tossed his hat on a peg and noted the kitchen table was set for one. A piece of parchment sat under his plate. He lifted it and read the note:

I've decided to meet Mama in St. Louis as she requested. I'm busy making plans for my trip. Your supper is in the pot on the stove.

Letty Sue.

Chase took a long pull of air, then dropped the note on the table. He stared at it for a time, scrubbing his jaw with a hand.

Her leaving was for the best, he thought, but he hadn't expected this, and it stung a bit.

His *wife* was leaving him.

Well, it'd be better for Letty Sue to be the one to leave. Then she could hold her head up high in this town. He'd wanted to protect her name and her reputation, but he'd also unintentionally hurt her. At least this way Letty Sue could save face.

He'd planned on dissolving the marriage anyway, then taking off, perhaps to rejoin Seth Johnston at his spread in Abilene.

Yep, it was better this way.

On impulse, Chase walked to Letty Sue's bedroom and knocked sharply. "Letty Sue," he said, "I'd like to speak with you."

A minute passed, then the door jerked open. She smiled warmly, surprising him. "Chase."

"I, uh, got your note."

"Yes, well," she began airily, "sorry I couldn't join you for dinner, but I have much to do before I leave. I'm composing a telegram to send to my folks. Arrangements must be made."

He nodded then, pinning her down with his gaze. "When will you leave?"

"I—I don't know. I have to check out stagecoach and train schedules. Tomorrow I plan on going into town and sending the wire." She smiled sadly then, causing a knot to twist in his stomach. "I should be out of your way soon enough."

He pursed his lips. His head told him to leave it be, that this was a far better solution for her. For them both. But his heart told him other things. Things Chase didn't want to hear, like the fact that Letty Sue could very well meet some refined gentleman of breeding in the East. With her beautiful face and body and feminine ways, no doubt she'd have men standing in line for her favors. Men would court her, fawn over her, shower her with presents.

Chase scowled. His fists clenched. He squeezed his eyes shut, pushing away the vivid pictures his mind conjured up.

He desired her like no other. As much as he'd tried to refuse lust-filled thoughts, they were always there, a constant companion, filling his mind with perplexing images. His fingers itched to caress her smooth skin. His mouth wanted to devour each and every inch of her. His body craved her with dire need.

He wouldn't allow himself the pleasure. There was no future for them. It was all he could do to send her away.

She was his wife, albeit in name only, yet she was still a married woman. He wondered if that would mean anything to her, once she was with all those fancy gents.

It hadn't meant a thing to Marabella that he had professed his devotion, Chase thought irrationally, comparing the two women. She'd used his love to gain ground with a more prominent man, and once that was achieved, had hastily turned her back on him.

The woman he'd gotten over quickly; the betrayal stayed with him always.

Yet if marrying Letty Sue had been a mistake, *not* marrying her would have been an even bigger blunder.

"Letty Sue, it's probably best that you go."

"Oh, I agree. Why, I've always dreamed of visiting the East. I've wanted to for as long as I can remember. Silly me, I should have answered Mama's wire sooner, but I...I—"

Brightness left her eyes then, replaced by a defeated, regretful look, and Chase had the uncanny feeling he was witnessing Letty Sue's true and honest feelings.

"You didn't want to leave the ranch. You wanted to make things work out."

Her lips tightened and she nodded.

Nothing much had worked out, he noted ruefully. He stepped out of the doorway and turned to leave. There wasn't anything left to say.

"I'll let you know my travel plans as soon as they're made," she offered softly before closing the door.

Three days later, Chase squinted against the morning light streaming into the kitchen, and finished the coffee Letty Sue had left for him in a pot on the cookstove. The early rays brought warmth to the room, casting it in a cheerful golden glow. By rights, it was a glorious morning, but not even such a lovely day could shake Chase from his foul mood.

He'd not slept well again.

Thoughts of his wife plagued and perplexed him.

She'd be leaving soon. She'd come to him the other day with her travel plans. In just five days, Chase would bid farewell to Letty Sue and watch her head out of Sweet Springs and out of his life.

He set down his mug and stared out the window, watching the livestock awaken to the light of day. Then his gaze traveled farther yet, to the horizon, and with mild interest he watched the sun rise up over a stand of cottonwoods.

With a deep sigh, Chase realized he'd resigned himself to Letty Sue's leaving, couldn't in good conscience ask her to stay. But he'd not been able to truly settle it in his mind.

Nothing about his dealings with Letty Sue had ever been simple.

He wondered why the people he had cared about in his lifetime always seemed to leave him. He'd never known his father, his mother had died young and heartbroken, Marabella had caused him a barrelful of grief and then turned her back on him, and now Letty Sue was planning to leave.

When would he find the life partner his mother had spoken about? Was there really someone out there who would stand with him as one? For the first time in his life, Chase was beginning to doubt his mother's wisdom.

Letty Sue barged into the kitchen and stopped short

when she saw Chase peering out the window. "Oh, I thought you'd be gone by now," she said.

He turned to give her a long, curious stare. "What in high heaven are you wearing, woman?"

Letty Sue flinched at his brusque tone.

She took a biscuit from its toweling and brought it to her lips, commending herself on its softer texture. This biscuit didn't thud when dropped onto the table. "I didn't get all the wash finished, just the clothes needed for my trip, so I borrowed some. I'm all packed and ready. I thought I'd take Starlight out for an early ride." She took a bite and washed the biscuit down with a sip of lemonade she'd made yesterday.

"Borrowed from who?" he asked, none too politely.

"Well, these britches are Mama's and the suspenders are Jasper's. I didn't think they'd mind. And, well, Sam was kind enough to lend me this plaid shirt."

Grim-faced, Chase glared at the shirt. Letty Sue wondered if she'd put it on backward or something. But no, she thought, fidgeting with the buttons, she was sure she had everything on right. Yet it seemed Chase would burn a hole right through the shirt, the way he was looking at it.

"Wait here," he said, and left the room. Minutes later he returned. He strode purposefully toward her, stopping only inches away. He pulled down the suspenders she wore, then yanked the shirttails out of her britches and began undoing the buttons. His fingers worked quickly, nimbly, and once done, he pushed the fabric off her shoulders. The shirt fell to the floor.

Stunned, Letty Sue stood frozen to the spot, vulnerable now to his gaze. She wore only a thin silky camisole under the shirt. "W-what are you d-doing?" she asked, her voice a high squeak.

His hand stroked her throat, then skimmed lower in a soft, intoxicating caress. She felt the slightest touch of his fingertips along the edges of the lace, just above her breasts. Her heart skipped suddenly. She held her breath, waiting, wondering.

He brushed his fingers across her breasts, making the nipples poke against the thin fabric. Oh Lordy.

Chase cupped her breasts in his hands, feeling their weight through the garment, then moved his palms down along her ribs until he clasped her waist. He applied gentle, torturous pressure. "You're my wife, Letty Sue. Any borrowing you need doing, you come to me." With a gentle shove, he pushed a shirt against her chest—one of *his* shirts. With its plaid design it didn't look much different than the one Sam had loaned her.

Chase plopped one of his hats on her head, too. "I'm riding out to find some wild mustangs I spotted the other day up along the east ridge. Join me. It'll be a nice ride."

"O-okay," she answered, confused by Chase's peculiar mood.

"Fine, then. Meet me outside in five minutes. And be sure to button up."

Numbly, she remained on the spot, her body humming from his touch and from his appreciative gaze. She clutched his proffered shirt to her chest.

"I'll be waiting."

Letty Sue watched him walk out the door, then proceeded to do exactly as he'd asked. She buttoned up. Once done, she dipped her face to the shirt collar and breathed in his scent. Earth and leather and man mingled and filled her senses. A thrilling tingle worked up her spine.

She liked being encased in Chase's clothes.

As she lifted the suspenders back up to her shoulders, her lips began an involuntarily curl.

His hat. His shirt. *His wife.*

Letty Sue smiled for the first time in three days.

Warm wind whipped wildly at her hair, Chase's hat unable to withstand both the force of nature and the speed with which she rode. The Stetson bounced against her back now, and she tossed her head and laughed as Starlight's swift stride matched Tornado's. Chase, too, had a rare smile on his lips as, body bent low, he traveled the open grasslands with grace and agility. Riding with single-minded purpose and unquestionable confidence, her husband almost became one with the stallion.

The animals needed this release almost as much as their riders, she mused, as Chase brought his horse to a trot. They'd ridden hard for quite some time, leaving Double J land far behind.

Tension oozed from her body, a welcome emancipation of the pressures robbing her of sleep. She'd needed this ride, and although she traveled alongside the cause of all her recent woes, and her heart still ached at Chase's quiet acceptance of her leaving, she couldn't place all the blame on him.

He'd done right by her.

He'd kept his promise to Joellen, taking excellent care of the ranch, as well as the rancher's daughter.

They slowed their horses to a walk now, Starlight and Tornado content to move at a more sedate pace.

"Do you think if we'd met under different circumstances, Chase—well, do you think things would've worked out?" she ventured to ask.

Chase took a long time answering, but when he did, he looked her straight in the eyes. "If you'd been a woman in my village, I'd have set my sights on you. Years might have gone by before I took any action. Then I'd ask a relative, most likely my grandmother, to approach you. She'd bring your family gifts. She'd plead my case and then leave you to speak with your family. If your family approved, then you'd dress in your finest buckskin, baby soft and nearly white from being worked expertly, and an elder woman would bring you to my house on your family's best horse. I'd be waiting, hoping. My family would place you on a ceremonial blanket and carry you across the threshold."

Her heart warmed at the notion of being Chase's wife for real. He would ask for her and she'd not hesitate to come to him. "Sounds lovely, Chase. I think I would have liked that."

Chase cast her a dubious, yet soft look, and nodded.

"Of course, I did get the threshold part," she said cleverly, her voice laced with amusement. Now that it was behind her, she saw the humor in her wedding night. Nothing about it had been real, so why be distressed over it? From the falsity of their marriage to the uneventful honeymoon, Letty Sue had to make light of it, because there hadn't been a genuine emotion behind it.

Chase grinned with devilish intent. "You did at that."

His gray eyes gleamed liked liquid silver and she knew he was recalling how he'd picked her up in that hotel lobby, carried her over the threshold, then proceeded to dump her onto the untried marriage bed.

Letty Sue sobered. "But I think I like the Cheyenne way better. I'd have come to you, met you over that threshold, and I do believe we might have even been happy together."

She clicked her heels lightly and Starlight took off again in a run. She left Chase in a tunnel of dust to ponder that thought.

Minutes later, he caught up to her. They rode in silence toward the long canyon ridge.

Chase pointed when he spotted the wild herd. "Look, there's the band. Spanish mustangs."

They dismounted, Chase leading her behind some low-growing brush. "There's so many of them," Letty Sue commented.

"But it's the band stallion I want," he said, his gaze trained on the horses calmly grazing nearby. "He's their leader. Look at him—he's pacing, watching, protecting the herd."

Letty Sue peered at the regal animal, his stance

clearly stating he was in charge. "He's beautiful." The spotted paint had incredible markings.

"He's the strongest, smartest. The band obeys him."

A pony and another horse joined him. The three moved together. Every so often the stallion would nip at the pony. "Why's he doing that?"

"It's his foal. He's teaching him to graze the land. Biting and nipping is their way of showing what's expected. That mare is the mother."

"You mean, they're a family?" Letty Sue asked incredulously. She knew the ways of cattle, having been raised on a ranch, but she realized she had very little knowledge of horses, other than how to ride them. Chase had an uncanny ability to read them, understand them.

"Uh-oh," Chase said, watching the stallion. "He's spotted us. He's moving up behind the others, at their back. See his ears twitch? It's going to be harder now to catch him. He's too intelligent."

They watched the horses run off, the lead mare at the front and the stallion following protectively. Chase came out from behind the bushes. "Another day," he said.

"But Chase, you can't separate him from his family. They need him. It's cruel and unthinkable."

"Cruel? You think it's cruel?" He paced alongside Tornado. "He'd make a fine stud, Letty Sue. And I'd be doing him a favor. These horses starve when there's a drought. They have to scavenge for food, and much of the time other herds have already used up the best grazing lands. Only the strongest survive.''

"Then bring them all in. The foal, the mare, all of them. But don't separate them. Promise me, Chase.''

"Why, Letty Sue?''

"I can't bear it. A family should stay together, no matter what.'' There was irony in her words, since in essence, she and Chase were a family, and she would be leaving soon. But Chase didn't seem to care, and Letty Sue felt she had no choice in her leaving. The horses were different, however. They were an actual family. The mare and the foal depended on the stallion. They needed each other.

Chase studied her face and inhaled the dry dusty air. "I'll bring them all in,'' he said.

Each silent and thoughtful, they rode toward the ranch. Chase stole a glance at Letty Sue in that getup, realizing that no matter what the woman wore she always managed to look enticing. The britches fit her rounded derriere to perfection and his shirt, though loose, followed the contours of her full bosom when the breeze blew by.

Chase removed his hat, then ran a hand through his hair. Damn fool thing to do this morning, he thought, touching her the way he had. He couldn't help it, though. When he'd seen her wearing another man's clothes, fury had overcome his good sense. It was as if he had to lay claim to her somehow, and since bedding her was out of the question, he'd done the next best thing.

For his benefit alone, he'd had to remove Sam's shirt from her body. Astonished at the overwhelming sensation he'd felt seeing another man's clothing touch her skin, he'd wanted to rip it off the moment she'd said whose garment she wore.

Whether Letty Sue read any meaning into what he'd done, he wasn't certain. But it'd been a rash thing to do, one that, if examined too closely, would surely show evidence of feelings Chase did not want to admit.

Good thing she was leaving.

"Chase, it's so peaceful here," Letty Sue said with a sigh, minutes later.

They rode along the crest of the ridge, where intermittent shadows blocked the sun's heat. "You getting tired? Want to rest a bit?"

She smiled and shook her head. "No. I feel fine. Gloriously alive today, Chase." She rode out of the shadows, lifting her face to the sun.

Watching her, Chase swallowed, hard. An uninvited thought entered his mind. He would miss Letty Sue, once she was gone.

"I think coming with you today was a great idea. I wish we could do this…" She stopped and bit down on her lip. Chase recognized her discomfort. They'd never again have this chance.

"For what it's worth, I'm glad of it, too."

She gave him a genuinely honest, beautiful smile, and his heart tripped over itself.

"You know, we don't have to—"

"Shh," he said abruptly, putting up a hand. "Do you hear something?"

Letty Sue clamped her mouth shut, grateful that Chase had stopped her from saying what she had on her mind. That maybe, when she returned, they could try to make the marriage work. It had been an impetuous notion, borne of a moment just shared. Letty Sue had to learn to lock her lips and think, really think before she said something foolish.

She listened, watching Chase carefully search the land. "I think so," she said, as a distant mewling sound caught her attention.

"Sounds like an injured animal."

"Do you think it's far?"

"No, not too far." Chase reined Tornado toward the sound. With rapt attention he listened, his entire body alert.

They traveled for a time, the whining sound, coming in spurts, growing a bit louder.

Letty Sue followed behind, a prickling fear raising bumps along her arms. "What kind of animal do you think it is?"

Chase was quiet for a time, listening keenly. "Maybe it's not an animal at all."

Then his gaze sharpened. He'd spotted something. He dismounted and Letty Sue did the same. They ground tethered their horses and walked toward the moaning sound.

"Here," Chase said. He shoved aside a thorny shrub and lifted the downed animal in his arms. Once

Letty Sue reached him, she let out a horrified gasp. It wasn't an animal at all.

In his arms, Chase held a badly bruised and battered little boy.

"He isn't dead, Chase, is he?" she asked, her stomach clenching violently at the sight of the young child's limp and bedraggled body.

Another pained sound stole from the boy's lips. "He's breathing, but he needs help. We've got to get him home…quick."

Chapter Thirteen

Letty Sue mopped the boy's forehead gently with a damp cloth, brushing back the blond hair matted there. He lay in her bed with a soft feather pillow under his head. She sat beside him, watching him with anxious eyes, hoping he'd awaken. His breathing was shallow, his face, behind the bloody scratches and abrasions, pale and ashen.

Chase stood by the side of the bed.

"What do you suppose happened to him?" she asked in a whisper.

"Don't know, exactly. Maybe he wandered off from his folks and got lost. Maybe something worse. Looks like he's been afield for days. Let's get some more water down him. He's dry as a bone."

Chase tipped a spoon and dripped the liquid onto the boy's mouth. Instinctively, his parched, shriveled lips parted. He took in the water, then swallowed so hard he coughed up most of what they'd given him.

"He's in a bad way, Letty Sue. I hope Sam hurries Doc Ramsey along."

She nodded slowly and continued to wipe away as much dried blood as possible from the child's face. "How old do you suppose he is?"

"Looks no older than two, I'd say."

Letty Sue couldn't tell the boy's age, so she took Chase at his word. She didn't know much about children, never having had siblings. "He's so still, Chase. And sometimes I think his breathing's stopped."

"He'll make it, Letty Sue. He's a strong boy, judging by the way he's held up so far. No telling what he's endured, but he's alive, and soon he'll have the doctoring he needs."

Letty Sue rose from the bed then, glancing once more at the boy. Weary from the long ride home and exhausted with worry for the child, she turned and fell into Chase's arms. "Oh, Chase. I'm afraid for him."

He closed his arms around her. Tears moistened her eyes. She blinked them back.

"We're doing all we can, darlin'. Don't cry."

She brushed a fallen drop from her cheek. "I'm not."

Chase pressed his lips to her forehead, stroking her hair gently. "Why don't you rest a spell? I'll watch out for him until the doc arrives."

She moved away from Chase and sat back down on the bed. She couldn't fathom leaving the boy, no matter how tired she was. "No. I'm fine, Chase. Truly I am." Rinsing the cloth in a bowl, she dabbed at the child's face once again.

Letty Sue silently prayed for the boy's recovery.

Whatever happened to him, she knew he didn't deserve the pain inflicted on his young, delicate body.

"Poor child," she murmured quietly.

Standing beside her, Chase laid a hand on her shoulder. The comfort he offered soothed her. She reached up and covered his hand with hers. The strength she felt from the contact brought an overpowering sensation of peace. She was amazed how the touch could nearly completely subdue her desperation. Chase had the power to calm her with just a thoughtful word, a tender touch. She glanced up at him then, and he returned her gaze with a warm, reassuring smile.

That was how Sam and Doc Ramsey found them when they entered the room. "Oh, thank heavens!" Letty Sue stood and rushed over to the doctor. "Please help him. He's hurt badly."

Doc Ramsey peered at the boy through his thick spectacles. "I'll do what I can. You'd best leave the room now, Letty Sue."

"No, no. I—I want to stay."

He lowered his head to peer over his glasses. "Now, Letty Sue, we all know you don't have the stomach for these things. I can't have you collapsing dead away."

The doctor was right; normally, Letty Sue wouldn't have been able to handle the bloody sight. But it was different today. She felt the boy needed her there. He was so very alone, in an unfamiliar house, among complete strangers. She grabbed hold of the doctor's arm and guided him toward the bed. "I promise I won't faint, and I'm not leaving, so please examine the boy.''

Letty Sue stood with Sam and Chase against the wall, watching the doctor administer to the child. Ten minutes later, Doc Ramsey rose from his place on the bed, stretched his arms and twisted the kinks from his neck. He muttered something about not being as young as he once was.

He turned to them and said quietly, ''Well, he's not as bad off as he appears. Most of the bruises are what you see, on the surface. I don't believe there's internal bleeding. His ribs will pain him, but not a one appears to be broken. He's lost a great deal of body liquids. Dehydrated, I'd say. It's important that he drink water, broth, anything you can get down him. He's exhausted and catching up on the rest his body needs. Now, can you tell me who he is? Where's the boy's family?''

Chase explained the situation, answering Doc Ramsey's questions the best he could. In truth, they didn't know a thing about the child.

''It'd be best not to move him around too much,'' the doctor instructed, once he'd been given all the facts, limited as they were.

''He'll stay right here,'' Chase announced.

Letty Sue's head snapped up. ''He will?''

''Yep.''

''But I, uh—'' She tugged at her bottom lip. She wanted the boy to survive, prayed for it, but having him stay meant she'd be responsible for him. She'd have to tend him day and night. She'd never cared for another human being before, much less a small injured child.

"We'll keep him until his parents are found, Letty Sue," Chase said quietly. And as if reading her thoughts, he stated with certainty, "You'll do fine." He glanced down at the child. "It'll be best for the boy to stay, since he's already here and shouldn't be moved. I'll ride out today and talk to the sheriff. Maybe the boy's parents have contacted him by now."

It was all settled in Chase's mind. Letty Sue still had doubts, yet she couldn't refuse to help the child.

They listened to Doc Ramsey's instructions, noting the most important thing was to give the child fluids. The doctor promised to come by tomorrow to check on his progress. Letty Sue prayed there would be some.

Once they saw Doc Ramsey out, Chase turned to Letty Sue. "I'm heading to town now. I'll find out what I can. Are you sure you're all right with this?"

She nodded, realizing Chase would be gone most of the day and she'd be solely responsible for the child's welfare. A tingle of fear rose up, but the child's needs outweighed her own uncertainties. "I'll take good care of him, Chase."

He studied her intently, piercing her with his gaze, then nodded. "I'll be back as soon as I can."

Letty Sue watched the boy sleep. She'd been able to get some water down his throat earlier. Color began to rise in his pallid cheeks and Letty Sue felt somewhat encouraged. This afternoon, she'd made broth from beef stock and vegetables. The boy needed the nourishment, as much as he could tolerate.

She lifted his head gently, propping another pillow behind him. "Here, sweet little one, try to sip this."

With her fingers, she parted his lips and spooned in a scant amount of broth.

The boy's eyes opened.

Big, sad, beautiful blue eyes.

"Hello," she said softly. Relieved that he'd finally awakened, she smiled broadly. With his eyes open, which somehow defined his features more clearly, Letty Sue thought the boy handsome, adorably so.

He stared up at her.

"I'm Letty Sue. We found you a ways from here. I know you hurt now, but soon you're going to feel much better. Do you think you can drink some of this broth? Doc Ramsey said you need lots of nourishment."

He didn't move or make a sound.

"Can you open your mouth like this?" She showed him what she wanted him to do.

Slowly, his lips moved, opening enough for her to spoon the broth in. The boy's dire hunger must have kicked in, because from then on, feeding him became much easier. Once all the broth was gone, he stared at the empty bowl with obvious longing.

Nothing could have made Letty Sue happier. "You want more? I'll be right back, I promise."

She dashed from the room, filled the bowl quickly, then, balancing it precariously, hurried back to the bedroom without spilling a drop. "Here we go," she said, out of breath.

But the boy had fallen back to sleep.

Letty Sue smiled and set the bowl down. She fingered soft blond locks of hair resting on his forehead. "Rest, little one." Then a deep yawn stole from her mouth. She scooted down next to the child and, overcome with fatigue, closed her eyes, certain she'd hear him if he awakened again.

Chase entered the darkened house. Not one lantern burned in any room, which seemed curious. He managed to make his way to the parlor and strike a match to light the closest lantern. With the dim yellow beam as his guide, he made his way to Letty Sue's room.

There, on the bed, lay two sleeping forms. Letty Sue's body curled around the young one's, her hand resting on the boy's shoulder.

Chase couldn't help but smile.

Yet the news he had wasn't good.

He wondered if he should waken them both.

The boy needed liquids.

Chase pulled up a chair and sat down. The movement was enough to cause Letty Sue to stir. Her head lifted and, through the shaft of dim light, she squinted until her eyes focused on him.

Lifting her skirts carefully, she rose from the bed.

Chase stood and, taking her hand, guided her out to the hallway.

Letty Sue, looking sexily rumpled, spoke with excitement. "He woke up, Chase. I fed him some broth.

He took the entire bowl. He's got the most amazing eyes, soft and blue like shallow lake waters.''

Chase thought *she* had the most incredible blue eyes he'd ever seen, but now was not the time to say it, much less even think it. "Did he say what happened?"

She shook her head. "He didn't speak, not one word."

Chase rubbed his jaw, the spiky stubble reminding him he was in need of a shave. "I don't have much to tell. The sheriff hasn't heard anything about a missing boy. No one's come looking for him. I asked around town. Not one soul knows a thing about him. Sam and I rode back out to where we saw the mustangs, and searched for signs of his folks. We didn't find anything."

"Maybe, now that the word's out, we'll hear something in the next few days."

"That's what I'm counting on. But the boy woke up. Now that's good news. Should we wake him to give him more liquids?"

Letty Sue shook her head. "He's so fatigued. The morning's soon enough. I'll make up another batch of broth and hopefully he'll get some strength back."

"You look tired. Go on back to bed."

She nodded. "I'll sleep next to him. There's plenty of room, and if he wakes up, I'll hear him."

"Want me to sleep in there, too?"

Letty Sue's brows lifted and her face flushed pink. She searched his eyes then, confused.

He explained, "I meant on the floor. I can watch out for him, too."

Her cheeks went rosy red and, apparently chagrined, she protested, "No, no. You've been out all day. You must be exhausted and you need your rest. I'll care for the boy. We'll be fine."

Chase thought it a good notion, too, because sleeping in the same room with Letty Sue, breathing in her scent and watching her sable tresses spill over the pillow, would most likely not allow him much sleep at all.

And he was just too doggone tired to fight those cravings tonight.

Chapter Fourteen

Morning sun streamed into the kitchen through blue checkered curtains. Letty Sue squinted, adjusting to the golden light as she entered the room. Chase sat at the table sipping coffee.

"Morning," she mumbled, then stretched reflexively. Her cotton robe opened. Chase's gaze followed her movements, his eyes focused on the open flap. With a quick pull, she brought the fabric taut and tied it up.

Tired as she was, she found herself not in the most cheerful mood today. She'd spent the last few nights with the boy, tending him. She wasn't sleeping as soundly as she was accustomed to, but it was worth the effort, because the child was recovering. Doc Ramsey said he'd be out of bed in just a few days.

"I was thinking about asking Sally if her family would take the boy in," Chase said, taking a sip from his coffee mug.

"Why in heaven would you want to do that?" she snapped.

Chase's lips pulled down in a frown. He turned the mug around in his palms. "I've given the situation a good deal of thought. So far, no one's come to claim him, and I can't run the ranch and watch out for the boy at the same time."

Appalled at the notion, Letty Sue fixed him with a stare. "*You* don't have to. And he's certainly not going to the Hendersons. They have enough children of their own to fill up Fort Worth."

Chase brought his palms up. "Then who? The town has no orphanage and I doubt—"

"Me, Chase, who else? I've been tending him the last few days, in case you've forgotten."

Clearly irritated, he shook his head. "I haven't forgotten, Letty Sue. But your stage leaves day after tomorrow. Or have *you* forgotten?"

Letty Sue had forgotten, momentarily, but she'd also failed to tell Chase her new plan, one she'd conjured up last night. "Chase, I'm not leaving. I couldn't possibly. I'm sending a wire today to inform Mama."

Along with a long letter of explanation about the turns her life had taken in the past few weeks. Letty Sue could barely believe she was a married woman now, with a child to raise. As much as she'd like to, she couldn't keep certain truths from her mother. But she didn't explain everything in detail, either. Mama would have to wait for the rest. Letty Sue had enough to think about at the moment, rather than worrying over her mother's sensibilities right now.

"You're not leaving?" Creases lined Chase's forehead and his eyes narrowed. "How come?"

"The boy. Oh, and I think since he's going to be living with us, we should give him a name. Since he hasn't spoken to tell us his real name, I'd like to call him Jake, after my father, Jacob."

Chase blinked. "You're staying because of the boy?"

"Yes, well, someone has to care for him. He's so sweet, and fragile still. Until we find his folks, Chase, he'll stay at the Double J. I'll raise him."

"You?" The dubious look he cast her injured her feelings. He didn't believe her capable of too many things, much less raising a child.

Twisted-foot Woman.

The name still gnawed at her, and although Chase hadn't teased her recently, she knew he still thought of her as a bungling, inept child.

Shaking his head, he protested, "You don't know a thing about children, Letty Sue. You've admitted that already, and tending him for a few days is quite a bit different than actually raising the boy."

Letty Sue's temper flared. Challenged now, she boldly met his gaze. "I know I'm probably not the best person for the job, but mind you, Chase Wheeler, what I don't know about child rearing, I'll learn. You and I both know what it means to be raised by one parent—the difficulties, the feelings of rejection, not really fitting in. Jake has no one…except us. I won't turn him over to anyone but his real parents."

Chase glared at her, a cold metallic look she recognized from their initial meeting weeks ago. She stared back, determined to press her point. Chase Wheeler could not and would not change her mind.

As he contemplated her arguments, his anger abated considerably, softening the angry lines contorting his face. "You're giving up your trip East."

"I know. This is more important. *He* is more important."

"It won't be easy."

"I know that, too. The child needs a home."

"That's a fact, but—"

"The boy is staying, Chase, and so am I."

Chase stood, taking one last gulp from his mug. He jammed his hat on his head and strode toward the back door. "The boy needs a home, Letty Sue. We'll give him one. But don't go getting fancy notions about all this and don't give up your heart. The boy's parents might show up any day to claim him."

Relieved, Letty Sue sighed wearily once Chase walked out the door. At least he hadn't put up much of a fuss about her staying. But he'd known betrayal from a woman he had once trusted, and it was clear he'd not allow anyone into his heart. The wounds caused by Marabella's duplicity were still too raw.

Perhaps in time Chase might learn to trust Letty Sue some, but the boy had already softened the hard edges of the man's tough outer core. She saw it every time he looked at little Jake, every time he ruffled his sunny blond locks. There was no mistaking the fact that he cared for Jake.

Don't give up your heart.

Chase's warning echoed her own dismay.

As far as Letty Sue was concerned, that might have already happened. She may have given up her heart to one adorable, golden-haired boy as well as her mule-headed, handsome husband.

Letty Sue fretted terribly over Jake, who was sandwiched between her and Chase on the buckboard wagon.

"Relax, Letty Sue. He's not going to fall out."

"I know," she said, keeping a hand on the boy's thigh. When the wagon jolted from a pothole in the road, all she could think about was how easily her lunch basket had flown off on the day of the social. Heavens, Jake couldn't weigh much more than that overstuffed basket. "But this is his first time off the ranch since we found him."

"It was your idea to take him to town. You wanted to get him fitted with some new clothes."

"He does need clothes, Chase. With him being so small, it's best I have him with me to make sure of the fit. And he'll see Doc Ramsey while we're in town." Letty Sue worried over taking Jake out today, although he did appear to be much stronger. It had been a week since they'd found him out on the range. "I think he's strong enough to travel, don't you agree?"

Chase let out a long-suffering sigh. "I told you so, yesterday, about half a dozen times." He peered at her over Jake's head. "He's going to do just fine."

Letty Sue nestled the boy closer to her and glanced

at his sweet face. Many of the bruises had healed, and he seemed more than interested in the scenery, his big blue eyes wide with curiosity, as they headed to town.

Less than twenty minutes later, Chase pulled the horses to a stop, setting the brake on the buckboard once they reached the livery. He jumped down, then reached up for Jake. When the child hesitated, looking to Letty Sue, she nodded her encouragement, and then Jake flew into Chase's arms.

Chase held him with one arm while helping Letty Sue down with the other. But instead of setting the child down, Chase chose to carry him.

"He's a bit unsettled right now. I think some candy from the emporium might help that situation."

Letty Sue agreed and they walked in that direction.

A short time later, Jake was busily chewing on salt-water taffy, his hands and face a gooey mess. Prancing through the emporium, he eyed many of the items on the shelves with a sense of wonder. Letty Sue picked up a few trinkets she noticed him viewing with longing, tucking them under the clothes she'd already chosen for him. She'd surprise him with the small toys later.

Measuring britches up against Jake's body, Letty Sue tilted her head, imagining them on the boy's slim form. "I think these will fit with suspenders."

Chase's smile was slow and easy. "He's going to have more clothes than an Eastern dandy, Letty Sue."

She chuckled, glancing at all the clothes she'd picked out already. "Well, he needs more than one pair of britches, and some underthings, shoes and socks. And of course, he needs something nicer for church on Sunday.''

Chase's face paled. ''Church?''

''That's right. It's only fitting we take him to church. Wouldn't hurt you, either, Chase Wheeler,'' she said, smiling coyly.

Chase frowned and decided to wait for them outside. He leaned against a thick post and lit a cheroot. Puffing hard, he contemplated his life on the Double J. He hadn't bargained on any of this when he'd agreed to help Joellen out with the ranch and her troublesome daughter.

Now he was married to her and had a boy to raise. At least until Joellen returned. But the boy complicated matters. If they didn't find his folks, Chase wondered how he could turn his back on them and walk away.

He hadn't planned on a family when he took this job.

Now, through unforeseen twists of fate, he had one. Temporarily, at least.

Chase was certain Joellen and Jasper would provide a loving home for Jake, and Letty Sue completely adored the child. They would become Jake's family, if his own weren't found.

But the question remained, could Chase walk away?

He had other troubles as well, keeping his hands off Letty Sue being first and foremost.

He'd had mixed-up, jumbled feelings when she'd decided to leave for the East, but had been relieved that at least the temptation would be gone. She'd not be there for him to witness her attempts at cooking a decent meal, hearing her softly muttered curses when supper didn't turn out as planned. He'd not have to endure the long nights, knowing she was in the next room wearing a next-to-nothing cotton gown to bed. He'd not have to witness the soft look glowing in her eyes when she glanced at the boy.

Letty Sue had a body made for loving. Chase was her husband and by law had every right to claim her as his. But he'd vowed not to touch her, not to compromise her innocence.

He cursed the day he'd married her.

Yet he couldn't fathom the thought of her in another man's arms. He couldn't abide the notion of Letty Sue one day giving to another man what he so desperately wanted for himself.

He was sentenced to living with a beautiful wife he couldn't have and raising a boy who could easily steal his heart.

Chase flicked the cheroot to the ground and stomped it out. If only it was as easy to extinguish the burning he felt deep within.

Letty Sue strode up, lacing an arm through his and holding Jake with the other hand. "I think we bought out the store," she announced gaily, wearing a cheerful smile.

Chase took her parcels.

"We're ready for Doc Ramsey now."

Jake's head snapped up at the mention of the doctor, his clear blue eyes round with fear.

Chase lifted the boy carefully, bracing him on his hip. Jake wrapped one tiny arm about Chase's neck. "Doc Ramsey's all right, Son. He's just going to make sure your bruises are healing just fine," he told the boy. Then he added with an exaggerated wink, "And that your...Letty Sue is doing right by you."

"Well!" Letty Sue feigned indignation. She punched Chase gently in the arm. "I'm doing just fine, Jake. Don't you worry about a thing."

The playful banter brought a smile to the boy's lips, and his eyes, no longer fearful, beamed with joy.

Chase didn't think anything could have reversed his foul mood just then, until the boy smiled.

He hoisted Jake up onto his shoulders and strode with purpose toward Doc Ramsey's office. "C'mon," he said, leaving Letty Sue behind. "Last one to Doc's has to cook up a big batch of fried apples."

The fried apples were good, even if a bit undercooked, Chase thought as he sat in a chair in the parlor, watching Letty Sue read to Jake. Chase hadn't thought Letty Sue would follow through and cook them up, but after supper, she'd dished up the steaming-hot dessert. He guessed she hadn't known how to make it, but had probably managed to pry the recipe from Emma at the diner in town today.

Chase leaned back and closed his eyes. The low-burning fire in the hearth heated the room enough to take off the chill. Clouds had blanketed the sky this afternoon as they rode back from town, and just minutes ago a storm had erupted. The rain beat down steadily now in a constant rhythm, and every so often a blast of thunder shook the windows.

"It's just a silly old storm, Jake," Letty Sue said. "It won't hurt you."

Chase cracked his eyes open a bit to peer at the child. Jake stared out the window with trepidation. Letty Sue snuggled him closer and pointed to a picture in the book to distract him. He peered down at the pages, but every so often Chase caught him sneaking a peek at the window again.

Chase wondered what had happened to the boy. What strange sort of occurrence had left him out on the range, vulnerable and alone? Sheriff Singleton had had no answers for him today. It was as though the boy had magically appeared in that field that day, but there'd been nothing whimsical or fanciful about it. Jake had gone through a rough ordeal. If they hadn't found him when they did, he would not have survived. Heat and starvation would have done him in.

Thankfully, they'd found him before it was too late.

During their visit today, Doc Ramsey had shed some light on Jake's inability to speak. He'd told Chase that sometimes a terrible trauma would inhibit children, causing them to withdraw into their own world as a form of defense, the experience being too frightful for a young one to bear. Doc also believed the boy capable of speech, seeing no real signs of damage to his throat. Yet he couldn't be sure, having no history on the child or his family.

Time would tell, the doctor had said.

Letty Sue's whisper brought him out of his thoughts. "Chase, he's asleep."

Chase rose quietly from his chair and lifted Jake from Letty Sue's lap. The boy weighed next to nothing, he mused, carrying him to Letty Sue's bed. Gently he laid him down. Letty Sue followed behind, as had become the ritual each night. She tucked him in and kissed his forehead.

Chase said good-night to Letty Sue and backed out of the room. He knelt by the fire in the parlor, adding a few logs.

"Do you mind if I watch the fire for a little while?" Letty Sue stood beside him, rubbing a kink out of her neck.

He shook his head. "I don't mind, but you had a long day. I thought you'd be exhausted by now."

"I am, overly so," she said, with a small, weary sigh. "I don't think I can sleep just yet."

Chase noted the signs of fatigue on her face. She hadn't bargained on any of this, either—a marriage and motherhood in just a few short weeks. Yet she'd held up, better than he would have guessed. He positioned himself behind her and placed his hands on her shoulders. "Just try to relax."

Letty Sue let out a soft, pleasured moan when he began massaging the knots from her shoulders. She lowered her head, giving him access to her neck. He ran his hands up and down, his fingers sifting through her silky sable hair.

Chase's body went tight. It was a fool thing to do, touching her like this, but now he had no choice. He worked at her shoulders some more, until tension eased out and once again she moaned in delight. "Oh, that feels so good, so very good."

Chase agreed silently, gnashing his teeth. He spent the next five minutes working her shoulders, caressing her throat, massaging gently—touching, smoothing, rubbing at the contours of her lovely form. Holding back all the while, he couldn't help wishing he could explore every inch of her. When he didn't think he could take another second of it, he stopped and whispered in her ear, "Think you can sleep now?"

She turned in his arms, her eyes bright, searching his. "I think so," she said, unmoving.

She looked so damned beautiful in the firelight, her radiance far outshining the dim glow from the hearth. Rain pummeled the roof, reminding him of another time he'd touched her intimately—in the supply shack that very first day, to warm her and keep her safe.

"Thank you," she said, her voice barely audible.

Chase grasped her slender waist with both hands. With a slight tug, he brought her close.

"Uh-huh," he said, brushing his legs against hers. Fire broke out instantly, a fierce flame that needed a quick and effective dousing. But the contact felt too good, too right to be denied. Chase didn't have the strength to refuse himself one kiss.

"I should get on to bed." Nervously, she licked her lips, staring at his.

"Uh-huh," he answered, lowering his head.

"It's late," she mumbled.

Chase smiled, bringing his mouth inches from hers.

He had to agree. It was late, *too late* for him. He crushed her lips with his, smothering Letty Sue's astonished gasp.

He thrust into her mouth then, the honeyed taste nearly buckling his knees. He drove his tongue deeper, claiming possession of the one part of her he could have, his rigid need against her belly reminding him grimly what he could not.

Little moans escaped her throat and she pressed closer, returning his kiss. Instinctively, he knew that if he laid her down on his blanket and made love to her in the fiery light, he'd not be disappointed.

Letty Sue would match his passion touch for touch, stroke for stroke, thrust for thrust.

But that would never happen.

With a deep, guttural groan, Chase slanted his mouth over hers one last time, relishing the powerful impact. Then, seizing every ounce of his willpower, he broke off the kiss.

Letty Sue's chest heaved, her breathing as labored as his. Her lips were a rosy pink, and moist from his kiss.

He cursed silently. "You're right," he said tightly, "you should get to bed."

He turned away from her then, facing the snapping flames in the hearth.

Letty Sue, calm and self-assured, said quietly, "One day, Chase Wheeler, you're going to see what's right in front of your eyes. I only hope it won't be too late."

He waited until the sound of her footsteps dimin-

ished and the door to her bedroom closed before striding outside. He stood out in the rain, letting the cool
drops wash over him, hoping they would extinguish
his powerful, all-consuming desire.

Chapter Fifteen

With the corral gate slammed shut behind him, Chase leaned against the fence, eyeing the three horses he'd been tracking since dawn. "That wasn't easy. Appreciate the help."

Sam nodded. "It's been awhile since I ran against wild mustangs. But we got them."

"Yep, we did. Took us the better part of the day, though. We must be aging, Sam. Used to be able to hunt down a whole herd before noon."

Sam chuckled. "Must be married life slowing you down, 'cause I'm fit as a fiddle. Don't feel any older than sixteen."

The wild stallion penned up in the corral snorted long and deep, then pranced nervously around the perimeter, as if looking for a way out. "The stallion's a beauty. I suppose he'd jump fence if it weren't for his mare and colt. He's smart enough to know the colt wouldn't make it and the mare wouldn't leave him behind."

Sam peered up at the blazing Texas sun. "Seems

to me he's a mite smarter than some folks I know."
He slanted Chase a glance.

Chase drew in a sharp breath. "Meaning?"

"I don't claim to know the whole of it and I don't
like interfering, but you and Letty Sue might want to
work some things out, for the boy's sake."

Chase tore off his work gloves, shoving them in
his back pocket. He chose his words carefully.
"There's no guarantee the boy's parents won't show
up soon. And I'm not fool enough to believe Letty
Sue wants to be my wife. Not in the real sense, any
more than I want to be her husband. When Joellen
gets back, I'm leaving, just like I planned. We made
a deal."

"Is that a fact? Well, turn around, friend. And tell
me your first honest reaction to what you see."

Confounded, Chase turned slowly from the fence,
glancing first at Sam, who was grinning smugly, like
a bank robber counting his plunder, then toward the
house.

A rush of blood-boiling heat welled up, threatening
to burst from his veins. He hated the reaction almost
as much as seeing Letty Sue, dressed in frilly blue
lace, entertaining a young dandy on the porch. Their
heads together, they were sipping lemonade, and the
sound of her sweet laughter grated in Chase's ears.

"Well?" Sam asked.

"Who is he?" Chase demanded.

"His name is Jimmy McCabe and he's just returned from Virginia. Been schooled at William and

Mary University. He's going to partner with old Mr. Halpern, the attorney.''

''He's a lawyer?''

''Yep, a new one. He and Letty Sue go way back.''

Chase eyed the dandy up and down. He disliked the man on sight, three-piece pinstripe suit and all.

''And she saw fit to entertain him, right out here in front of all the ranch hands?''

Sam laid a hand on Chase's shoulder. ''Chase, we just now got back from rustling up those mustangs. No telling how long he's been here, visiting. She's sitting with him outside. It's the proper thing to do.''

Chase pursed his lips. Sam did have a point. At least his *wife* hadn't brought the man into the house.

''Jimmy always said he'd come back to marry Letty Sue. I imagine he was quite surprised to find someone beat him to it.''

Chase grunted and folded his arms across his middle, eyeing the man who laughed so easily with his wife. One day Chase would leave, and no telling how many men would line up to court her then. ''He might just get the chance, one day.''

Sam burst out laughing. ''Chase, judging by your reaction, I do believe it would be over your dead and buried body. Come on, she's waving us over. I'll make the introductions.''

Letty Sue paced in the parlor, wearing thin her mother's Oriental rug. ''You were extremely rude to Jimmy today, Chase.''

Sitting on the wing chair—*his* chair, as Letty Sue

had come to think of it—Chase dragged a hand down his face. "I had work to do. I can't afford to waste time entertaining your…" He waved his hand in the air, agitated.

"Guest, Chase. Jimmy was our guest. Why would you be so rude to someone who was a guest at the ranch?"

"He was *your* guest, Letty Sue, not mine."

"He's a family friend. I haven't seen him in years."

"You mean he was your beau, don't you?"

"Hardly. He was sixteen when he left town."

Jimmy had made overtures to Letty Sue, but she'd never thought much of it, since she knew his intention was to leave Sweet Springs and go to law school one day. He'd dreamed of becoming an attorney ever since he was a young boy chasing her around the schoolyard. He'd always teased her about how he'd return and they'd get married, but Letty Sue had put no stock in his friendly banter.

Chase rose from the chair. His eyes burned hotly, their silvery rims gleaming. She stopped pacing to face him directly.

"What you do when I'm gone from here is one thing, but while you carry my name I expect you not to disgrace it," he stated.

Letty Sue's mouth dropped open. Stunned into silence, she blinked rapidly, his words sinking in. "I would never—"

"Enough said, Letty Sue."

Her denials, her pledges of faith, would go unheard. Chase wouldn't trust her; he didn't have it in him. He'd seen her with another man and assumed the worst. Yet she'd been innocent of any wrong-doing.

Anger began in stages, fitting her like an intricate coat of armor, layer upon layer, until she was fully dressed, ready for battle. She pointed a steady finger at him. "Don't you dare imply I'd be anything but faithful to you and our marriage!" Her voice was little more than a hiss, since she didn't want to wake Jake and frighten him. "I've done nothing to give you reason to doubt me or my intentions. I've tried to be a wife to you, Chase Wheeler. Too bad I can't say the same about you. You've not been a husband to me, not in any way that really matters."

Chase reached out and grabbed her wrists. He pulled her close, his voice tight with restrained anger. "What way really matters, Letty Sue? You want me to rip off your clothes, drop you down to the floor and make love to you until we're both so damn spent we can't draw our next breath? Is that what you really want? Is that what makes a marriage?" He released her so quickly, she fell back a step.

She inhaled sharply, drawing in much-needed air. "I do know what I want, Chase. And it's certainly not a man who won't face the truth."

"What truth, Letty Sue? Tell me what you think I can't face."

"Me, for one. You want me."

"I told you once before that any man would want you. You're a beautiful woman."

"You have feelings for me."

He turned his head away, refusing to respond.

"And for little Jake."

He snapped to attention. "I told you, his parents might come back for him."

"And they might not."

Chase's chest heaved. It was a long time before he spoke again, this time with trepidation. "You're saying you want a real marriage?"

Letty Sue's shoulders fell. Yes, she wanted a real marriage. She'd only just come to that conclusion recently. But a hefty dose of pride wouldn't allow her to beg a man who'd constantly made it clear he couldn't wait to leave her. With her chin up, she kept her pride intact. "I'm saying that, when the time comes, Chase, and Mama returns, I won't ask you to stay."

Chase strode out of the house, his mind muddled, confused. Letty Sue was one exasperating woman. He couldn't begin to figure her out. Just when he thought he knew her, she'd up and change her ways.

He wanted her, and that was just plain enough to drive him crazy, but these stirrings he harbored for her went beyond lust. He couldn't afford them. He'd met her kind before, hadn't he?

Walk as one. Stand together.

His mother's wisdom, like a spiritual guide, stayed with him always. He'd made a terrible mistake with the wrong woman once before, and he'd not do it again.

Yet seeing Letty Sue with another man brought forth certain undeniable emotions, feelings so powerful, Chase needed a justifiable outlet for them. He'd waited and watched for the lawyer to touch his wife. One touch would have laid the man on his backside. The attorney would have trouble practicing law without his front teeth, that was for damn sure. But he hadn't made any covert gestures, and Letty Sue, Chase had to admit, had kept a proper distance.

Glancing up at the late afternoon sun making a slow descent toward the horizon, he rubbed tension from the back of his neck. The day had started out pretty doggone good, he thought, with catching those mustangs. With Sam's help and a few others, they'd brought in the best of the band of horses. Chase had been eager to rush home and show them off to Letty Sue, hoping for her approval and a big beautiful smile.

It niggled at him how much he looked forward to her smiles, to coming in after a day's work to see her fidgeting in the kitchen, hoping her meal was edible. He'd come to relish the quiet evenings, too, sitting by the hearth watching her entertain little Jake.

Being married to her was beginning to feel comfortable, too damn comfortable even though he'd not received the rewards of sharing her bed. For a man who'd been hell-bent on dissolving the marriage, doubts were creeping in, slowly sneaking up on him, like a rattler stalking its prey.

The Spanish mustangs in their corral at the end of the pens caught his eye. Chase walked over to them, stopping by the fence. The stallion's deep-set, dark eyes bored into him, daring him to make a move.

Chase stood his ground, not moving, only watching.

The lead mare nestled next to her colt. Both the male and female stood alert, protecting their young one.

They were a family.

Chase was glad Letty Sue had convinced him to bring them in together. He wouldn't separate them. They belonged together.

But Sam's words rang in his ears.

Was the stallion a lick smarter than he was? At least the spotted paint knew his place: he belonged with the mare and colt and would protect them with his last breath.

The glorifying sound of a child's quick and sudden chuckle had Chase turning swiftly around.

It was little Jake.

And he was laughing.

A wide grin spread across Chase's face. Letty Sue, rubber ball in hand, was playing a game of catch with the boy. Jake reached for the ball and flung it hard, hitting Letty Sue smack in the nose.

She made silly contorted faces, exaggerating her movements before falling to the ground. Jake rushed over to her, his smile as bright and happy as any young child's should be. He stared down at her, giggling.

It was the first time he'd made happy sounds.

Letty Sue grabbed him about the waist and wrestled

him down, tickling him. His joyous, youthful laughter filled the air.

Chase had a sudden urge to join them, but he held back, watching instead the love shining in his wife's eyes for the boy who might very well be taken from them.

He'd warned her not to give up her heart.

But that might not have been possible.

Letty Sue led little Jake up the porch steps, dusting him off before they entered the house. She turned suddenly at the door, and her eyes met his. A flush of rosy color stained her cheeks and her face beamed with delight.

Chase drew in a deep breath and turned away.

The sight of her with the boy made his insides churn with a need he'd not felt before.

Perhaps he should heed his own warning.

Don't give up your heart.

And he wondered just then if that were at all possible.

Chapter Sixteen

≈≈≈≈≈

"For it is written, 'He shall give his angels charge over thee, to keep thee. And in their hands they shall bear thee up, lest at any time thou dash thy foot against a stone.'"

Letty Sue sat in church, listening to the commanding sermon Reverend Davidson was preaching today about angels and their offerings. His voice boomed against the walls and long, narrow, stained glass windows of the church. Surely, it seemed an angel had been watching out for Jake the day they'd come across him on the range, because the boy would not have survived if Chase hadn't heard his anguished cries. And perhaps, just as surely, an angel had been watching over her the day Chase Wheeler had entered her life. Though their union had hardly been made in heaven, Letty Sue had a feeling about her and Chase, that they belonged together. Perhaps it was destiny or fate that had brought them together all those years ago. He'd saved her life when she was just a mite older than Jake, and since then, he'd come to her rescue more times than she could count.

Little Jake's squirming pulled her attention away from the sermon. He shuffled his small body across the weathered pew to climb up Chase's chest. Her husband shifted and turned to accommodate the wiggling boy, but Jake was full of vinegar today. He knocked his head full force into Chase's jaw, causing him to flinch back, stifling a curse. Letty Sue cupped her hand over her mouth, muffling a laugh. Chase slanted her a stern glance and she giggled again.

Finally, Chase settled the boy on his knee, after bribing him with half a licorice stick. Chase claimed it helped calm the boy when he was fidgety, but Letty Sue knew differently. Jake positively glowed with happiness, a bright smile crossing his face the first time Chase had given him the candy. From then on, her husband began carrying a handful of sticks in his pocket, surprising Jake with a treat every so often.

Chase cuddled the boy close to his chest. More relaxed now, Jake was content to chew on his licorice stick.

Both boy and man wore white today. Chase's billowing shirt was tucked into fine trousers, and Jake's own snowy cotton garment fit into his finest linen britches, held up with black suspenders.

Letty Sue's heart warmed at the sight of them. Chase was more handsome than ever, with his dark hair groomed back, his chiseled jaw and proud features enhancing the silver-gray of his eyes.

And Jake—no child was more adorable.

With a silent sigh Letty Sue admitted to herself how difficult it was caring for a man who claimed he wanted no part of her, or their marriage. He wouldn't stay after Joellen got back. Their sham of a marriage would be dissolved.

Letty Sue's heart broke at the prospect of his leaving. No man could measure up to Chase Wheeler in her mind, stubborn and noble as he was. She doubted she'd find happiness after he left, but at least she had Jake, and the boy was making clear progress.

Just the other day, and for the first time, he'd laughed. Since then, Letty Sue had done everything in her power to get him to continue. The sounds of his joyous laughter brightened her days. Now if only she could coax him to speak. Deep within her heart, she believed that he could.

And selfishly, she prayed that no one would show up to claim him. The thought of losing both the men in her life was far too painful to bear. She shoved those unwelcome thoughts out of her mind, listening once again to the sermon.

After the service, Chase, Letty Sue and Jake met Sam and Sally on the lawn in front of the church. Letty Sue had witnessed the whole Henderson clan taking up the first three pews in the church, directly in front of Reverend Davidson's pulpit.

"It's good to see you all here today," Sally said, her voice holding a particularly joyful lilt. Sam stood beside her and the two exchanged a conspiratorial glance, both looking extremely smug, but happily so.

At Sally's nod, Sam took hold of the conversation.

"We're especially glad to see you all this morning since we have something to tell you." He reached for Sally's hand, bringing her closer. "Sally has agreed to become my wife."

"We're getting married!" Sally's delighted voice carried in the early morning air. Many of the other churchgoers turned smiling faces their way.

Surprised and delighted, Letty Sue reached for Sally first. "Oh Sally, you're getting married." They embraced, hugging with heartfelt exuberance and deep emotion.

Chase shook Sam's hand. "Congratulations, Sam. You're getting a great gal."

Sam agreed. "I do believe you're right, Chase."

Chase placed a kiss on Sally's cheek, and Letty Sue stepped into Sam's outstretched arms. They'd been best friends on the ranch for years. Letty Sue had always hoped Sam would find happiness, she'd just never thought that it might be with her good friend Sally.

Funny how things had a way of working out, it seemed, for everyone but her. But Letty Sue wouldn't let her own melancholy mood spoil her friend's excitement. "When's the wedding?" She had a barrelful of questions, but this one was first on her mind.

"Well," Sally began, taking a big breath of air before resting a loving gaze on Sam. "We've decided to make it sooner rather than later. Papa and the boys are heading out next month for a cattle auction in Fort Worth. Mama is going, too. It's to be sort of a special trip for them."

"We don't want to wait till after they get back, so the wedding's in two weeks," Sam interjected. "It'll be close friends and family at the Hendersons, and you two are the first to know—except, of course, for Sally's folks."

"Two weeks!" Letty Sue jumped, bumping into Jake. Automatically, she picked him up. "Did you hear that, little Jake? We have a wedding to plan and we only have two weeks." She pressed her face to Jake's and he giggled.

"Whoa, slow down, darlin'. I don't remember Sally asking for your help," Chase said, teasingly.

Sally smiled warmly at him. "We'd always agreed that, when the time came, she and I would help plan each other's wedding."

Her words hung in the air and an awkward silence ensued. Chase eyed Letty Sue with a look of new-found knowledge, a softening in his smoky gaze that she couldn't possibly return. She turned away from him, her heart plummeting. Her wedding hadn't been planned, wasn't even real, and that humiliating fact was clear to all who stood in the semicircle.

Perhaps it was the first time Chase realized what Letty Sue had missed out on. A woman always dreamed of her wedding day, of making preparations, of having her family present at the ceremony. Letty Sue had had none of those things.

She fumbled with Jake's collar, straightening it with a hand, then setting the boy down. "Well, since we only have two weeks, we'd better get to the plan-

ning. Why don't you and Sam come to dinner tomorrow night? We can talk more then and celebrate.''

"We'd love to," Sally said quickly.

"Guess it's settled." Sam shrugged helplessly. "It
appears my intended has taken to making decisions
for me."

"A wifely duty," Sally said, "and I'm just warming up."

Her wide grin eased the tension and they all
laughed.

With farewell hugs, they parted, Letty Sue just realizing she'd invited company to dinner.

Her mind reeled. What on earth could she possibly
cook without disastrous results?

And with little Jake underfoot, the task would be
even more challenging.

"This is the barn...*barn*." Letty Sue pointed at the
building as she and Jake passed by. "It's the first
thing my papa built on this land, even before the
house. I was too young to remember, but Mama says
we slept in the barn for months while the house was
being built. *Barn*," she repeated to Jake. "Let's go
see the horses."

She led the little boy to the corral, hoping to catch
a glimpse of Chase. She needed just an hour or so of
free time to prepare the evening meal, and hoped
Chase had the time to spare. As much as she enjoyed
having Jake around, she doubted she'd be able to concentrate on cooking while he was turning the kitchen
inside out.

And she so very much wanted this dinner to be enjoyable. She'd looked forward to helping Sally plan her special day since they'd been pigtailed schoolgirls together.

Letty Sue was also on a mission to teach Jake some new words, hoping he'd catch on one day and actually voice his thoughts aloud. He had such soft, expressive eyes, and she felt a kinship with him, as though she knew what the boy was thinking or feeling by looking into them.

When he jumped delightedly and pointed at the new colt in the pen, she walked over there with him. Careful not to get too close, she lifted Jake onto her hip. Guiding his hand, she made him point. "That's the colt. He's the baby." The mare trotted up and sidled next to her colt. "That's his mama. *Ma-ma.* And that big one over there, watching us carefully, is the papa. *Pa-pa.* He's strong and protects his family. He wants to make sure his family isn't in danger. Look how his ears twitch."

Jake chuckled and smiled.

"Can you say papa? *Pa-pa,*" she said again.

Jake turned his attention toward her and opened his mouth as if to speak, but no words came. He'd simply mimicked her, but at least it was a start, she thought. She hugged him tightly and kissed his cheek. "It's okay, sweet boy. You'll get it soon."

The mustangs in the corral continued to fascinate Jake, so they stayed there watching them. A short time later Chase rode up into the yard with a few of the ranch hands, and Letty Sue waved him over.

"Thought you'd be in the kitchen cooking up a storm by now," he said with a grin. Tornado side-stepped, then snorted, showing his high-strung nature.

Protectively, Letty Sue shifted Jake onto her other hip. "Well, I plan to, but I need help."

Chase put up his hands in surrender. "What I know about cooking fits into a small fry pan, darlin'. Can't help you much there."

"I just need an hour or two. Do you have time to care for Jake?"

Chase stared at her, then a dazzling smile crossed his features. "Sure thing. That, I can do. Give him to me."

Letty Sue hugged the boy tightly. "You don't mean to put him up on Tornado?" She made no attempt to hide the panic in her voice. She couldn't fathom having the child atop such a big, dangerous animal.

Jake must have caught on, because instantly, he nearly crawled out of her arms, reaching for Chase.

"You see?" Chase said smugly, pointing to Jake. "He wants a ride."

"He's two years old, Chase. He doesn't know any better."

"But I do, Letty Sue. I wouldn't put the boy in danger. Give him to me."

He bent down, and reluctantly Letty Sue transferred Jake to his arms. He set Jake in front of him and placed both his chubby hands on the saddle horn. "Now hold on tight. I've got you."

Jake nodded obediently.

Tornado began a slow walk around the perimeter of the yard, Chase guiding him with soft commands. Letty Sue's gaze remained fastened on the boy, who seemed to be immensely pleased, showing no fear whatsoever.

"Better get to cooking," Chase said. "Company will be here before you know it."

Letty Sue stood a moment longer, watching them. Jake appeared safe enough, she thought, sighing deeply. "You just take care with him, Chase Wheeler," she admonished mildly, "and don't get him dirty. He's already had his bath today."

Chase planted his Stetson on Jake's blond head, causing the boy to break into giggles, then shot Letty Sue an innocent look. "Yes, ma'am."

Not two hours later, Letty Sue came dashing out of the house, striding purposefully to the corral. "Chase, have you gone completely mad?"

With a lazy roll of his head, Chase greeted her. "Not the last time I checked, darlin'. Finished cooking?"

"No, not yet. But you've got that boy too close to the mustangs. They're wild, Chase. No telling what will happen."

Chase stood directly behind Jake, gripping the child, who sat on top of the corral fence just inches from the new colt. The animal's tawny coat was a few shades darker than little Jake's sunny blond locks.

"It's all about trust, Letty Sue. Watch this." Chase leaned over, stroking the colt's neck, just under its mane. The pony's mouth opened slowly and his tongue lolled to one side.

"He's learning to trust, isn't that right, little fella?"

Chase's singsong voice was light and sweet. Letty Sue had never heard him use that tone. It had a soothing effect on her as well. She stared as Chase gained the colt's trust, giving his own.

"Nothing's more important than trust, darlin'," he said softly, speaking of the mustangs. Or was he?

At the back of the corral, the mare rubbed against her stallion and the stallion snorted, then began prancing, his dark, watchful eyes never wavering.

"He's not liking this," Letty Sue said in warning.

"The mare's worried a bit and she just let the stallion know. But they'll see soon enough we mean them no harm."

Letty Sue had to admit the colt seemed to be enjoying Chase's soothing voice and his deliberate stroking. She swallowed hard, wondering if her husband's gentle nature was solely restricted to his horses. Or would he pamper his woman that way? Would he speak soft words and stroke her tenderly with those strong hands until he gained her full trust?

Letty Sue's body tingled with awareness, her heart thumped hard against her chest and she prayed her expression wouldn't give away what she was feeling inside. More and more, she wanted Chase. There was a growing need inside her that knew no pride or humility. Sadly, she thought, she might never get more from Chase than the memory of his kisses, stolen during forbidden moments in their lives.

"Okay. Now Jake," Chase said quietly, and Letty Sue was immediately brought back from her errant wanderings. What was Chase planning now with her boy?

He leaned the child toward the colt's snout, and Letty Sue held her breath. The mare, too, seemed to stand perfectly still, both mothers watching their young. Letty Sue bit her lip to keep from crying out. She had to learn to trust Chase with the boy. He knew what he was doing.

Still, she said a silent prayer.

"Breathe into his nose and he'll breathe into yours."

Whether by choice of simply by nature, the boy and colt shared the same air, breathing in and out in their greeting. "That's it, Jake. You're doing fine," Chase said again in a soft, lilting tone, one hand wrapped tight around the boy, the other sliding up and down the colt's neck. He spoke again to the horse. "You're kinda sweet, little fella, and you like my boy, Jake here, don't you? Yeah, and he likes you, too."

After a few long moments, Chase pulled the boy away from the colt's snout. "I think you've made a friend, Son. The colt's going to like having you around him now." He ruffled Jake's hair.

"Chase, look," Letty Sue said softly, peering at the mare. The bay had begun walking slowly toward the colt. "She's coming over."

Chase's smile was wide with gratification. "Looks

like I've made myself a new friend as well." He winked at Letty Sue. "A female one."

"Humph," she grunted, "*that* doesn't surprise me."

Chase chuckled, mischief in his eyes. "Jealous?"

"Never," she said, and stomped away, but Chase's solemn voice stopped her.

"Letty Sue?"

"What?" She turned around to search his eyes.

He drew in a deep breath, then set Jake down. The boy ran off when he spotted a jackrabbit by the barn. Chase's face wore no humor now, but instead looked pensive and somber. "I'd like the boy...well—" he took his hat off and jammed his hand through his thick dark hair "—I'd like Jake to have the colt one day. I'm sure Joellen wouldn't mind and I'll work with them both while I'm here...."

While I'm here. Letty Sue's stomach clenched tightly, her insides roiling with raw emotion. Her eyes burned hot. "I—I think...that's a f-fine idea."

She turned briskly, picking up her skirts, and dashed back to the house.

There was no use denying it; Chase was leaving soon.

Chapter Seventeen

"This is really delicious stew, Letty Sue," Sam said, lifting a spoonful to his mouth. "I'm impressed. Seems like married life agrees with you."

Sam glanced at Chase, then shifted in one of the dining room's cane-back chairs and helped himself to another biscuit. A fluffy, evenly cooked biscuit. Chase had to give Letty Sue credit, she'd done a fine job with the meal. Everything tasted mighty good tonight. But hell, Sam was rubbing salt into fresh wounds, bringing up their marriage. Sam knew why Chase had married Letty Sue. Everyone pretty much did, so why was he forever trying to make it seem as though the union was real?

Chase had no such illusions. Yet every time he looked into Letty Sue's deep blue eyes, viewed her near perfect face and stared with longing at her tempting body, he had a gut feeling she wasn't the same woman he'd married all those weeks ago. The thought didn't settle well. He needed to cling to the notion of leaving soon, but each time he did, an uneasy sensation crept up his spine.

Letty Sue granted Sam a gracious smile. "Thank you, Sam. I appreciate the compliment. But Petey Mayfield gets credit for my cooking abilities. He's been giving me lessons."

A look of astonishment crossed Sam's features. "So that's where you go when you steal away in the evening. And to think Chase here thought—"

Chase warned Sam off with his most deadly stare.

"What did you think, Chase?" Letty Sue's full attention was on him, her eyes coaxing out an answer—trying to get him to admit he'd been plagued with jealous notions, no doubt.

"Nothing, Letty Sue." He turned to Sam. "Not one blasted thing."

"Well, I did go out one night, but Chase made me promise to take my lessons during the day, when he can drive me into town."

Sam's laughter filled the room. "Is that so?"

"Sam, what is so funny?" Sally asked, her face registering confusion.

He took her hand and placed a soft kiss there. "I'll tell you later, sweetheart."

Chase pursed his lips before lifting his glass of wine. He stared at the ruby liquid, wishing instead it were a stiff shot of whiskey.

Damn Sam and his meddling ways.

Just because he was getting hitched didn't mean he knew everything there was to know about the subject.

Letty Sue picked up their plates, Joellen's finest,

refusing Sally's help. Then she brought in the dessert, a precisely cooked, golden-crusted pecan pie topped with Letty Sue's steaming-hot fried apples. Even the coffee tasted great.

Chase frowned, glancing at the three happy faces before him. Letty Sue had already put little Jake to bed, feeding him his meal earlier. Apparently, Chase had worn the boy out today, and now the two couples sat drinking coffee and nibbling on pie at the fancy dining room table.

Letty Sue was the perfect hostess, serving up the food and refilling coffee mugs, a charming smile on her face.

Chase wanted to make love to her tonight. He wanted to undo those tiny pearl buttons she wore and free up the restraints so her ample bosom would spill out. He'd peel her out of her pretty ivory dress and lay her down gently, feasting on her creamy skin. He'd make long, slow, torturous love to her all night, easing the anguish of his taut and tense body.

He wanted all those things. Now. Tonight. And he cursed his nobility, his honor and the vows he'd made to Joellen and his own mother. Vows he'd also made to himself.

Her soft hand on his shoulder stung like wildfire as her sweet jasmine scent surrounded him. "Chase, would you like some more pie? Coffee?"

She stood close by his side—too close. On impulse, he shoved his chair back and stood abruptly. "No thanks, darlin'. I need a smoke. Sam, want to step outside and let these two get to planning your wedding?''

"Sure thing," Sam said, taking a last bite of pie and a large gulp of coffee. "Ladies," he said, standing. "Excuse us."

He followed Chase outside.

Letty Sue watched them go, then let loose a slow, woeful sigh.

"He's crazy about you, Letty Sue."

"Who?" Letty Sue wouldn't even entertain the notion that Sally might be speaking of Chase.

"Chase, that's who. You know, the man you married? Your husband."

Letty Sue cleared away the dessert dishes, bringing them into the kitchen. Sally brought out the cups and coffeepot and set them down in the wash bucket.

"There's no truth to that, Sally."

"I'd say there is. That man's eyes fairly smolder when he looks at you. And he does it often enough. Why, a body wouldn't think there was anyone else in the room when you're around, the way those silvery eyes follow your every move."

Letty Sue shrugged. "What difference does it make? He as much as told me today he's leaving. He wants little Jake to have the colt he and Sam brought in the other day."

"He cares for that boy, too, honey. It's a fact."

"I know he does. He spoils him, but won't admit to that." Letty Sue's heart lifted at the thought of Chase and Jake today with the pony. They'd been so close, had had so much fun together. Anyone looking at them would think them father and son from the way they were acting this afternoon.

"When's your mama due back home?" Sally kept her tone light, but Letty Sue knew what spurred her thinking.

"First of next month. She'll be sorry she missed the wedding."

"I wish she could be here, too, but honey, that's less than a month away."

"Twenty-five days, to be exact." Letty Sue had been counting the days, wondering if she could continue living in this house, without Chase, once her mother and Jasper returned.

"Letty Sue, I've never seen you give up on anything before. What's got into you? Why, just about every man in Sweet Springs would almost die for a chance at your attentions."

She shrugged, unable to hide a grim smile. "Every man but one."

Sally sidled up to her, whispering, "Have you ever tried to, um," she began, then cleared her throat, "You know."

Letty Sue knew immediately what Sally was intimating. But seducing Chase would only lead to more heartbreak. "It wouldn't do any good, Sally. Chase would only turn me away. He's done it many times in the past. He's headstrong and willful. He's got notions in his head and I can't change them."

"Sounds like someone else I know," Sally teased, bumping her shoulder. But Letty Sue didn't laugh or smile. Her fate was almost upon her.

"Still," Sally said, her eyes filled with mischief, "if he was my husband, I wouldn't give up."

Letty Sue balled her fist and set it on her hip. Sally certainly had her curiosity sparked. "And what exactly would you do?"

"I'd let that man know exactly what I wanted from him. I'd show him what he'd be missing without me."

"I c-can't, Sally, because in the end he'd still leave. His mind is set. And all I'd be left with was a broken heart."

"How can you be so doggone sure?"

She lifted her shoulders, then let them fall. "I just know."

"Still and all, twenty-five days is a long enough time."

"For what?"

"For the man to realize he's in love with you."

Letty Sue felt better a little later, after helping plan Sally's wedding. Excitement stirred the air with all the fancy ideas they'd both come up with. The ceremony would be held inside, since the Henderson home was large, and Sally would walk down the curving staircase to greet her groom in the parlor by the hearth. Sally's aunt Bessie would play the piano.

They'd decided to decorate with flowers, since so many were in bloom now, and Sally would wear some of the paler ones in her hair. She'd wear her mother's cream-colored taffeta-and-lace gown. Her mother, thank heavens, had preserved it in a cedar chest all these years, hoping one day Sally would have an opportunity to wear it.

They planned to hire Emma and her diner crew to cook up the meal, and afterward, they would celebrate out back under the mesquite trees.

Letty Sue was in charge of the entertainment. She would round up the best musicians in Sweet Springs and they'd have dancing and singing.

How perfect Sally's wedding would be! Both she and Sam deserved such a fine celebration. Letty Sue couldn't be more pleased for her friends, but she realized during all the planning that she didn't need any of that to make her happy.

No, what would make Letty Sue happy was far different than flowers and dancing and a fancy celebration.

Chase entered the kitchen after seeing Sam and Sally off. "I've never seen two people better suited for each other."

Letty Sue smiled in agreement and walked into the parlor. It was late, she was tired, and most of all, she needed some time apart from Chase. Tonight especially, after entertaining their friends, the marriage felt almost real, but Letty Sue had to let go of those feelings. She knew that now. "I know. I'm so glad they found each other. Some people go their entire life and don't find what they're looking for."

Chase stepped closer to her, searching her eyes. "Sam found Sally, your mother found Jasper. Sometimes it works out."

"And sometimes it doesn't," she said softly. "I'm tired, Chase. I'm going to bed."

She turned to leave, but his arm snaked around her waist, pulling her close. He had a look about him tonight, a dangerous, dark, seductive look. Letty Sue didn't want to delve into what that look meant, not now. She just wanted to shut her mind off, close her eyes and lose herself in sleep.

"You did real good tonight. The meal was wonderful."

She nodded and pried herself out of his arms. "Thank you. I've been working at it."

When she stepped back, he followed her, his eyes gleaming, calling to her. She landed smack against the parlor wall. He moved in closer, trapping her with his legs widespread. "You look real pretty tonight, too." His index finger traced the edging of lace around her bodice, until he met the first of her pearl buttons, just above her breasts. He toyed with the button and dropped his gaze to it. "I like this dress."

Letty Sue's body stirred. Every time the man touched her she had to subdue the rapid rumblings of her heart and the incessant tingling his every caress evoked. "Chase, don't."

"Can't a man compliment his wife?"

"I'm not really your wife, remember?" She spoke in hushed tones, her back pinned against the wall.

"Sometimes I forget."

"Well, it's best you remember because I—"

His finger brushed her lips. "Shh. No more talking,

darlin'." And his mouth replaced his finger, covering her lips in a fiery kiss.

Letty Sue thought she'd melt from the heat, the flaming fire of his kiss was so potent, so incredibly intense. He pressed his body close, his solid strength overwhelming her. She could get lost in him, in his power and vitality.

His mouth consumed hers, commanding her to respond. And she did respond, thrilling to his nearness, his absolute, unyielding passion. The intimate way he possessed her, parting her lips and driving inside as though staking his claim, made her head spin crazily.

His arms wound around her, pulling her in tight, the carnal need in him evident and breathtaking. He didn't try to hide his desire, and there was no mistaking it.

The top button of her dress popped open under his nimble fingers. And then the next. He drove his hand inside the material, cupping her breast and letting out an anguished groan of pleasure.

She felt it, too, this pleasure, this unwavering spark of passion. She closed her eyes and allowed herself to know him this way, to give herself up to him. His kisses were hot and heady as he continued his primal assault. She relished the feel of him stroking her, making her tips go pebble hard. Oh, it felt so good, so right.

Did he not feel the love pouring out? How could he not see what his touch did to her? How could he not see how much she wanted to be truly his?

Lordy, Letty Sue, she thought frantically.

I love him.

She did, and there was no more denying it. A sense of futility set in. No matter what occurred, Chase would leave the Double J. He'd leave as soon as her mother returned. Letty Sue wouldn't fool herself into thinking otherwise. He'd spoken of lust many times in the past. That was all he felt for her.

There was no grand love or devotion on his part. She might wait a lifetime and not hear the words she so desperately needed from him. She feared she never would. She'd give him her all and in the end she'd be left, once again, with nothing. No marriage, no husband, no heart.

As right as his caresses felt to her, the whole of it was wrong, because love did not enter into the picture. At least, not for him.

Letty Sue wanted his love.

She was proud enough not to settle for anything less.

With all her might, she shoved at him. Catching him off guard, she was actually able to move him off her. He fell back a step.

Stunned, he simply stared.

She redid the buttons on her dress with trembling hands and pleaded, "Don't compliment me, Chase. Don't say nice things. Don't kiss me until I want to die from the pleasure and don't touch me so tenderly my heart nearly bursts from my chest. Just don't do it. I really can't take it anymore."

"Letty Sue—" he began gently, but she interrupted, pointing her finger.

"And don't...don't say my name like it means something to you. I'm asking you, Chase. Please, just leave me be."

She pushed away from the wall, leaving the parlor and an astonished, dumbfounded husband behind.

Letty Sue closed her bedroom door, slumping against it. "And most of all, Chase Wheeler," she whispered in her dark, desolate room, "don't make me fall deeper in love with you."

Chase stared at the empty hallway, his body still tight with undisguised desire. He dragged a hand down his face, wondering what had just happened.

He had entered the house after seeing Sam and Sally off, fully intending to say a brief good-night to Letty Sue before turning in. But then he saw her—looking so damn beautiful, wearing a pride-filled, satisfied expression—and realized he, too, had been proud of her accomplishment tonight. He'd only wanted to tell her so, but then something had fairly snapped in his brain—or farther down, below his waist, more likely—and he'd nearly seduced her.

He'd wanted to.

She was his wife, dammit.

But Chase didn't think he'd ever lose control that way. She hadn't tempted him or teased him. She hadn't connived or played havoc with his mind, and Lord only knew, she certainly could if she wanted to. But she hadn't done any of those things.

Instead, she'd been sincere in her efforts, making for a most pleasant, entertaining evening. Chase enjoyed watching her bustle about the dining room. He couldn't quite get that vision out of his head, of her sweet smiling face, her cordial ways, her courteous behavior. She was a true friend to Sam and Sally, wanting only to please her friends with helping to plan the wedding.

The spoiled, inept woman he'd married, Twisted-foot Woman, seemed to no longer exist. Maybe she'd grown up. And if that were the case, Chase was in real big trouble.

He let loose a weary sigh and began to undress. Tossing aside his shirt, removing his boots, then undoing his pants, he laid his blanket down and cursed his predicament.

He had a wife and child.

He couldn't keep either of them.

He was leaving in less than a month.

That was the way it had to be. Besides, Letty Sue had told him she'd not ask him to stay even if he had a mind to. She didn't want this marriage any more than he did.

It'd be smart to remember that. He'd have to keep his distance. There were only weeks left before Jo-ellen returned and life would get back to normal.

Whatever that was.

Chase lay down on his blanket, vowing to uphold the pledges he'd made. He'd not lose control again. It wasn't fair to Letty Sue; he could see that now. He couldn't ease the lust in his body, no matter how much he wanted to, and then simply walk away.

She was right to push him away.

At least one of them had kept a clear head. Surprising that it had been her this time.

Half an hour later, Letty Sue appeared in the doorway. Her sweet scent wafted into the room before he'd lifted his head to confirm her presence. Her eyes were bright red, holding back tears. She held an agitated little Jake in her arms.

Chase stood, throwing on his pants quickly. "What's wrong?"

"He's having nightmares. I can't seem to settle him down. Don't let us disturb you. I thought some warm milk would help." She headed past him toward the kitchen with little Jake rubbing his eyes, moving restlessly in her arms.

Chase strode toward her and reached out. "Let me have him."

She hesitated, clearly uncertain whether to give him the boy. Chase lowered his voice, stroking Jake's head, using the same smooth tone he did for his horses. "I bet you'd like to hear a Cheyenne legend or two, wouldn't you, Jake?"

Slowly, with eyes rounded, Jake nodded.

Letty Sue peered at Chase cautiously, then kissed Jake's forehead and turned the boy over to him. Jake was clammy, sweating, clearly upset.

"He didn't make a sound, but thrashed and thrashed in the bed. I think he's remembering something awful," she whispered.

Chase nodded. "Let's sit him down. Letty Sue, would you turn up the lamp a bit?"

As she did so, Chase sat down on the sofa and

cuddled the boy in his arms. "My grandfather told me this legend for the first time when I was just a mite older than you, little Jake."

Jake gazed up at him silently, but his eyes seemed to clear a bit, the fear Chase witnessed there vanishing. "Letty Sue, go on to bed. Me and little Jake here, we're going to get to sleep a bit later."

Letty Sue hesitated a moment, appearing downcast, and Chase wondered if what had happened earlier was still on her mind. She had trouble meeting his eyes, but apparently Jake's welfare far outweighed her own discomfort. Quietly, she said, "I'd rather see that he's settled first before turning in. I'll just sit with you both for a little while."

Chase nodded and turned his attention back to Jake. He felt the sofa sag just a bit, and was surprised when Letty Sue sat down next to him. But then, when she stroked Jake's hair lovingly, he realized she only wanted to be near the boy.

"A long time ago the great spirit Nesaru had charge over all of creation," he began, feeling Jake settle more comfortably in his arms. "And below his blue sky was a lake that went on for as far as the eye could see. In this beautiful lake two ducks swam ever so peacefully. But then the ducks saw Wolf Man and Lucky Man approach them. They asked the ducks to bring up mud to make the earth and…"

Jake's head fell onto his chest, his eyes closed.

Softer now, Chase continued, "Wolf Man made a great prairie for the animals to live in, but Lucky Man made hills and valleys where the Indians could hunt and find shelter.''

The scent of jasmine invaded his senses. Letty Sue. She'd closed her eyes moments ago, and now her head dropped onto his shoulder. She made sleepy sounds and he smiled. He wound his arm around her, carefully tucking her against him. She snuggled close.

''And between these two regions, a great river began to run....''

Chase slumped down lower on the sofa as he finished the story, careful not to awaken either of his two sleeping charges.

He, too, closed his eyes then, knowing sleep would surely claim him as well.

For Chase had never known a greater peace.

Chapter Eighteen

Letty Sue handed Sally her wedding bouquet, made up of colorful springtime flowers, then fluffed her blond curls. They stood inside Sally's bedroom, waiting for the wedding music to begin. "You're absolutely beautiful, Sally. Sam's a lucky man."

"I think I'm the lucky one, Letty Sue," the bride-to-be exclaimed, her face beaming. "Who would have thought I'd find such a fine man right here in Sweet Springs? Oh, I do love him so."

Letty Sue smiled graciously. "I'm happy for you both. Just think—my two best friends, married. Those little ones you're going to have had better call me Auntie."

"Oh my gosh! Children? Bite your tongue, my friend. I've had about enough of raising my brothers and sisters for a while. I want Sam and me to have...time, before a little one comes along."

"Hmm," Letty Sue replied wistfully. "Sometimes fate takes that out of your hands."

"You mean, your little Jake?"

Letty Sue brightened. "Yes, he's so…"

"You love him, don't you, honey?"

"How can anyone not love that sweet child? He's precious to me."

Sally adjusted the taffeta skirt of her wedding gown, swishing when she turned to face Letty Sue in the cheval mirror. "I sneaked a peek at Chase and Jake sitting up in the front row. What a handsome family you have, Letty Sue."

"Th-thank you," she murmured, unable to meet Sally's eyes in the mirror. Instead, she smoothed out the back of Sally's gown. Letty Sue didn't want to dampen Sally's special day with her own troubles, but inside, her stomach churned. Three days ago she'd gotten a wire from her mother. Joellen and Jasper had had enough of the East and decided to shorten their trip. They could be home as soon as the end of the week. Letty Sue wondered if they truly were tired of traveling, or if her news was responsible for their early return. After all, learning that their daughter had a husband and a child certainly would raise a barrelful of questions.

Deliberately, Letty Sue hadn't elaborated on either situation, but Joellen had wired her back, congratulating her on her marriage to Chase. Her mother had said Chase was a fine man and it gladdened her heart that they'd married.

Joellen's homecoming meant only one thing of importance to Letty Sue. Chase, her husband, the man she'd fallen in love with, would have no more reason to stay.

She had balled up the wire in her fist when she'd received it, denying its contents in her mind. She'd thrown the telegram into the fire that evening and hadn't told a soul, Chase especially. But the reality of her destiny could no longer be ignored.

Faint sounds of music from downstairs wafted up to the room. Sally jumped to attention. "Oh my! This is it!"

Letty Sue momentarily forgot her own distress and embraced her dear friend, kissing her cheek. "I'll be going now. It's time. Give me a minute before you come down. I want to watch your entrance coming down the stairs. Oh, Sally, I'm so glad this has all worked out for you."

Sally grasped her hands tight and said quietly, "It'll work out for you, too, Letty Sue. I have a good feeling about you and Chase."

Letty Sue didn't allow her smile to falter, yet in her heart, she knew nothing at all was working out the way she wanted.

Chase sat next to Letty Sue in the front row of chairs set up for the invited guests. Wearing pale blue satin, the color more than bringing out the deep-sea hue of her misty eyes, she'd never looked lovelier. A fancy matching hat no bigger than a flapjack sat on her head, over dark sable curls as big and round as sausages.

She dabbed at her eyes as Sam and Sally said their vows. Little Jake squirmed in his seat, and Chase put a hand on the boy's shoulder to calm him.

He had an urge to take Letty Sue's hand to comfort her, although he hoped her tears were ones of joy for her friends. She'd been so quiet lately, almost sad. He'd seen a forlorn look on her face for days now and wanted to ask what was wrong, wanted to console her. But since that night in the parlor when she'd pleaded with him not to touch her, he hadn't.

Not once. Not in any way.

And it was killing him.

His fingers itched to entwine with hers and squeeze gently in reassurance. He wanted to wrap an arm around her shoulder and bring her close. He did none of those things.

Once the vows were spoken, the festivities continued outside, under thick, shady mesquite trees decorated by the Henderson clan with paper hearts and colorful streamers. Food and spirits were in abundance, and after they'd all filled their bellies, the music began.

Jake ran off to play with two of the younger Henderson boys. Chase kept a vigilant eye on the lad, but his attention was also on his wife, dancing a polka with Bud Henderson, the young man closest to Letty Sue's age.

Chase stood rigidly, watching man after man cut in and whirl Letty Sue around the dance area. Her hat was gone now, and the sable curls bounced against her cheeks and along her throat. Chase drew in a deep, sharp breath.

"Do you dance, Chase?" the bride asked. He hadn't noticed Sally approaching until just then.

"Some."

"Well then," she said gaily, "I do believe this is our dance."

The music slowed to a more sedate tune, and Chase glanced once more at Letty Sue, who was just starting to dance with the groom.

"I do believe it is," he replied with a smile, taking Sally's hand.

They moved to the music, Chase guiding her smoothly. "It was a nice ceremony, Sally. You and Sam look happy together."

"Mmm. We are. It's amazing how we only just got to really know each other. If his horse hadn't thrown him that day, we might never have gotten together. Sam says sometimes what we want is under our very nose and it just takes some looking to find it."

Chase arched a brow. "Sam says that, does he?"

"Oh yes. 'Course, he was just speaking about me and him, nobody else." Sally cast him a coy smile.

"Of course," Chase agreed.

After a minute, Sam sidled up next to them. "I'm cutting in, Chase. Switch partners. I want to dance with my *wife*." He grinned when he said the word, as if enjoying the sound of it on his lips.

Chase turned Sally over to him, then stared at his new dance partner, Letty Sue. He had an uncanny feeling he'd been set up by the groom, or the bride, or maybe both.

"Care to dance, darlin'?" He would let her decide if she wanted contact with him. They'd hardly spoken all week, except for polite conversation, most of it regarding Jake.

Her skin glowed from the exhilaration of dancing, casting a sheen of moisture to her face, but her eyes held a cautious look. She hesitated for a brief second before answering. "I—I'd like that, Chase," she answered softly, and nearly floated into his arms.

Together, they moved and swayed gracefully to the music. Chase tucked her head under his chin, bringing her closer, and waited to see if she'd pull back.

She didn't. Instead, she sighed into his chest. "It was a glorious wedding day for Sally and Sam."

"It was. Different than ours," he said, then wished he hadn't. He didn't want to dredge up the past, but rather relish the feel of Letty Sue's pliant, giving body in his arms. He'd ached to touch her, to hold her, and didn't want to destroy the moment. He'd have to hold this image in his mind and keep it there to bring up on cold, lonely nights.

"Ours was…" she began, but didn't finish.

"Pretty bad?"

"That's not what matters. Not really, Chase."

Letty Sue wouldn't elaborate. There was no need. She'd already decided it wasn't the ceremony that bound two people together, but the love between them. She knew Sally and Sam had that, and tonight they would share their hearts, their bodies, their souls. It's what marriage was truly about—loving and being loved.

Being in Chase's arms, feeling their hearts beat in

rhythm and their bodies blend so remarkably together, felt so right to Letty Sue.

She thought of Sally and what she would learn tonight in the arms of her husband. It was what Letty Sue wanted as well. She'd often thought that giving in to Chase would be settling for less than what she truly deserved, but now she knew differently.

Giving herself to the man she loved wouldn't be "settling" at all, but rather a precious gift she could hold in her heart forever, a reminder of what might have been. She wanted to help mend Chase's heart, but if that wasn't going to happen, at least she could show him love, true love, and hope that one day he would recognize it as such and trust in her enough to believe that they had a future.

Time was running out.

Tonight, Letty Sue decided, she would know her husband in the real sense.

And she silently prayed that the man she loved wouldn't turn her away.

Letty Sue put Jake down to sleep. His nightmares had ceased, thankfully. He'd had several more after that first one, and each time, she and Chase would calm and console him with love and tenderness. Chase had many stories to tell, and she would read to the child or placate him with a treat.

She stared down at Jake, sleeping peacefully in her bed, and sudden panic welled within. The uncertainty of her future involved the two males in her life—her

husband, who was out seeing to the horses, and this
one trusting little child.

She'd made her decision about Chase tonight, yet
her feet were suddenly unable to move. Her heart
raced erratically, thumping against her chest, the full
impact of what she'd planned finally settling in.

If Chase cast her aside, the hurt and humiliation
would be too much to bear. But if he didn't, then
maybe she'd have a chance at gaining his trust and
healing his heart.

It was what she wanted, more than her next breath.

Spurred on by her bold resolve, she kissed Jake
softly on the cheek and strode purposefully to her
mother's bedroom. She found the key Joellen kept in
a sculpted mahogany jewel box, then moved to the
foot of the bed and bent to open the large rectangular
chest there. The pungent scent of cedar filled the
room.

From amid the collection of finery, china plates and
odd pieces of silver, Letty Sue lifted out a snow-white
lace-and-gauze nightdress. With a silent gasp, she
stroked the exquisite gown, running a finger along the
lacy edge of the bodice.

The nightdress was a special gift from her mother,
to be included with Letty Sue's dowry. Joellen had
commissioned a French dressmaker she'd once met
in Fort Worth to design the gown for Letty Sue in the
event of her wedding.

Letty Sue couldn't think of a better time to wear
it.

With swift efficiency, she removed her clothing and

donned the beautiful gown, buttoning up the tiny front buttons, which barely came to the top of her ribs. The bodice dipped tight and low, barely containing her bosom.

Oh Lordy, Letty Sue.

If words failed her, Chase would certainly know what she had in mind with just once glance.

The back door closed with a slight thud. Chase had entered the house.

Right then, sudden realization dawned, like a storm cloud parting, allowing golden sunlight to peek through. Letty Sue knew that to earn Chase's trust, she'd have to lay the truth out before him. There was no other way she could come to him, no other way to start clean and fresh.

She straightened her gown needlessly, the fabric flowing to the floor with smooth grace. She dabbed jasmine water onto her throat and shoulders, a bit between the valley of her breasts, then drew in a deep, steadying breath of air, calming her jittery nerves. Leaving her mother's bedroom, she walked down the hall to the parlor door.

Her fate and her future lay on the other side.

Chapter Nineteen

Chase crouched down by the hearth and, with a long iron rod, poked at the fire he'd just built. A startling burst of blazing light illuminated the room before quickly dying to a low even flame. Deep in thought, he stared into the fire, recalling how he'd held his wife in his arms and danced with her at Sally's wedding earlier.

It was a good memory, one he could take to his grave, as his grandfather would say. When you got old, the memories were what you had left, he'd often advised. Chase hadn't understood his grandfather at the time, his young mind filled only with "todays," but now he understood what the old man had meant.

"Chase?" Letty Sue's soft voice filled the room.

He didn't dare look at her, not now, when he was still reeling from having her in his arms. "Is it the boy? Another nightmare?" He kept his focus on the dancing flames.

"No, Jake is sleeping peacefully. I, uh," she began, "I wanted you to know Mama is returning home. She wired that she'll probably be home at the end of the week.''

Chase squeezed his eyes shut, a deep pain slashing his gut. He'd known this day would come, he just hadn't expected the impact to feel so damn miserable. Hell, he should be letting out a whoop of joy. He'd be free soon, his commitment to Joellen more than served, his vow to keep Letty Sue safe honored.

But he didn't feel like celebrating.

Far from it.

"Chase?"

"Thanks for letting me know," he muttered, still facing the hearth. "You can get back to bed now."

"Chase, I intend to go to bed…with you," she said quietly, her voice trembling.

Confused, Chase turned his head from the fire, then rose slowly, his gaze caught by the vision standing in the doorway. His mouth went bone dry and his chest heaved, tight and heavy, as he viewed his wife. She looked like some lovely, unearthly spirit, dressed in white. "Letty Sue?" he managed to croak. The vision stole almost all of his breath.

Her chin went up, but she spoke tenderly. "I want a wedding night, Chase."

He blinked back his surprise, but found himself moving toward her, his willpower as charred and hollow as the timber he'd placed in the fire long minutes ago.

When he reached her, he took her hands in his, then let his gaze travel the length of her, lazily drinking in her luscious body with his eyes. The nightdress did nothing to hide her figure. She was exposed to him, through fine lace. He'd known she was beautiful, but tonight she was so much more.

She was pure, coming to him like this, giving him claim to her body. And honest, telling him of Joellen's return.

"This is between the two of us," she whispered boldly. "No one has to know."

She was giving him a way out, letting him know she wouldn't protest when the time came to dissolve the marriage. Her courageous act warmed his heart. But he couldn't think of that, or anything else beyond the woman he'd wanted since he'd set eyes on her two months ago.

He brought her close, cupping her face with his hands. "Sweetheart, I couldn't deny you tonight if I wanted to." He kissed her briefly on the lips, then bent to lift her into his arms. "Where?" He headed toward the only unoccupied bedroom.

Letty Sue shook her head. "No, here, where you sleep, Chase."

Chase smiled and set her down on his blanket in front of the fireplace. She lay before him, her nightdress fanning out around her and dark sable curls teasing the rosy peaks of her high, full breasts. He stretched out beside her, his body ready and taut with need. "Are you sure?" he asked, searching her blue eyes.

"I'm sure. Make me your woman, Chase."

His groan was long and deep, coming from the

depths of his chest. He wanted this woman, there was no doubt about that. But was she *his woman?*

Walk as one, stand together.

It was too much thought for a man whose body had been denied all these months. He bent his head and kissed her full on the mouth. She wrapped her arms around his neck and pulled him close, thrusting her tongue into his mouth, turning his mind to mush.

He broke off the passionate kiss minutes later, to whisper in her ear, "Sweetheart, tonight you're mine."

Letty Sue wanted to be his forever, but if tonight was all he was offering, she'd wouldn't complain. She'd love him with the whole of her heart, hoping to heal his wounds. Hoping that, one day, he'd love her back.

He slid his hand down her throat to her chest, where he caressed the swells of her breasts. His touch sent her senses reeling. And when he unfastened the tiny buttons of her gown, parting the fabric and lowering his head to her awaiting peaks, she closed her eyes from the sheer pleasure.

"Chase," she murmured, when his stroking became too much. She needed more from him, the heat deep within her escalating, building in intensity.

"I know, sweetheart," he whispered, "trust me."

She did trust him, perhaps foolishly, but he held her heart. "I do," she said softly, "so very much."

Chase kissed her again then, his passion sweeping her away in a swift and sudden storm. She'd never felt this way before, as if her heart and body were in rhythm, as if senses she'd never experienced before.

She could feel his heat, his desire. It filled the air and consumed her. She needed this man, and the time was right.

With gentle pressure, she pushed until he slid to the floor at her side. She reached for the buttons on his shirt and with trembling fingers managed to undo all of them quickly. Spreading his shirt open, she laid her palms on his chest, finding his skin sleek, smooth and so very hot. With her hands, she sought every inch of him, stroking gently, her fingertips moving with precision. Then she pressed her lips to his skin, kissing and drawing her tongue over both flattened disks. His body tightened.

He ground his teeth and a pleasured groan escaped his throat. "You trying to kill me?"

Letty Sue smiled as she continued to explore her husband's powerful body with her mouth. The strength of him astounded and thrilled her all at once. His hands went into her hair, a loose mane of un-tamed curls. He pulled her up higher so their lips could meet once again, then he guided her back onto his blanket.

His kisses were hot now, wildly so, but it was when he cupped her womanhood with his hand that Letty Sue nearly burst into flames. A low, aching moan of pleasure poured from her throat as he pressed, tenderly massaging her female core.

There was no describing the sweet ache building. Letty Sue had never known such pleasure existed.

The heat, the tingling, the arousing sensations continuing to heighten until she thought she could die from it all. She arched up instinctively, her body attuned to Chase's steady stroking.

Then the stroking ended. She witnessed her husband shrug out of his pants and kneel proudly before her, his eyes savage yet tender upon her. The sight of the man about to claim her was breathtaking to behold. "I won't hurt you," he said. It was a vow, and she believed him.

She parted for him, and slowly, with restraint that cost him much, he entered her, filling her fully. This sharing of their bodies, their remarkable joining brought tears to Letty Sue's eyes. She'd never felt so complete, so wonderful.

Chase's face fell when he noticed her tears. He began to pull away.

"No, no. It's just so beautiful, Chase," she said adamantly, tugging him close again.

He exhaled in relief and moved inside her. She met his stride, thrust for thrust, slowly, then more rapidly, his body urging hers on.

Letty Sue matched him time and again, the pace fast and heady now. She felt a building pressure, an unrelenting need, potent and powerful. Chase kissed her then, long and hard, bruising her lips. She returned his kiss and called out his name, the pressure releasing, shattering her senses. Chase, too, ended the pleasing torture—with one final thrust and a low guttural sound that came from the depths of his chest.

Moisture coated his bronzed skin as he stared down

at her, brushing aside a lock of hair that had fallen onto her cheek. His dark smoky eyes glimmered.

He looked more like Silver Wolf now, untamed and primitive and so very appealing.

She was his woman.

Silver Wolf's woman.

If only he could see that.

"You didn't hurt me, Chase," she said softly.

"Tried damn hard not to, sweetheart, but you're one hell of a tempting woman."

"I'm your wife, Chase."

He rolled off of her and lay on his back, taking her with him. She fell onto his chest, her naked body pressed against his. "Tonight, I'm glad you are."

She wanted to ask, "And what about tomorrow?" But she couldn't break the spell, the magic of the moment, being in his arms so intimately. She wanted to relish this time they had together. "Me, too," she said truthfully.

"Are you sure you feel okay, darlin'?"

Although it warmed her that he might worry over her well-being, a wicked notion struck, and Letty Sue couldn't resist. She pressed her breasts against his chest, causing torturous friction against his taut skin. "Don't I *feel* okay, Chase?" she teased softly.

He groaned aloud. "Damn woman, you *are* trying to kill me." He rolled her over onto her back and grinned devilishly. "But I know exactly how to take out my revenge."

Letty Sue savored every bit of his expert, erotic retaliation.

* * *

Chase stroked little Jake's head tenderly, watching the boy sleep. He smiled down on him, grateful he seemed to have accepted his new home without much fuss. Although he'd had some nightmares, they had ebbed, and Jake had effortlessly become a part of their family, taking easily to the ranch and the newness of his situation.

When the boy stirred slightly, Chase made his way out of the bedroom, carefully closing the door. He strode back to the parlor and to Letty Sue. She'd tossed off her blankets and was sitting up, waiting for him. "Is Jake all right?" she asked, her expression a mixture of sated woman and concerned mother. Her nightdress had slipped off her shoulders, the material parting in a most tempting way.

"Jake's just fine. Sleeping soundly."

"Come back to bed then," she whispered, patting the spot where he'd slept earlier in the night, holding her in his arms.

He shook his head and rubbed at his jaw. "Don't think so, sweetheart."

Her face, full of eager expectancy, fell, her sweet mouth turning down in a frown. "Why not?"

It hurt him to disappoint her in any way, but she needed her rest. He'd taken her innocence tonight and her untried body would need time to heal.

"If I come back to you, neither of us is going to get much sleep."

He didn't trust himself to keep his hands off her.

With regret, he'd decided to sleep the rest of the night outside.

Letty Sue rose up on her knees, reaching for and grasping his hands. She tugged him down to her level without great effort, since Chase wasn't putting up much resistance. Her eyes, so blue and honest, shone in the dim firelight. "I need you here with me, Chase."

"But if I touch you…it won't stop there."

"I was sorta hoping you would," she said sweetly. "And I do ache, Chase. For you. Come back to bed."

Chase prided himself on his iron will, but her soft smiles and beckoning eyes assured him like nothing else ever could, and it wasn't as if he *wanted* to sleep apart from her. Hell, he'd call himself every kind of fool for a lifetime if he refused her invitation.

"Move over, sweetheart," he said, taking up most of the space on the blanket, so that the only room left was on top of him. He hoisted her up gently. "I don't think this is going to get us much sleep at all," he said, then brought her lips to his, kissing her deeply.

Her swift acceptance and overwhelming passion stunned him. She kissed him fervently, holding nothing back. Chase was at a loss to protect her from his desire. And when she removed her nightdress and straddled him, all rational thought left his head. He guided her down onto his manhood and watched as she closed her eyes, her face a beautiful blend of innocent woman and sexy vixen. She moved on him now, slowly, her bare body learning to adjust to his size. Her hair, loose and untamed, teased the tips of her breasts with each unhurried thrust. Moisture coated her creamy skin, radiating a brilliant glimmer. He let her set the pace, entranced by her beauty, this woman, his wife, as she rode him, nearly conquering him.

Chase had never *wanted* like this before. He'd never lost himself in a woman, not this way. Not as though his very life depended on taking her, pleasing her, making her his. He didn't know what it all meant, couldn't fathom the intense feelings swelling in his gut.

And when she moaned his name, a soft, low, anguished caress to his ears, he cupped her bottom, speeding up the pace and acknowledging her need, for it matched his own. They thrust together now, as one, Chase giving to her all that he possessed. They met at the top, a perfect sensual joining of two bodies, two souls.

Letty Sue fell onto him, spent. He held her tight, feeling her heart pound erratically. He stroked her skin tenderly, until they both calmed. Then she rolled to the side and gazed up at him, the soft glow in her eyes revealing her heart.

"Chase," she whispered, "I—"

He kissed her quickly, stopping her from saying what he read in her eyes. He needed time to figure it all out. He couldn't bear to hear her words, not until he knew what he was feeling, what was in his own heart.

He had closed himself off for such a long time, he couldn't abide making the wrong decision, not now, and not just because she'd given him a hell of a good time in bed.

Things would become more clear to him tomorrow. He simply needed the time. "It'll be dawn soon, darlin'. We should sleep now. We'll talk in the morning."

She nuzzled his neck, her breath tickling his throat, her naked body a temptation he could scarcely resist. "Promise, Chase?"

He ground his teeth. The woman was getting to him again. "It's a promise." He set her aside gently and stood, reaching for her hands. "It's best you get back to your own bed now."

"But I don't—"

"Jake will be waking soon. You'll need to be there for him."

That convinced her. She dressed quickly, then took his hand. He walked her to the bedroom door. "I wish we could sleep together tonight," she said, regret evident in her tone.

He smiled and stroked a finger along her swollen lips. "We tried that. Doesn't work, sweetheart."

"I'll miss you."

Hell, he'd miss her, too. He doubted he'd get a wink of sleep, his mind reeling, his body still humming from their lovemaking. "You need to get some rest."

Her eyes beseeched him. "Until the morning, Chase."

He nodded. "Good night, Letty Sue."

* * *

Chase couldn't believe he was standing face-to-face with Marabella Donat. He'd awakened later than usual this morning to a sharp knocking at the front door. Marabella's driver had stood at the threshold, claiming that the woman needed to speak with him. Chase had dressed and splashed water onto his face, then headed outside.

She'd been leaning on the corral fence, admiring his stallion, Tornado. "I knew he was yours the minute I saw him. He has a strength about him, a certain pride."

Chase rubbed his neck, glancing at his once would-be bride. She was as stunningly beautiful as he recalled. Long golden hair wound up in a fancy bun touched the collar of her emerald velvet traveling suit. The color brought out the wintergreen in her lustrous eyes. Chase once thought that he'd never seen a lovelier creature in his life. "Marabella," he began, then glanced around, noting many of the ranch hands looking on with interest, "I doubt you came here to admire my horse."

She laughed and took hold of his arm. "Heavens, no, Chase. Perhaps I came here to admire you. Shall we take a walk? I've been riding in that buggy quite a while."

Chase didn't want to play her games. He'd played enough of them back in Abilene. He stood rooted to the spot. "Why'd you come, Belle?"

"Oh, Chase," she said with a long, wilting sigh, "you have missed me, haven't you?"

"I'm married, Marabella. You have to know that." And it surprised Chase how much he meant what he'd said. For the first time since that day at the picnic, Chase felt as though he were truly married, bound to another by vows hastily spoken, but vows nonetheless.

"I know you were heartsick when you left the ranch. I know I made a terrible mistake, Chase. We can rectify that." She brushed her body against his. "Won't you give me another chance?"

"Marabella, did you lose your hearing? I'm a married man, with a…a son."

Chase glanced back at the house. Letty Sue, looking rumpled and tired, holding a sleepy little Jake, stood at the porch rail.

"That's your wife, Chase? Did I hurt you so badly that you had to pick out the most needy woman to take to your bed?"

Chase unfolded her from his arms, pushing away. "It's time you left, Marabella. Sorry I can't offer you some refreshment, but town's only an hour's ride away. You'll get a good meal there and then you can head back to Abilene."

"Oh, I don't think so, Chase," she said, undaunted by his rude behavior. She smiled sweetly. "You see, I did come with a purpose. Seth is sick. Seems my stepfather needs to speak with you. He's been asking for you. He's dying, Chase. I don't think he's going to last much longer."

Chase's gut twisted. "Marabella, if you're lying—"

"My, I did cause you damage, didn't I? No, Chase.

I'm not lying. I thought it best to come and explain personally. Seth *is* dying. There isn't much time.''

Chase cast her a long hard look, blowing out a deep gust of breath. Damn, but he believed her. He didn't want to, but his instincts, which he'd always relied on, told him that she spoke the truth.

"I'll pack up a few things and be ready to leave soon. You can go on ahead."

"No need, Chase. I'll wait for you."

There wasn't time to argue. If what she'd said was true, then he'd need to get to Abilene as quickly as possible. "Suit yourself."

He headed to the porch, took a curious Letty Sue by the hand and led her inside.

"Chase, what is it? You look very upset. And who was that woman?" Letty Sue set Jake down, to give Chase her full attention.

"Marabella."

Letty Sue's face collapsed. "Oh."

"I have to head back to Abilene, darlin'."

"You're going back…to her?" Her voice trembled, but rose with disbelief.

Chase's mind spun as he began gathering his clothes. When he rolled up his blanket, her scent still lingered on it. "It's not what you think, Letty Sue. I have to go. Seth Johnston's taken sick. She claims he's dying. He's asked to see me. There's not much time left."

"I'm sorry to hear that, Chase, truly I am. But what about us?"

What about them? He didn't have time to think it

through. He'd been hit with all this too suddenly to make sense of any of it.

"I'll make sure the boys watch out for you. Talk to Sam and Sally. Let them know I'm gone. You'll be fine, Letty Sue."

"When will you be back?" she asked, her eyes misting up.

He didn't have answers. All he had right now were questions. "I don't know."

She nodded bravely. "I'll take care of little Jake. We'll be fine."

He kissed her then, a quick meeting of lips. "Goodbye."

Chase crouched down to Jake. He hugged the boy tightly. "I have to go now, Jake. You listen to…to your ma and be good." He ruffled Jake's hair and kissed his forehead. "Bye."

Chase stood and picked up his gear. "I'm sorry, Letty Sue. There's no help for it."

She drew in her lower lip and nodded. "Goodbye, Chase."

He was halfway to the door when a small, unsteady voice called out. "Papa!" Jake came barreling full force toward Chase, grabbing his legs.

Stunned, Chase looked down at the boy first, then lifted his gaze to Letty Sue. She'd been working with Jake every day, hoping, praying for his speech to return. She'd never given up. Now, the sound was bittersweet. Jake had spoken, but was it out of pain at his leaving?

"Chase," she said, her eyes round and full of tears,

her voice filled with awe, "he spoke. I can't believe it."

Chase bent to lift the boy up.

"Papa," Jake repeated, tugging on his neck.

"That's right, Jake. I'm your papa." He glanced at Letty Sue. Tears streamed down her face now. He handed Jake over to her. "And this is your mama. She's going to take good care of you while I'm gone." Chase hated to leave. He wanted to stay, to revel in the sound of Jake's voice, to watch Letty Sue's face flush with excitement when the boy spoke.

Jake nodded. "Mama."

"That's right, Jake," Letty Sue replied with a trembling voice. "I'm your mama."

"Papa go?"

"Yes, he has to leave us right now." Letty Sue pressed the boy to her chest.

"I'll be back, Jake," Chase said, "so you practice up on all that talking, you hear?"

"He'll be talking up a storm by the time you get back, won't you, little one?"

Letty Sue's brave smile pulled at Chase's heart.

"Mr. Wheeler, Miss Donat says it's time to go," the driver called out from the front door.

Chase glanced once more at Letty Sue, then at Jake, before whirling around and striding outside.

He couldn't help feeling he was turning his back on them both.

Chapter Twenty

If one good thing came from Chase's leaving, Letty Sue mused, it was that Jake started speaking again. She'd spent the next day coaching him with words, just as she'd always done, but this time the boy responded. His words were unsure at times, but so very endearing. It was a balm to her ears, and his sweet voice helped to soothe her aching heart.

"Papa horse," Jake said, pointing toward the empty corral.

"Tornado?"

Jake nodded and pointed again. "'Nado."

"Tornado is with Papa," Letty Sue said quietly, turning Jake's attention to three young chickens wandering about the yard. She couldn't very well tell the child that Chase would be coming home soon, since she held no faith in that happening. She'd not subject Jake to any disappointment.

In truth, Letty Sue held little hope of Chase's return. He knew Joellen would be home shortly, his services no longer needed on the ranch. He'd always planned on dissolving the marriage. And even though their lovemaking had been wonderful, he'd not once claimed to love her.

Lust was the word he'd often used. She'd known he wanted her in a purely natural way, but she hoped that she hadn't imagined his tenderness, a warming of his cold, unyielding heart. When he'd held her and kissed her and joined their bodies, he'd seemed to truly care for her. She'd given herself to him fully, completely, knowing no other way to show him her love. She'd planned on telling him in the morning how she felt, how much she loved him, and pride aside, she would have asked him to stay, to try to make their fake marriage real.

But then Marabella had shown up. Beautiful. Elegant. Refined. Letty Sue would never forget the heart-stopping emotion she'd felt watching that woman touch Chase. She'd laced her arm through his while they spoke, as if staking her claim, and it was as though a boulder had crushed Letty Sue's chest, making it hard to breathe. Chase hadn't backed off from the woman, either, not until he'd glanced at the house and seen Letty Sue watching them.

Anguished images came to mind, of Marabella and Chase reuniting. What if she wanted to patch things up with Chase, make amends? What if after Chase left the Double J, he'd found it in his heart to forgive Marabella her deceit? After all, he'd *wanted* to marry her. Unlike their marriage, which had been nothing but a way to uphold Letty Sue's reputation. Chase had been honor-bound to marry her.

Letty Sue closed her eyes to the deeply entrenched pain within. She'd lost Chase, she was certain.

Jake tugged on her hand, pulling her out of her self-imposed misery and toward the barn, where baby chickens scurried throughout the yard.

"Chicks," she offered.

Jake chuckled when one sunny-yellow ball of fluff nipped at another, putting on a bit of a show, before scampering off. "Chicks," he repeated.

"That's good, Jake."

Jake smiled, beaming with pride.

Sheriff Singleton rode up and Letty Sue's breath caught. The sheriff never came to the ranch unless there was bad news. Immediately, she thought of Chase. Had something happened to him?

Then her mind went to Jake. What if the sheriff had word of the boy's parents?

A welling sense of dread crept up her spine. It was all she could do to welcome the sheriff with a smile.

"Hello, John," she said, taking hold of his horse's reins as the man dismounted.

"Letty Sue. You're looking well. Marriage agreeing with you?"

"Yes," she replied quickly.

"I hear your ma's due home any day now."

"Yes, should be quite soon."

"That's good."

The sheriff removed his hat and fingered the rim. "I, uh, got some news for you." He glanced at Jake, who'd latched on to her leg. "It's about the boy."

"Oh?" Letty Sue's stomach clenched. She bent to

Jake's level. "Jake, why don't you wait for me on the porch? We'll have ourselves a molasses cookie in just a minute. Okay?" She turned him by the shoulders and patted his bottom. He took off running, eager for his treat.

Letty Sue didn't think she'd ever feel like eating again, if the news the sheriff had was what she feared it'd be. "Did you find Jake's parents?"

The sheriff drew in a big breath. "I'm afraid we have."

Letty Sue squeezed her eyes shut. "And they want him back."

"No, Letty Sue."

Her eyes flashed opened. "They *don't* want him? Why, I've never heard of such an awful—"

"They're dead, Letty Sue. One of Toby Mc-Farland's ranch hands found a wagon about five miles past where you picked up the boy. It had careened off a cliff and got covered up by some tall brush. That's probably why no one's seen the wagon until now. Three bodies were found. Probably the father, mother and an older child. Appears that the boy was thrown deliberately, to save his life, or else he flew off that wagon before it went over that ridge."

"But how can you know it was Jake's family?"

The sheriff reached into his saddlebags and brought out a Bible. "This was found in the wreckage. According to the inscription, there were four in the family. Name's Swenson. Olga, Johann, Elise and the boy's name is—"

"No, don't tell me. I can't bear to hear it right now.

He's Jake. Named after my father, Jacob. That'll be his name from now on."

The sheriff looked at her curiously. "You mean to keep the boy?"

"I do."

"Then I suppose I should give you this." He handed the Bible over. "He might want something of his family, when he's older."

"We're his family now," Letty Sue announced, a sense a relief mingling with sympathy over lives lost in such a terrible tragedy. There wasn't anything she could do about Jake's family loss, but she could offer him a loving home from now on. "I'll see that he gets this, when the time is right." She flipped through the front pages of the Bible. "There's no mention of any other family."

"No, doesn't appear he has any. We think they were planning on settling west of here, maybe California. It's a shame about his folks. That boy was real lucky you found him when you did."

Letty Sue smiled, grateful she wasn't losing Jake. "I think both of us were lucky, John."

Chase stared down into the light gray eyes of Seth Johnston. The once vital man appeared defeated, his face pale, his eyes watery. He'd opened them just moments ago when Chase entered the room and pulled up a chair by his bed.

"Seth, it's Chase Wheeler."

"Thank God, you made it, Son." Seth's hoarse

voice displayed his weakened state. He reached for Chase's wrist. "I'm glad you're here."

"Marabella said you wished to speak with me." Chase spoke softly, amazed at how this apparently healthy man had taken ill so quickly.

"I know I don't have much time left on this earth. I have things to say to you. I must ask for your patience, and your forgiveness."

"My forgiveness? Seth, you've been nothing but fair and generous with me. I have nothing to forgive you for."

"Yes, you do." Seth drew in a breath slowly. Chase could see how hard the simple act of breathing had become for this man. "You see, many years ago, I was bushwhacked and left for dead in Indian country. A Cheyenne woman found me, nursed me back to life. We fell in love and married. I loved her very much, Chase, but she wouldn't leave her tribe and I, well, I know now I should have found a way to keep us together."

Chase listened patiently, as Seth had asked, but his gut knotted with each word the man spoke.

"Her name was Snow Cloud." Seth's gaze sharpened on his. "Your mother."

"Then, are you saying—"

"I'm your father, Son."

Chase drew in air. Unable to speak, he nodded slowly, taking it all in, trying to absorb the import of what he was hearing.

"I didn't know about you. Snow Cloud and I parted and never spoke again, but then this tall, proud young man came looking for work on my ranch. He had my gray eyes, and my grandfather's name.''

"Chase Wheeler was your grandfather?'' Chase's mind spun, thinking back to the time when he'd tried to come up with a white man's name for himself. Snow Cloud had suggested it. She said it was strong and powerful.

"That's right, Charles Wheeler Johnston was my grandfather. He was known as Chase. When I heard your name and looked into your eyes, I knew Snow Cloud must have sent you here.''

"She did. She mentioned that she'd heard of a white man who was fair-minded, who would give me a job.''

Seth had a fit of coughing then and Chase grabbed for the glass of water on the bedstand. He held it up, carefully dripping the liquid down Seth's throat.

Seth calmed, resting his head on the pillow. He took many deep breaths, then continued. "I didn't know you existed...I left well before you were born. But when you came here that first day, I knew who you were.''

"And you didn't say anything.''

Regret filled the sick man's eyes. "No. I'm not making excuses for that. It was wrong. I should have welcomed you, like a father would his only son. But you see, Marabella's mother wouldn't have understood. She was already ill and I feared upsetting her with the news.''

"And after she died?'' Chase asked. He wanted to

know why he hadn't been acknowledged all those years.

The man slumped even further down in his bed, shamefully admitting, "I lost my nerve. I should have told you, but so much time had already passed. And then Marabella and you seemed to hit it off, and I thought you'd be in the family, anyway. It thrilled me to see you two together."

"It didn't work out, as you know."

"Yes, I do know. It's a pity. But I understand you married. That's good, Son. Keep her close. Love her. Or you'll regret it the rest of your life."

Chase listened, only half hearing, the newness of the situation still dawning. Seth Johnston was his father. Chase had lived on the ranch, worked here for ten years, and only now, on his deathbed, had the man decided to share the news.

"I hope one day you'll forgive me."

Chase could only nod. There wasn't much he could say right now. "You need to rest. I'll be back later."

Seth called to him before he reached the door, his voice a strained whisper, "Chase, I really am sorry, Son."

"I know."

Chase made his way down the staircase to the parlor. He helped himself to a glass of smooth amber whiskey and sank down on the plush velvet sofa. He thought of all he'd heard today, the magnitude of it slowly sinking in.

He had a father.

The man was dying.

Could he find it in his heart to forgive him?

Liquid poured into his emptied glass. Chase glanced up. Holding the decanter in her hand, Marabella smiled, a charmingly sexy lifting of lips that turned men's heads. Her charm no longer worked on him.

"Care for some company?" She didn't wait for his answer, but sat down beside him. "So Seth told you?"

He turned sharply to face her. "You knew, too?"

"Yes, I knew," she said, stroking his arm. "Seth explained your parentage after you left the ranch. He was heartsick that you and I, well, that it didn't work out. Then when he took sick, he asked me to come get you."

"All those years, wasted," Chase said aloud, shaking his head. He braced his head in his hands.

Marabella ran her hand through his hair, fingering the locks. "It was wrong of Seth. He should have told you. I can only imagine how you're feeling, darling. Let me help ease the pain." She whispered in his ear, "Like I used to, remember?"

Chase removed her hand from his hair and stood abruptly. "I need to be alone right now, Belle. Leave me be."

"I understand, Chase. But I'm here, whenever you need me."

"Marabella, it's over. There's no going back." Chase strode out the door. He had enough to think about right now—his father, his mother. And his mind kept returning to Letty Sue, his wife, and the way they'd made love. She'd been everything he could ask for and more. Surprisingly.

And seeing Marabella again sparked in him no interest, no feeling at all. He didn't need her. It was Letty Sue he wanted right now. Only she could help comfort him. She'd been on his mind since the moment he'd ridden off the Double J. She and little Jake.

His family.

Chase took a long walk, heading west along a low ridge. Seth Johnston's spread was large, ten thousand acres, but Chase had always liked this area the best, where a shallow stream splashed against the rocks and moved fluidly, turning and twisting, not entirely unlike his life. Certainly the past few years had changed course, and the path he'd chosen had twisted unexpectedly.

He thought of his mother now, and how much she'd loved his father. Chase had seen it in her eyes on those rare occasions when she'd spoken of him.

He knew her to have a tender heart.

She would have wanted Chase to forgive the man his wrongs.

Chase decided he wanted that as well. He couldn't send the man to his maker without a clear conscience. Seth could die in peace, knowing Chase held no animosity for him.

It was the honorable thing to do.

Chase switched directions and strode purposefully toward the house. He only hoped it wasn't too late.

* * *

I forgive you, Father.

Chase stared down at Seth Johnston's grave in a small picketed cemetery on the ranch, recalling the last words he'd spoken to his father. Chase was glad they'd had a chance to speak one last time by his bedside, Seth doing most of the talking, reliving the past and relieving himself of ten years of guilt. There'd been a peaceful look on Seth's face at the end, as he'd uttered Snow Cloud's name quietly and left this earth.

They were together now, Chase believed, for two souls so much in love should share everlasting life. That thought brought with it a sense of peace. It helped to ease Chase's mind and give him more than a bit of solace.

He returned to the house slowly, breathing in the crisp night air, reflecting back somewhat and also thinking of the future, his future. He owned the ranch now, a startling revelation that he'd only found out this morning when his father's attorney came by to read the will after the funeral. Chase could hardly believe it. Seth Johnston had left the majority of his holdings—the house, the ranch, his great wealth—to Chase. Aside from a comfortable allowance provided for Marabella, Chase had pretty much inherited everything.

He entered the house quietly, noting shadows dancing along the walls in the parlor. A feminine scent, strong and exotic, wafted to his nostrils. Marabella. Chase kept walking, heading up the stairs to the bed-

room next to Seth's, which she'd insisted he take in
case the ill man needed him during the night. Chase
hadn't argued, since Marabella did have a point.

But tomorrow he planned on heading back to the
Double J and to Letty Sue. There were things that
needed clearing up, words that needed saying.

"Chase, is that you?"

Chase hesitated only briefly on the stairs. "I'm going up, Marabella. It's been a long day."

"May I have a word with you? Please, Chase."

Chase rubbed his neck, frowned, then turned and
strode back down to the parlor.

She stood in the firelight, wearing a pale green
nightdress full of frills and lace, her blond waves curl-
ing down past her shoulders, a beckoning look in her
eyes. "Have a drink with me, Chase?"

She walked up to him, placing a snifter of brandy
in his hand.

"I'm leaving in the morning," he said, taking a
sip. He'd been gone four days and was itching to get
back to the Double J.

"That's what I want to speak with you about." She
set her glass down, came closer and laced her arms
around his neck. Her voice was sugary sweet. "Don't
go, Chase. Stay with me. Remember how it was between us? We can have it all again—the house, the
ranch, all of Seth's wealth. Lord knows we deserve
it."

Chase set his drink down and unfolded her arms
from about his neck, but she clutched his hands.
"Marabella."

"Think of it, Chase. We'd be rich and together. I can't think of anything more perfect." She tightened her grip.

Chase broke her hold. "No."

Her tone reached a desperate pitch, losing all that sugary sweetness. She spoke rapidly now, with determination. "We don't have to stay here. We can travel, go East if you'd like, or west to California. Anything you want, Chase. As soon as you dump that trollop of a wife, you'll be free, and we can be married."

He shook his head. "We tried that once, Belle. But you set your sights higher than a half-breed ranch foreman, as I recall."

"Pierce was a mistake. He was nothing but a down-and-out gambler posing as a refined gentlemen. He wooed me, but he was only after Seth's money. That's why I got rid of him."

"You got *rid* of him?" Men seemed to turn up dead when Marabella was around. Chase shook off that niggling thought, dismissing it as a result of sheer fatigue.

With a wave of her hand, she replied, "You know what I meant. I broke off our engagement."

"Too bad, you two seemed suited for each other."

She brushed her body up against Chase, crushing her chest to his. The intimate contact stirred in him nothing but disgust. "We're suited for each other, you and me. Chase, don't make me beg. Stay with me tonight. You won't want to leave in the morning." She began unfastening the buttons on her nightdress.

He halted her. "I *am* leaving in the morning. I'm

going back to my wife," he announced, before stepping away.

"You couldn't possibly want that woman over me, Chase. You don't love her!"

Chase turned his back on Marabella and headed for the staircase. "That's where you're dead wrong, Belle," he muttered under his breath, realizing now just how much he did love Letty Sue. She was who he needed right now. And who he wanted. And by tomorrow night, he hoped to make her his, forever.

The next night, Marabella stood over Chase as he lay in his bed. She shook her head. "Poor Chase, you seem to have caught the same virus Seth had. I sent for the doctor, but he's delivering a baby across the county. He'll be here in the morning to see to your affliction, I'm sure. Have some more broth. I made it up special for you."

Chase's mind felt like mud, a thick layer of it clogging his senses. His last recollection was of sipping coffee that morning, as he was ready to leave. Then the world had spun around him, he'd lost all sense of himself, his knees had buckled and he'd collapsed. Next thing he knew, he was in bed, with Marabella watching over him.

Now his stomach clenched as if a giant snake was squeezing it tightly. He didn't think there was much left of his gut, since he'd emptied it so many times. Sweat poured down his face, his body was soaked and his legs felt like Letty Sue's oatmeal, cold and mushy. There was no strength in his limbs. Weak and exhausted, Chase could only lie on the bed.

Marabella wiped him down with a cloth. "Chase, it could have been good between us. Pity you didn't see it that way."

Dizzy as he was, Chase couldn't lift his head off the pillow. But keen instinct told him not to take any more broth. *Don't eat, don't drink, Chase.*

If only he could get himself off this bed.

Chapter Twenty-One

Letty Sue sat in a crimson, tufted velvet chair facing a beautifully sculpted oak desk waiting for Jimmy McCabe to greet her. She glanced around his office, noting the finery. He'd done quite well for himself, this young man who used to tease her unmercifully and chase her around the schoolyard. She'd always held a special place in her heart for him, that being one of the best memories of her childhood.

He entered, looking trim and professional in a three-piece, pinstriped suit. Funny how she preferred a man *with* mud on his boots now. She preferred a man of strength. She preferred…Chase.

No other man would do.

But Chase wasn't the reason she was seeking her friend out. She needed legal advice. This was most important to her.

"Morning, Letty Sue. You're looking as lovely as ever." Instead of a stiff handshake, the way he'd greeted her at the ranch when Chase was about, he bent to kiss her cheek. She watched him circle around to the other side of the desk and take a seat.

"Jimmy, this is such a fine office. I hope you do well in Sweet Springs."

"Thank you, Letty Sue. People tend to trust one of their own. My law practice is growing and I'm happy here. Now, what can I do for you, since marrying you is out of the question," he said with a teasing glint in his eye. "Seems you've done quite well for yourself."

"Yes, I suppose," she replied, although she wasn't at all sure what he meant by that. And she wouldn't mention that perhaps Jimmy would have to tend to more unpleasant legal affairs for her, if Chase chose not to return. He'd always vowed to dissolve the marriage. With pain in her heart, she'd come to accept that fate, if that was what Chase really wanted.

Letty Sue straightened, getting back to her reason for seeking Jimmy out. "I'd like to adopt Jake."

"Ah, I see." He leaned back in his chair and she witnessed a softening in his eyes. Jimmy really was a nice man. "I'd heard the boy's family was found. All of them are dead."

"Yes, that's right. It's unfortunate, but Jake has a home with me. He's very happy on the ranch now. Did you know he started speaking again?"

"No, no. I certainly didn't. Does he have any recollection of his folks?"

"I don't know for sure. He doesn't ask about them. Doc Ramsey thinks he's put the whole tragedy out of his mind. Says he might never remember. His nightmares stopped weeks ago. He really is adjusting well and I hope to see that continue. I want to adopt Jake officially. Do you see any problem with that?''

''I'd have to check into it, but no, I don't see any problem. The boy has no family and you're willing to give him a home. Besides, with your husband's wealth now, that would play in your favor.''

Letty Sue took a big swallow. ''Excuse me? My husband's wealth?''

''Yes, his inheritance.''

Letty Sue blinked, trying to hide her shock. ''I don't understand.''

''I thought you knew. Pardon me for speaking out of turn.''

''My husband was summoned back to Abilene. Seems his employer is dying and wanted to speak with him.''

''His employer? Then you don't know the whole story,'' he said, more to himself than to her.

''Jimmy, just tell me what you're talking about!''

Jimmy rubbed his nose, hesitating. There was a debate going on in his head, she surmised, but finally he dropped his professional tone and continued. ''A few days back, a woman came by my office speaking of a will she'd read. Pardon me for saying so, but I've never laid eyes on a more striking woman.''

Letty Sue frowned. ''Marabella Donat?''

''Yes, that's her name. She had spoken of her stepfather's last wishes and wanted to know if there was any way around it. Seems the dying man is your husband's...'' Jimmy stopped and twisted his lips. ''You didn't hear this from me, Letty Sue. I shouldn't be repeating it.''

Letty Sue's heart pumped hard in her chest. She needed to know what Jimmy had to say. ''It'll go to my grave, Jimmy. I swear. This is important. I need to know. Please go on.''

With a wary nod, he continued. ''Seth Johnston is Chase Wheeler's natural father.''

She gasped aloud. ''Oh my!''

''Yes, and I've never seen a more enraged woman. Seems this Marabella wanted to know if the will was legal and binding. She was fit to be tied when I told her that, yes, from what she'd told me, Chase Wheeler had every right to his father's holdings. She started ranting about the unfairness of it all. And that—again excuse me for saying this, Letty Sue—that no filthy half-breed bastard should get what was her due. The woman walked out of here with murder in her eyes.''

''Oh!'' Letty Sue was speechless after that, her mind reeling with all she'd just heard. The man Chase had worked with for the past ten years was his true father. Chase hadn't known. The shock must have devastated him. And what of Marabella? If what Jimmy said was true, she'd be out for revenge. Yet the woman hadn't seemed vengeful when she'd come to the ranch that day. No. She'd appeared more the temptress. Was she hoping to ingratiate her way back into Chase's life, just for the money? Either way, Chase might encounter trouble with her.

''Letty Sue?'' Jimmy walked around the desk to check on her.

"I'm fine, Jimmy. Really. This is all such a shock."

"Yes, well, I hope it all works out. But I'd be careful with that woman. She didn't strike me as the kind to let this drop."

"I was thinking the same thing, Jimmy. Thank you," she said, reaching for his hand, "for trusting me with this news." She rose from her seat, amazed at how wobbly her legs felt. Taking a deep breath, she mustered her strength and smiled.

"I'll get working on the adoption today," he offered. "Can I walk you out?"

"No, Jimmy. I'm fine. I can see myself out."

He kissed her again on the cheek. "Letty Sue, should I be worried about you?"

"Oh, Jimmy. You are a dear. Just see to the adoption and I'll take care of the rest."

The concern on his face escalated. "That's exactly what I'm afraid of."

Letty Sue was afraid, too, of what she'd heard today and of what it all meant. But most of all, she was afraid for Chase.

"I can't thank you enough, Sam. This is asking almost too much of our friendship, pulling you away from your wife of less than a week." Letty Sue reined in Starlight at the foot of a hilly rise. Faint predawn light fought off the night. Letty Sue's sore backside reminded her how far she'd traveled in a scant amount of time. "And I made her take little Jake in, when she's got her hands full with her own siblings."

"She offered, Letty Sue. And her brothers love playing with Jake."

Letty Sue let out a deep sigh. "I know. You two are the best friends in the world."

They were just outside of Seth Johnston's spread near Abilene. She could see over the entrance to his property the wide arches with the initials S.J. carved out of cedar. Chase was there, somewhere. She didn't know if following him here had been wise or just plain foolish. She might very well humiliate herself if Chase turned her away in favor of his first love.

But if that wasn't the case, he might need her now, more than ever.

Either way, she had to know. She wasn't fighting just for herself anymore, but for little Jake, too. Chase had to know that Jake was theirs now. They could be a real family.

Sam steadied his mare with a soft whisper, then added, "Besides, Sally wouldn't have it any other way. With all that talk of you riding to Abilene in the dead of night alone, she insisted I come."

"So did you, my friend. I know you worry about me."

"Geez, Letty Sue, when are you and that husband of yours going to get it right, so *he* can do all the worrying over you?"

Letty Sue rubbed wearily at her neck. "I'm working on it, Sam. That's why I'm chasing that man down. He could be in trouble."

"All the more reason to let me come along. I could lend a hand if needed."

"Sam, you've already done enough by giving me a quick lesson in shooting, and leaving Sally last night to bring me here."

Sam grunted. "You sure you remember how to shoot, Letty Sue?"

"Mama made me learn when I was a young girl. Of course, I haven't had much use for a gun recently, but yesterday you helped me recall all that my mother taught me. Heavens, I'm not planning on shooting anyone. It's just a precaution."

"All the more reason you should let me come with you."

"No, Sam," she insisted, as kindly as she could. "I've let others do for me all my life. This is one thing I must do for myself."

Sam finally seemed to understand, nodding solemnly. "Okay, but I'm not leaving. I'll get a room in town. You just give a holler if you need me."

Her body quaked uncontrollably and Letty Sue recognized it as pure panic, not because Sam was letting her do this her own way, but because, soon, she'd know her fate. If Chase sent her away, pride wouldn't allow her to plead.

She'd leave with her chin held high.

And never lay eyes on him again.

Letty Sue peered down the rise at the ranch, which seemed to beckon her. Dawn was on the horizon now, a bursting golden-orange blaze. "It's time for me to go."

Sam reached over to cover her hand. "Remember, I'm not far away."

She squeezed tight, then released him. "I know."

Within minutes, Letty Sue was on even ground, approaching the large, opulent ranch house.

The only sound she heard was the faint rumbling of men just coming to in the bunkhouse. The smell of strong bitter coffee flavored the air. Quickly and quietly, Letty Sue knocked on the front door.

When there was no answer, she went around to the back of the house. The door to the kitchen was open. She stepped inside cautiously, but when she heard footsteps approaching, instinct told her to hide inside a dark storeroom. With her ear to the door, she listened intently.

"It's okay, Rosalee, I'll take Mr. Wheeler his morning coffee."

"He is better this morning, yes?" The woman who asked had a Mexican accent.

"I'm afraid not. The poor man's just as sick as my stepfather was. I'm afraid he's not long for this earth."

"*Dios!* I shall pray for Mr. Wheeler. He is such a nice man."

"You do that, Rosalee. Why don't you take the morning off to say your prayers? I'll tend to him and sit by his side today. A man shouldn't be alone when he dies."

"Oh, Miss Marabella, I hope he does not die. I will pray for him."

When one set of footsteps faded off in the distance, Letty Sue heard Marabella's voice ring out. "You can pray all you like, Rosalee." Her wicked chuckle pierced Letty Sue's ears, "but it won't help Chase Wheeler. Nothing will."

Letty Sue stepped out of the storeroom with all the stealth of a panther. She hid behind the doorway leading to the kitchen, slanting her body, pressing against the wall. Bravely, she peered around the corner in time to see Marabella slip two leaves of a plant Letty Sue didn't recognize into a steaming pot of coffee.

"That should just about do it. But not to worry, Chase. I'll be sure to dig your grave right next to Seth's," Marabella said gaily. "Won't be long now before the bastard son joins the father."

Letty Sue didn't have to know the particulars to understand that Marabella had tainted the coffee with poison. She'd heard tales of certain plants being deadly, especially if one brewed the leaves or any part of the stem and added the mixture to a drink.

"There, we'll just let that brew a bit, while I tidy up."

Letty Sue leaned back out of view quickly and heard the door slam.

Aghast, she shook all over, and it was a full minute before she calmed. Marabella was a killer? She'd poisoned Seth Johnston, and Chase was next on the list.

Not if she had anything to do about it.

Letty Sue knew she had to find Chase fast. From the sound of it, there wasn't much time. Her hand fumbled inside the pocket of her riding skirt, where she kept the small derringer Sam had given her.

She climbed the stairs quietly, darting her gaze about, watching for Marabella. She listened outside each door before opening it. By the time she reached the second to last door, her patience had just about run out. Where was Chase? Why couldn't she find him? Her heart raced with a panic she'd never known before.

She opened the door to a darkened room. All the others allowed bright sunlight in, but this one had the smell of...death about it. It was dark, dank and dreary. She stepped inside and heard a moan, low and anguished, barely human.

With fear clutching her belly, she went to the window and gently pulled open the drapery.

She gasped when she saw him.

Pale, sallow and weak, with dazed eyes, Chase lay sprawled out on the bed. She rushed over to him.

"Chase, it's me, Letty Sue. Chase, Chase. Wake up."

He tried to focus on her and she saw how difficult that was for him. "Letty...Sue?" His mouth was dry. It obviously troubled him to swallow.

Tears sprang from her eyes, but she didn't have time for them. "Chase, sweetheart, yes, yes, it's me. I'm here now and I'm going to take care of everything."

"Don't take the broth," he mumbled nearly incoherently. "Don't eat a thing."

"Chase, you have to listen to me." She took his face in her palms and made him listen. "I have a plan."

Chase's nod, a slight movement of his head, obviously brought him such pain that he winced. She prayed for him, and prayed that her plan would work. She hid behind the drapery clutching tight the little derringer she hoped she wouldn't not have to use today.

It was only minutes later that Marabella entered the room. "Good morning, Chase. I have a tray for you and lots of hot coffee. Why, your father never went a day without drinking at least half a gallon of the brew. You must have some today. You didn't drink enough yesterday."

Letty Sue stepped out from behind the curtains. "I have a better idea, Marabella. Why don't *you* drink the coffee?"

Marabella turned and let out a shriek. "Oh!" Then she seemed to have recognized her. "Whatever are you doing here? And don't you dare point that gun at me. Can't you see this man is sick? He needs his nourishment."

"That man is my husband. And this gun will stay trained on you until you drink from his cup there." Letty Sue gestured with her gun. "Go on. I want to see you finish what's in that mug."

"No, don't be ridiculous. I wouldn't dream of taking his meal. Chase needs it."

"Like hell, Marabella. Either you drink it or I'll shoot. And I'm not bluffing."

Marabella looked at the tainted coffee with round, frenzied eyes. She shook her head and began to back away, as though the steaming liquid was a wild animal stalking her. She kept backing away, shaking her head. "No. No. Don't make me. I can't, don't you see? I can't. They had to have it, not me. They had to die."

"I didn't deserve the treatment I got on the ranch. I was tolerated, just tolerated, and once Mother died, he didn't care if I was happy or not. He ignored me most of the time. I hated it here. Mother should have never married him. She took me away from my friends." Marabella began to break down, her body trembling, her hands going into her hair. "I didn't have any friends here. Not one." Her head bobbed up and down. "I deserved that inheritance. It should be mine, not Seth's bastard half-breed. He needs to die. Then it's all mine. Mine!" Her voice elevated to a fevered pitch. "It all should be mine!"

She pointed toward Chase. "He wasn't even supposed to be here. He was supposed to hang for Pierce's murder. Don't you see? I had it all planned out so carefully!"

Letty Sue didn't let down her guard. "You killed Pierce Mainwarring and set Chase up for the murder?"

"Brilliant, wasn't it?" She grinned then, tugging at her hair again. "It would've worked perfectly, too. No one would believe a half-breed over the evidence. I used his Cheyenne ropes to tie the man up. He had no alibi."

"I gave him his alibi."

"You ruined my plans." Venom poured from her lips like hot lava. "I hate you, too." Suddenly, the woman pounced, clutching at Letty Sue's body, ripping her clothes. Letty Sue turned and twisted, her hand still firmly on the gun.

"Don't," she warned, but the crazed woman kept on with her attack.

With a firm, steady push, Letty Sue shoved her away with all of her might. Marabella went crashing against the window, and when she turned up, ready to attack again, pure evil on her face, a shot rang out.

The woman slumped to the floor, gripping her shoulder in agony.

Chase stood by Letty Sue's side, one arm wrapped around her waist, the other covering her hand, pointing her gun.

"Chase, I shot her."

"We shot her," he corrected, using her strength to keep himself upright.

"But how did you get up?"

"I couldn't risk her hurting you," he said, his body sagging against hers. "Can you tie her up?"

She nodded. "I think so."

"Good. I love you, Letty Sue...." he announced, then collapsed on the floor right in front of her.

Three days later, Letty Sue sat on the bed watching her husband devour his afternoon meal. Color had come back to his face. His body appeared strong and healthy again. Each day of nursing him had brought him a little closer to a full recovery. She'd never once left his side. "You've got quite an appetite today, Chase."

"It's all this fine cooking," he teased.

"Rosalee is giving me some help, but I insist on cooking all your meals from now on."

"I won't be arguing with that."

He set his plate aside and grabbed for her hand, pulling her closer. "Come here."

"Chase, you need to rest in bed."

"Letty Sue, what I need has nothing to do with rest and everything to do with this bed."

"But—but you're recuperating."

"What I need right now only you can give me." He kissed her soundly on the mouth, dragging her down beside him on the bed. "I love you, sweetheart, now let me prove it."

Letty Sue was powerless to stop him. He was her heart, her soul, her very life, and the thought that she might have lost him scared her senseless. And if she hadn't come here when she had, he surely would not have survived. Marabella, with all her deceit, had sought to destroy Chase. But Letty Sue wouldn't think of that venomous woman now. She focused all her attention on the man whose hot searing gaze was turning her insides to warm jelly.

She removed her clothes quickly, watching the appreciative gleam in her husband's eyes as they moved over her length. And when he touched her, his intimate caresses scorched her skin like burning, licking flames.

Chase loved her. She could hardly believe it, but his smoldering kisses and consuming passion could be nothing else. And she loved him back with everything she had.

The brave Cheyenne boy who'd saved her all those years ago had been her destiny all along. They were meant for each other. Fate had had a funny way of bringing them together, but they were together at last—now and forever.

"Oh Chase," she whimpered, when he moved his hand down to her most private region and stroked her. "Feels so good...so very good."

"Sweetheart, it's going to feel even better." And moments later they were joined, a beautiful blending of two bodies coming together as one.

Chase held her tight in the aftermath of their torrid lovemaking. This woman meant everything to him. His love for her was staggering.

Walk as one. Stand together.

His mother would approve.

Letty Sue was the woman he'd been waiting for, the woman who would be forever in his heart. It had just taken her longer to grow up, but she had, and now he felt like the luckiest man alive.

He kissed her forehead and shook his head, recalling how Letty Sue had fought off Marabella and saved his life.

"You took an awful chance coming here."

"I had to, Chase. I love you with the whole of my heart. You, me and little Jake, we're a family now. I had to fight for that."

"I do love you, but I didn't know just how much until I saw you that morning. Know what I thought?"

She curled up in his arms, snuggling closer. "No, what did you think?"

Chase drew in a deep breath and exhaled slowly. "I was so weak, I didn't know how to take my next breath. I thought I was dreaming when you entered my room. You were an enchanting vision I needed to cling to for survival, but when you came to the bed and spoke softly to me, I knew you were real. It was then I thought of a fitting name for you, one that will endure our entire life."

Letty Sue smiled sweetly. "Tell me it's better than Twisted-foot Woman."

Chase grinned and kissed her cheeks. She lifted her head up, waiting, her heart tripping over itself. Smoke filled his gorgeous silvery eyes. She knew the look, and finally knew what it meant.

"When I saw you, my mind cleared and I thanked all the spirits in heaven for bringing you to me. I thought, here she is, my beautiful wife, the woman I was meant to love, Leticia Suzanne...my Angel at Dawn."

Epilogue

Letty Sue lowered her two-year-old daughter down onto the bed, kissing her round cheeks and tucking her in. "Good night, Baby Jolie," she whispered, then turned to witness Chase brushing a kiss on Jake's forehead.

"He's out. Nothing's going to wake him till dawn." They peered at Jake, clinging to his pillow, taking deep exhausted breaths.

"Seems Barnum and Bailey's Circus tuckered our little ones out today," Letty Sue said softly, as they headed out the bedroom door of the New York hotel suite. This was their first trip East, their honeymoon. Chase had promised, and true to his word, as soon as he could manage to get away from Johnston Ranch—his ranch—he'd surprised Letty Sue and packed them all up for this journey across the continent.

Standing by the fireplace in the parlor of the suite, Letty Sue felt her shoulders slump with fatigue. This was the sixth hotel they'd frequented in as many weeks, and although she loved seeing the East with

her family, she felt herself yearning for the simpler
side of life.

"I think the circus tuckered you out as well."
Chase grinned, putting an arm around her waist.

"It was fun, but seeing those circus horses made
Jake long for his own pony. He misses the ranch,
Chase. And our sweet little Jolie misses her own
bed."

Chase brought Letty Sue closer, whispering in her
ear, "And what do you miss, sweetheart?"

She sighed deeply. "I never thought I'd say this,
but I miss Texas. I've enjoyed every minute of our
trip and I thank for you for bringing us, but would
you mind terribly if we headed home a bit earlier than
we planned?"

"I'm willing," he replied, struggling out of his
pressed suit coat and tie. He dropped them briskly to
the floor. "More than willing, darlin'."

Letty Sue took in the sight of her handsome husband. Her heart never ceased to pound more quickly
whenever he was near. After three years of marriage,
that hadn't changed. "You do look fine in your fancy
duds though, Mr. Wheeler."

She touched his starched white collar, then began
to undo the buttons. "But you'd look much better
wearing nothing at all."

Chase's grin was pure sin. "Is that an invitation?"

"An invitation?" She pulled the shirttails out of
his trousers, her fingers brushing the golden taut skin
of his chest.

He captured her hands, pressing them flush against

his hot flesh. "For me to make love to you all night long?"

"Why yes, dear husband," she breathed, "please do."

He wrapped his arms lovingly around her shoulders, guiding her to their bedroom. "And tomorrow?"

"Tomorrow, Chase, my love, you're going to take your family back to Texas...home."

* * * * *